WHEN GODS WAR (ROMAN CANDLE)

F. HOWARD BILLINGS

authorHOUSE®

AuthorHouse™
1663 Liberty Drive
Bloomington, IN 47403
www.authorhouse.com
Phone: 1 (800) 839-8640

Published by AuthorHouse 09/01/2017

ISBN: 978-1-5246-9205-6 (sc)
ISBN: 978-1-5246-9206-3 (hc)
ISBN: 978-1-5246-9204-9 (e)

Library of Congress Control Number: 2017907595

Print information available on the last page.

CHAPTER 1

Convergence

I N THE VASTNESS OF AN advanced system spins a simpleton, Zeon. It is the fifth planet in a nine planet system. With 70 percent covered by landmass and two unconnected seas, it carries life, but is a world still in development. The oxygen content is a meager 14 percent and the sea water is a tepid green; drinkable, but certainly not good, with insects and small aquatic life only. The land is mostly wild grasses and small shrubs. In another time there were forty large timbers, but long before any Zeons could remember, all forty were cut down to large flat stumps just above the ground. The Zeons use these stumps for assemblies and gatherings.

Zeon's most obvious feature is the great mountain Altai, a 40,000 foot snowcapped dormant volcano with a base thirty miles wide. On this small planet, Altai almost looks out of scale. At Altai's base are small mountains with their tops curled over away from the great peak. They are curled waves stuck in time, as if they suddenly cooled from molten to solid. The rest of Zeon is covered with these curled-over mountains, which provide good shade. The difference between Altai and the smaller curled peaks is due to their composition. The other mountains are limestone or sandstone, but Altai is solid granite.

Afloat in the seas are large leaf pads. With content levels that match the surrounding water, they never deteriorate; the lone remnants of a time before Zeons when the great timbers stood, but the most alluring features of Zeon are the gentle swirling breezes that blow through the grasses and across the seas. Their effect is sedating, giving Zeon a calming, comforting sereneness. In the sky, thin white clouds spiral upward like helixes, mimicking the ground winds, but the breezes are by no means warm as only the center third of Zeon is livable. The ice caps are substantial, and no Zeon is equipped to venture far north or south without certain peril.

There are two large groups of Zeons on opposite sides of the planet. On one side are the Nearside Zeons, with settlements of huts surrounding their sea, which from space on this small planet looks more like a very large lake. On the opposite side are the Farside Zeons with their own similarly-sized sea.

Adult Zeons stand about four feet tall. In the Nearside tribe, males have dark brown fur and females, light brown. This is in contrast to the Farside Zeons which are dark red and light red and want nothing to do with Nearsiders. Farside Zeons are also a bit larger, having a burly build and standing five feet tall.

Zeons' most telling features are their sizeable feet and big round eyes; eyes of innocence, curiosity and longing. There are families and little ones and all should be content, but a coming doom tempers all moods. The impending doom is the sixth planet Tareon, which orbits their sun in a direction opposite of Zeon. Twice each year their orbit paths converge toward each other and each time they pass, the larger Tareon pulls Zeon closer and closer to Tareon's own orbit path. Because of this twice-yearly convergence, Zeons talk among each other in half-year terms.

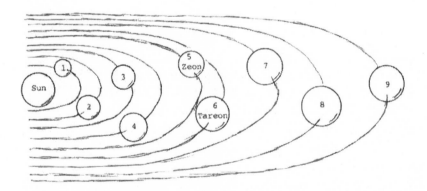

Adult Zeons remember the last pass-by and its three days of mayhem and tremors. Each passing of the planets has grown progressively worse as the planets are closer with each encounter. Nearside Zeons used to endure the calamity by hiding under the protection of the curled-over peaks, but after a few of their kind were sucked up into the atmosphere and killed, they have resorted to hiding in the caves on their side of the planet. Children try to block out the chaotic memories of past fly-bys, and parents try their best to not remind them.

The 600,000-strong Nearside Zeons are headed by their chosen leader, Scepter. Although not the most knowledgeable, when relying on recommendations of others his judgment is good. Other prominent Nearsiders are Elixor, a chemist/blacksmith with one silver tooth who has inhaled too much of his compounds, and the elderly Chronicle, a graying beard with two piercing silver eyes. Silver eyes are known for their ability to sense the feelings of others, and are very rare. Chronicle is the only Zeon with two silver eyes, and even *he* has forgotten how old he is. It is said that two silver eyes can etch stone - although Chronicle cannot remember doing so - and that the blood of two silver eyes is a purple so permanent that it will never fade. It is imperative for Chronicle to be present at all important Nearside events, as he is the official recorder of record.

Scepter was chosen the Nearsiders' leader based on his knowledge deciphering the cave paintings and symbols of Zeon's past. Zeons know enough about their recent past, but nothing reaching far back, as if all prior ancient history has been erased. Scepter's knowledge of the old symbols and language surpasses that of even Chronicle, who has forgotten some of his endless memories.

The Nearside tribe believes that in the days left, they should at least learn all that is possible about both their own planet and Tareon, their fast-approaching enemy. The Nearsiders' first landing parties sent to Tareon reported a very advanced world, yet no people. Maybe, just maybe, something about Zeon or Tareon would explain how their orbits pass closer together, twice each year.

The current half-year has been unusually short, because in the last pass-by – after being attracted to each other by their gravity - Tareon and Zeon slingshot past each other with great speed, reducing the current half-year by 30 days. Today is the 120th day of the current half-year, and this half-year is almost over.

Under this billion-star evening, Nearsiders Kairn and his son Trillo fish for aquatics with others on the last open "finger" of their sea. All adults know it is the last night of normalcy before the coming calamity, and try to stock up on food and rations. Nearby, Kairn's wife Rayelle oversees the Nearside Zeons' two great infrastructure projects which are both finishing tonight. The first is the working of naturally-secreted putrid green primordial ooze from below the wet sand into a thick, taffy-like 10-mile cord known as the Great Elastic. This kneading is done using sticks made from that same green ooze by thousands working from the shore up toward Major Cave.

The other project is the sewing of a thin translucent green cover over the entire Nearside Sea, which is attached to the ocean shore perimeter by a zipper-like strip of retainers. Kairn and Rayelle's daughter Evene – five years older than Trillo - is part of this Sea Cover effort. Thousands more Nearsiders are involved with this effort. The cover is made from a thin film of the same material as the Great Elastic. The cover's purpose is to prevent the Nearsider's ocean water from evaporating up into the atmosphere during the pass-by so there is something drinkable afterward, if there *is* an afterward.

This putrid green ooze is a staple for Zeons and the Nearsiders work it into all shapes and uses, from thin flexible fabrics to strong hardened- and dried- members, and during times of shortage, it even has redeeming food value, however wretched.

Elixor and his two aides – brothers Garl and Hark - toil at a small seaside foundry making special tools and metallic instruments using foot-powered saws, drills, grinders and lathes. They work mined metals into various small shapes and have a basic understanding of electricity, but make only limited use of it as only Elixor and his aides have been able to grasp it. Zeons do not have much, but they make the most of what they have.

"Garl, Hark, start tearing these tools down and take them to Major Cave," as Elixor barks out pertinent orders. "I don't want to have to rebuild them again."

"Yes, Elixor."

Under a starlit heaven that slowly scrolls from west to east across the sky, each family has two fishing lines suspended across the sea inlet with lured lines dropping down into the water. When an aquatic bites, that line is pulled to shore and the pizza-shaped flapper is removed, and the line re-lured and zipped back out over the water.

As the youthful Trillo gazes skyward through his father's simple sighting telescope – made of that same green material - "I wish I could fly and see what's up there," he says with complete innocence.

"All stargazers do," responds Kairn.

"And which is the one that will kill us," asks Trillo.

How does a parent answer knowing there is no future? This pensive mood permeates all adult Zeons, heightening the worried look in those big round eyes. Looking as if he's about to tear up, Kairn tries to stay on subject.

"Look just off the lower right corner of the triangle cluster, to the bright one that pulsates. That's Tareon."

"It doesn't look that scary."

"Not yet, but Tareon is steadily growing, and that rate of growth increases as we and it accelerate toward each other. Plus, Tareon is thirty five percent bigger than Zeon, so it exerts a larger gravity force, and anyway, who said it's going to kill us?"

"My friends' parents."

This does not totally surprise Kairn. There were two ongoing bets among his stellar sighting colleagues and in the first bet, forty percent believed a collision would occur during this coming closure of planets. Inwardly, Kairn is glad his son is finally showing an interest in the stars, the same interest that got Kairn his position as a stellar sighter. If they live and Trillo becomes a sighter, he would be a third generation sighter, starting with the greatest sighter of all, Kairn's father.

Trillo lowers the telescope and gazes upward and notices the slow movement of the stars across the sky from east to west, as they do every night. "Tell me again why all the stars move across the sky."

"They don't move. We do. All planets rotate to maintain their orbit around the sun. In our sky, all stars rise in the east and set in the west, and tomorrow night when we come around again, it'll all happen once more. Because our planet is small, it doesn't take long for us to rotate through a whole day."

"And is it true what grandpa told me? That our planet orbits our sun in the opposite direction of the other eight planets?"

"Yes, what little we know about our system indicates that we are the exception. We are also hearing that the other planets might be more advanced than us."

"If we orbited in the same direction as the others, would Tareon still be pulling us closer?"

"Since Tareon is so much bigger, it could, but not as often. Our planet and Tareon would pass each other, less often."

Just then, an aquatic bites and flaps on one of their lines.

"There's a bite! Pull it in," exclaims Kairn.

Trillo pulls the tugging line closer to the shore and removes the flapping creature. He writhes with it slightly before adding it to a line with other captured aquatics. Kairn watches almost nonchalantly out of the corner of his eye, but is actually looking closely for something, as he does every time they fish. Trillo re-baits the line and sends it back out over the water.

No sooner does Trillo send the first line out when, "There's another bite on the other line" notices Kairn.

Trillo reels the line in and grabs the next aquatic. As it squirms in his hands, he squirms with it, and an otherworldly voice not possibly his own, comes from his mouth: "Hey!" He quickly adds it to the line with others they've caught and looks at his dad with wide-eyed amazement. "What just happened?"

"Reach down and grab it again," advises Kairn.

Trillo reaches down and again squirms with the flapping creature. "Put me down" blurts from Trillo's mouth in the same ungodly tone. He again rises and stares wide-eyed at his father.

"It's finally happened," remarks Kairn. Trillo has always had one bright silver eye, a rare trait from his mother. Silver eyes are able to connect with- and sense- the feelings of others. This ability even works with Zeons who've recently died.

"We've caught enough," concludes Kairn. Let's pull our lines in because this last inlet will be covered later tonight, and we'll get your mother and sister and go home." Others fishing nearby also prepare to leave.

Moments later, "It's happened," opens Kairn, meeting up with wife Rayelle and daughter Evene. "Trillo's achieved his first link and gotten in contact with the aquatics."

"That's good. Now, if only we had a future where he could use it," as Rayelle quietly mutters with a tempered approval.

Kairn and Rayelle are a youngish couple who are well thought-of. Kairn is known for his knowledge of the sky and Rayelle for her silver eye sensitivity and quick judgment and reasoning. She has managed many projects which ended up successful and some think she may one day be chosen as Scepter's replacement, except that they are all doomed to die. Kairn and Rayelle's busy daily schedules have resulted in an increasing appreciation for their time together as a complete family.

As they prepare to leave the shore, the night crews take over on the Sea Cover and the Elastic, and Rayelle has pertinent instructions to give the night foremen.

"Foreman Nord, everyone is done catching our final aquatics, so this last inlet can be covered tonight. And Foreman Boll, two more loops over itself in Major Cave and the Elastic will be long enough. I'll see you all in the morning."

Together, Kairn, Rayelle and other families walk toward the hills and their reed-and-mud huts. Carrying green buckets of aquatics and root vegetables, they walk up the gentle slope leaving the shore. Looking like a never-ending anaconda, others nearby carry the lengthy Great Elastic in the same inland direction. The Elastic extends from the shore up over hills toward Major Cave, and Kairn and Rayelle walk home along its path.

"Father, when will we feel the first effects of Tareon approaching," asks Trillo as they walk.

"It's already begun," replies Kairn. "Do you feel our breezes?"

"They're gone," notices a suddenly astonished Evene.

"That's the first effect, and tomorrow will be warmer and the day after - much warmer, with strange winds growing ever stronger, and that's just the beginning." With the clock of normalcy quickly running out, it's a time for closeness. As they walk home, they would hold hands, but their hands are full.

Kairn and Rayelle's hut sits among others at a sizeable settlement just below the opening of Major Cave, where the green Elastic is being guided into. The cave opening is no bigger than any other cave, but the interior stretches more than three miles back into its mountain.

After setting down his buckets and reaching for his Sighting Scope to take one last look at Tareon for the night, "Ugh. Now see? I don't even need my scope anymore," mutters a dejected Kairn.

In the time they have walked from the shore to their hut, Tareon has grown to the size of a significant moon, and its rotating collage of purple-and-green is now plainly visible.

The next morning, "Dad, why is the sun coming up so early," asks a groggy Trillo.

"Let's step outside and see why."

As all four in Kairn's family step outside their hut, Zeon seems to have a huge new moon in the sky as Tareon has grown in size 800 percent, overnight.

"Oh no, we're coming together much faster than last the last convergence," exclaims Rayelle, who can't believe the rate of closure.

"Son, there's your answer," as they all stand together in closeness. "Do you see our sun rising a little faster than usual?"

"Yes."

"That's because as our planet and Tareon get closer, our rotation is speeding up, so the days on each planet are getting shorter and shorter, which means we each have to get going and shove off as these hot, dry winds are not Zeon-like."

"Today, the two projects finish up," Rayelle reminds Kairn as they prepare to split up.

"They'll have to. By nightfall, the winds will be furious and the Sea Cover must be secure."

A hug for Rayelle and Evene and a reminder to listen for disaster orders from leadership. Kairn holds one hand up – shaping his thumb and fingers into a half-circle shape. Rayelle does the same and touches her half circle to his, completing the connection. This is a family salute Kairn and Rayelle have created for themselves and their kids. A hug and touch-salute to all, and they split up. Rayelle and Evene head back down to the sea's edge and Kairn and Trillo walk over the hills to Kairn's work at Launch Control.

As Kairn and Trillo walk the trail leaving their settlement, the compacted ground transitions to a zone of sand dunes, and they soon walk along the ridge of the first of two large and deep sand craters.

With its soft sand and rocky outcropping at the bottom, the first is known as the Soft Sand Crater. It is treacherous and Nearside Zeons have had to be rescued from it. Kids can walk down it safely, but adults must wear webbed Sand Shoes which distribute their weight and prevent them from sinking in. The Sand Shoes – again made of that same green material - are scattered around the crater rim.

"I love this crater," blurts out Trillo, who does not always accompany his father to work. "It's always been my favorite playing place. How much bigger would I have to be to wear the Sand Shoes that would keep me from sinking in?"

"In another three years, you'd be too heavy and would need to wear the shoes." He doesn't dare say it, but in the back of his mind, Kairn knows that any thought of a future is a useless dream.

Just past the Soft Sand Crater is the adjacent larger Burial Crater. It has firmer sand and the Nearsiders have used it for eons to bury their dead. Thousands of small raised mounds are visible marking graves at the bottom of the burial crater. The sight of this crater prompts Trillo to ask another of his innocent, yet thoughtful questions.

"And there's our Burial Crater. If we all die, who would bury us?"

How is a father to answer?

"I guess Tareon would bury us all. We'd be gone and Tareon and Zeon would join in an infernal fusing-together of worlds, but let's not dwell on that. Let's enjoy our last days together."

Soon after passing the Burial Crater, the sandy zone gives way to solid soil and the prominent wild grasses and shrubs reappear alongside their trail.

Their journey ends at Kairn's work at Launch Control, which is on top of one of the curled-over peaks. This is the widest of the curled-over peaks, allowing many sighters to study the heavens and the valley beyond. Below its curled overhang is shade; a place to adjust both scopes and eyes which have seen too much sun.

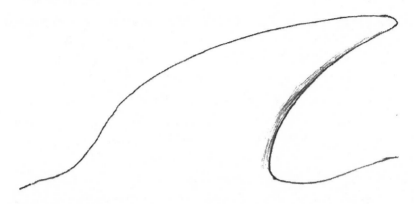

Launch Control has a commanding view of the valley beyond; a valley with a healthy river as each valley carries water from the substantial ice caps toward the sea. Across the valley is the first steppe of Altai, the great dormant volcano. The beautiful breezes of Zeon are gone now, replaced by a dry, warm unnaturalness, which is quickly melting and blowing snow off of Altai's upper reaches.

Atop Launch Control, other stellar sighters are busily taking measurements of Tareon's approach. As Kairn and Trillo walk up the overhang, "Father, you haven't been here in so long. And mom, you came too," as the first two Zeons Kairn sees are a surprise.

"I wanted one more look from up here before we have to retreat to the caves," responds Kairn's father. "And I haven't been here in years," adds Kairn's mother. "It's a special day for your father and I want to be part of it. And how is our grandson Trillo?" With doom fast approaching in the sky above, she tries her best to avoid the obvious.

As Trillo hugs his grandparents, Kairn begins his initial sighting by first reaching for – as he always does - his green Sighting Scope, but quickly realizes Tareon is much too close, and instead resorts to measuring Tareon with his outstretched fingers and thumbs.

"Ugh. In the hour we've walked here, it's grown substantially closer. And if its rotation wasn't speeding up, we could make out its features, but just look at those colors; deep purple seas and lush green land masses! It must be very unlike our planet."

Other sighters – including Kairn's most trusted Brill - and Scepter approach. As leader, Scepter wears a necklace adorned with polished metal stones. Scepter's wife Norl also walks up, with their two year old son Effy.

"Brill, are you monitoring the rotation increase of each planet," asks Kairn, while taking his initial sighting.

"Yes Kairn. The speeds are increasing at a faster rate than ever before."

"Scepter, the rate of closure is much faster than the last pass-by," advises Kairn after completing his initial sighting. "All past timetables are useless."

Overhearing this, the elder Chronicle and his wife Woon, walk up.

"Tell me you're inhaling some of Elixor's hagweed root," Scepter asks Kairn.

"I am not, but I'm afraid this convergence is going to be a very rough ride," replies Kairn, who notices his parents have led Trillo away and that Effy is too young to understand. "I hope we are prepared enough in all ten caves."

Scepter and Chronicle each walk with tall, ornately-carved Comstaffs, which can be used to talk into. The Staffs are a dried and hardened piece of that green ooze, with a green megaphone near the top. At the top of the Comstaff, a woven reed cover protects a small, simple, metal satellite receiving dish. Sound travels well through Zeon's crust, and stabbing the staff's sharp point in solid ground enables all with a Comstaff to hear out of their own similar speaker. Three taps indicates an important message. This crude messaging ability is not without its limits as there is no privacy, and everyone on the planet with a Comstaff can hear what's being said. Because of this, communication is reserved for only the most important of messages.

To Kairn's remark about being prepared enough, Scepter stabs the staff's sharp point into the ground and replies, "Well then, it's not too soon to begin evacuation procedures, so let's find out if all of our teams and parties are ready," but before Scepter can say anything into his Comstaff, his megaphone chimes with Rayelle's voice. She stands at the distant sea shore with her own Comstaff.

"Scepter! Status from the sea: The Great Elastic is looped 344 times over itself in Major Cave, and the last sea inlet is ready to be closed."

"That's just in time. Cut the Elastic, block off the ooze port, guide the Elastic into Major Cave, and close up the Sea Cover," replies Scepter.

At the sea, with that order over her own Comstaff megaphone, Rayelle directs Evene and others to cut the cord and begin hauling the lengthy, taffy-like Elastic cord for storage, and gives the order to finish covering the last finger inlet of the great sea. Within a few minutes, they cinch the cover tight and the entire Nearside Sea is covered with the thin translucent green envelope.

"The sea is covered Scepter, and the end of the Elastic is on its way to Major Cave," as atop Launch Control, Rayelle's voice is heard over Scepter's Comstaff.

Above the sea, while hundreds of Zeons hustle the giant Elastic toward Major Cave, each Zeon also carries a woven reed backpack with water, captured aquatics, and some root vegetables.

Just then, a strange warm gale cuts through everyone atop Launch Control. It's a foreign wind, nothing Zeon-like. The elder Chronicle does not take it well and now sweats profusely.

"The breeze is ominous," observes Chronicle. "This is going to be much worse than the last encounter. It's time to alert all."

"Very well. Cave teams, are you there," as Scepter speaks toward his Comstaff."

The Nearside tribe has three cave teams searching all known caves on their half of the planet. They are looking for any undiscovered old writings or carvings which might provide answers on how Zeon and Tareon have come closer over the years.

"All cave teams listening, Scepter."

"We're about to evacuate Launch Control and head underground. Make way to your assigned caves to be with your families."

"We will, sir."

Scepter turns his staff horizontal to reach up to the top and removes a woven reed cover over a crude metallic receiving dish, and points the staff and dish skyward. "Tareon teams one and two, are you there?"

The Nearside tribe has extended a small, metallic tethered relay dish high up in the atmosphere on a balloon, which relays signals to the scout teams on Tareon. The tether is a long thin piece of the lightweight Sea Cover material. The two scout teams on Tareon reported similar relay satellites are already in place above that planet.

"Tareon Team One, Drago here," replies Drago's voice, after a short pause.

"Tareon Team Two, Othar here."

"We are about to go underground, so this may be the last time we talk for awhile, if at all," responds Scepter.

"Very well, Scepter. It's a shame you all can't be here. Tareon is everything Zeon is not, but we can't find any beings here. We'll explain later. Since this planet is much bigger, it may not be affected as much as Zeon, but we are still going underground to be safe."

"Very well" replies Scepter. "And how's my bother Nax?"

"I am here, Scepter. Drago and Othar seem to know this planet well. We are following their lead."

"Excellent. We hope to talk again after the pass-by." Scepter then concludes with the Nearsider's customary sign-off. "Stay alert, stay smart, and forward with brilliance."

"Forward with brilliance," respond Drago and Othar in unison.

With that conversation done, Chronicle can't avoid asking Scepter the obvious.

"Aren't you going to touch-base with the Farside tribe?"

"Do I have too? I try to avoid their leader, Dorn."

"If we're all about to die, some last words might be good - however difficult," advises Chronicle.

With that, Scepter stabs his Staff tip into the hard soil three times. "Farside Zeons, this is Scepter."

The 1.4 million-member Farside Tribe lives on the opposite side of the planet, with their own sea. They are led by Dorn-22, anointed leader before his birth, simply by being his father's son. Like his father Dorn-21 and those before, he's adept at imposing fear on his people. For inspiring fear within others - when it comes to himself – he's beyond cocky, which is why Scepter tries to minimize contact. Dorn is so fearful that he is the only Farsider who is allowed to carry a Comstaff, which means his only gets used when talking with Nearsiders. Dorn and his lieutenants stand atop a command post on one of his side's curled-over peaks.

"Dorn, this is Scepter. It's getting warm and windy on our side."

"Likewise on our side, but we have faith that we will get through this."

"What precautions are you taking, Dorn?"

"We will nestle under the curled overhanging peaks."

"But you'll be killed! They are not enough protection. Take cover in your caves as we are."

As he speaks, Dorn doesn't notice other Farsiders listening around him. They are wondering if what Scepter says is true, that the caves are the only place of safety.

"Yours is not our way," proclaims and increasingly agitated Dorn. "We have confidence Tareon will pass by and leave us intact, and I have no time for doomsayers!"

"And if this is to be our last hour, why do you forbid your Farside Zeons from contact with us," as Scepter gets in one final question. "Are we not brothers?"

"To preserve our purity. We prefer isolation and control. That's enough of this talk. Dorn, out!"

With the communication abruptly ended, "Their leader is afraid of his own fur," mutters Scepter after he lifts his Comstaff off of the ground.

Nearby, "Father, mother, you'd better head to Major Cave," as Kairn approaches his parents while others start to leave Launch Control. "Trillo and I will be there, shortly." After hugs and kisses, his parents depart.

Suddenly, a very hot dry gust from across the valley blows across Launch Control. The gust is so dry that the fur of everyone remaining now stands erect. Elixor grabs Chronicle's arm to steady him and each is jolted by the snap of an electrical shock.

"Ouch! Is that spark, your doing," asks a squinting and wincing Chronicle. "And why is our fur standing up?"

What other planets would easily know as static electricity is totally foreign to Zeons. Their air is usually cool and moist.

"I know a little bit about electricity, but I have no idea," responds Elixor, who turns to Scepter. "Scepter, we'd better get to the caves."

"Agree" replies Scepter, who with three stabs of his Comstaff, "Command to all, it's time to enter your pre-assigned caves. Commence evacuation procedures immediately!"

As the others atop Launch Control waste no time gathering loose items and leaving, Trillo stays very close to his dad, eyes squinting in the warm dry wind. As Kairn and Trillo take one last look up at the bulbous elephant Tareon in the sky, "Father, I'm scared," admits Trillo.

Sighting a portion of Tareon through his thumbs and fingers and detecting a miniscule deflection in Tareon's path, Kairn can't hold back the truth. "So am I, and this is going to be very, very close."

In truth, most Nearside Zeons are already in their assigned caves. There are ten caves on their side of the planet. Caves One through Nine are known by those numbers. Cave number Ten is by far the biggest, and commonly known as Major Cave. It's the only cave big enough to house the Great Elastic, and also holds more than 300,000 Nearsiders. Kairn and Trillo go there, since Rayelle and Evene are there, and families are designated to gather together.

Scepter, his wife Norl and son Effy, Chronicle and his wife Woon, and Elixor head to Cave One. Cave One is small, but rather strong. A leader from each cave carries a Comstaff to stay in contact.

As they walk, Trillo notices something weird. "Father, why are our shadows already long?"

"Because our planet's rotation keeps speeding up and the day is getting shorter. As our planets get closer, gravity increases, pulling the planets together faster, and also speeds up our rotation. The same thing is happening on Tareon."

Zeon's crust also transmits electrical signals well. Each cave has one crude monitor, made of that same green material with a wires visible inside, which were cobbled together by Elixor and his aids in his seaside foundry. A lens on each monitor looks at those huddling within that cave. The lens transmits images to the monitors in other caves, as long as each lens survives and is working. Elsewhere, lenses are also aimed at the covered sea, Altai, and at the ever-growing Tareon. Farside Zeons don't know it, but Nearsiders have hidden a few camouflaged lenses on their side of the planet, overlooking Farside settlements.

Viewed from space - since each planet orbits the sun in an opposite direction – Zeon and Tareon spin methodically toward each other. Zeon - the inner planet of the two - can do nothing to avoid being pulled toward the larger Tareon. This convergence is a culmination of an eons-long twice-a-year ritual. It was over 20 years before that Kairn's father and other stargazers warned that the two planets would one day speed up and strike each other in a horrific fusion of worlds, killing all alive and creating a new larger world that would need millions of years to renew.

There is a strange obsession in each planet's approach, as in *"I am for you and you are for me,"* as their rendezvous with destiny nears. This is physics at work on a galactic scale. Being a simple people on a simple world, there is not much Zeons can do about the approach except huddle together and have the worry in those big round eyes get even worse.

Kairn and Trillo reach Major Cave Ten amid a now howling, roasting wind. Rayelle, Evene, Kairn's parents, and Rayelle's parents greet them at the entrance. Rayelle's mother also has one silver eye. The meeting *should* be joyous, but there is an abundance of worry in everyones' eyes.

"Rayelle, it's nice to see your folks again," remarks Kairn. "Kids, you and your grandparents head inside and mom and I will be right behind."

Kairn and Rayelle take two last looks before heading inside Major Cave. The first is out toward the sea. The translucent green cover is flapping wildly in the wind, but the perimeter shore anchors are holding steady.

The second gaze is one last look up at Tareon, its spinning blur of purple and green now filling the sky. Tareon is thirty five percent bigger than Zeon, but up this close, looks even larger.

At the mouth of Cave One with winds howling by, Scepter points his Comstaff skyward for one last message with those on Tareon.

"Tareon Teams One and Two, what's it like there?"

After a slight delay, "There's so much to tell sir, but we haven't got time," responds Drago with his own winds whipping wildly in the background. "It's getting very hot and dry here. We've found a good sized cave and are about to go under."

"Very well. If we don't make it and you do, carry on somehow. We wish we could be there with you. Stay alert, stay smart, and forward with brilliance. Scepter, out."

"Forward with brilliance," responds Drago.

Scepter enters Cave One and - with the help of others - rolls a thick slice of an ancient timber stump across the cave opening into a groove they've chiseled into the surrounding rock. The slab is bigger than the opening, so once in place, it is secure within its groove slot. The slab has a small window cover that can be opened, just big enough to peer out of. Each cave has a similar timber-slab door.

In Major Cave, the sizeable Elastic is wrapped hundreds of times over itself in the back half of the cave. In front of the Elastic, the cave is large enough that over half of the Nearside Zeons – more than 300,000 - are also gathered there.

"Can we play while we wait," Trillo and Evene in unison ask Rayelle.

Before Rayelle can answer, a sudden powerful outside gust slams the thick wooden door within its slot. The kids quickly then cower and look even more wide-eyed.

"Do you *still* want to play," responds Rayelle.

"No" reply the now-jittery kids.

"Find a rock to sit against" advises Rayelle. "If you don't, the gravity forces will press you to the ground."

As the kids step away, Rayelle turns back and notices a suddenly humbled Kairn peering out the small viewing window in their door slab.

"Honey, our home was just blown away." She joins him at the window and both watch helplessly as their hut and others below the cave are swept away by the sandstorms and winds. In a matter of seconds, their entire settlement has been blown to bits.

"But if we don't live, we'll never miss our home," reasons Rayelle. "Kairn, how bad is this passing going to be?

"Very bad, like nothing we've encountered before."

No one can see it but instead of holding hands, their thumbs and fingers are touching in their family circle salute. It's a time of worry and closeness.

In Cave One, Scepter, Norl, Effy, Elixor, Woon, and Chronicle have taken a seat against a boulder. Scepter sits next to Chronicle. On Scepter's other side are his son Effy and wife Norl. The boulder they sit against is across from both their monitor and one of the great cave paintings. The painting has symbols next to it of a past language, and a depiction shows their solar system – all nine planets. Zeon is shown as the fifth planet, with Tareon – the sixth, beyond it. There is a sizeable gap between them as if at one time, the planets were much farther apart. Scepter has spent countless hours studying these glyphs, so there is nothing new for him to learn. Still, he holds out hope that the markings will one day explain how these two orbs of destiny have come together.

In all ten caves, the entire 600,000 strong Nearside tribe sits with their backpacks of water and root vegetables. An occasional small sip of water, but no one dares eat. Most sit where they can see their lone monitor screen. They can't control or select what's on their screen, only Chronicle can in Cave One.

Built into the base of the Cave One monitor is a clear green vessel containing a recently deceased brain floating in a preservative fluid. Two wires from the brain connect to the monitor. With Chronicle's silver eyes and ability to get in touch with others, if he thinks *Sea Lens*, that image will appear on the screen, commanded by the brain attached to it. If he then thinks *Farside Lens One*, that image will appear. Scepter – sitting next to Chronicle with his hand on Chronicle's arm - can also command Chronicle on which view to check next. When Chronicle switches, all Nearsiders will be seeing the same view in their caves. This telepathic control method was employed when on a recent pass-by, a wired controller that Elixor was holding was blown out of his hands.

The winds outside are beginning to whip furiously and each cave's circular door now bounces within its slot, sending a concussive racket booming throughout each cave. Elixor – feeling heavy and barely able to stand - takes one last look out of the Cave One small viewing door.

He sees thick blowing dust storms and light which transitions to dark and back to light again as both Zeon and Tareon are spinning wildly now. He closes the small viewing door and awkwardly finds his way back to his seat, as if it takes great effort to remain standing. This is why everyone lies down or sits against a big rock. Their planet's faster rotation increases gravity, making everyone feel heavier, and all will be pressed against the cave floor.

One by one, all don simple goggles made of that ubiquitous green material, see-through, just like the Sea Cover, and large mud-and-reed earmuffs are also fitted. They each then pull from their backpacks a long green straw. Each straw is closed off at the top, but has holes just under the top to breathe through.

On the Cave One monitor, Chronicle selects a lens pointed at the *Sky* and it's filled with the now-giant Tareon, which often blocks the sun as both it and Zeon spin frantically. It would be nice if he could see Tareon's features, but it's now an imposing dark blur.

Cave One now rumbles loudly; so loudly that although Scepter sits next to Chronicle, he has to shout commands. "Check the Farside lenses!"

Chronicle selects *Farside Lens 1*, which shows a Farside village being blown away by the tornado-velocity winds. With a larger population, Farside villages are much larger than Nearside villages, yet within moments, the entire Farside panorama is wiped clean.

Chronicle then changes to *Farside Lens 2*, all Nearsiders see a sickening sight; their Farside brethren huddled under the overhangs of their curled peaks, holding onto what little they can grasp and to each other, but it doesn't last long as clumps of them are quickly sucked up into the dusty sky, never to be seen again. It happens over and over as thousands upon thousands are vacuumed upward. They never stood a chance. More than half of Zeon's population is blown away in mere seconds.

Chronicle changes to a lens looking at the *Farside Sea* and it shows another sobering sight: rain traveling upward in massive amounts, with the droplets quickly evaporating in the overheated sky. Added to that, the ancient leaf pads floating in the Farside Sea lift up and take flight, flapping like giant airborne manta rays before quickly drying and burning up in the hot, dry air. The Farside Sea is disappearing before their eyes. This prompts Scepter to yell, "Check our sea!"

Chronicle changes to their *Nearside Sea Lens* and all view the surrealness of their Sea Cover bulged highly skyward. It's arched up like a billowing green balloon, straining to hold the water underneath, but the shore anchors are holding it secure; the only hopeful thing seen so far.

A check of the *Mountain Lens* shows a completely snowless Altai, something Zeons have never seen as the entire snowpack has melted from the intense heat.

Outside of their caves, the wind has now reached the macabre tone of a siren of death, strong enough to feed off itself. Suddenly, multiple concussions slam the cave doors in their slots, and it continues; it never stops. The wind outside has now broken the speed of sound, and sound pressure bounces within each cave from all directions. Those not securing their belongings quickly lose them in the gusts.

From space, Tareon – the outer planet, and Zeon - the inner, approach each other as competitors sizing each other up; two fast-spinning tops methodically approaching each other in a solar system tango. Each planet's normal clouds have disappeared as the approach of the other has disrupted all normal weather patterns. A ghoulish umbilical of dust and death grows between the planets as each is infringing its atmosphere and gravity on the other.

And then comes the arcing. Sparks begin flying between the poles of each planet as each is now close enough that their magnetic fields interfere. A few stray sparks fly off in other directions, but most are reserved for the opposing invader. Zeon would like to slide by on its normal inner orbit path, but the pull of Tareon stretches out Zeon's orbit. This is not a bull and a bullfighter, its two bulls, with Tareon – the larger, inflicting the most damage. This is a violent part of space, no place to be.

The lightning striking each planet's poles causes flashes in the skies, and thunder echoes and bounces relentlessly throughout each planet's atmosphere. It's a strange sight, not a cloud in the sky of either planet, and yet there is lightning and thunder.

On Tareon, all eight in the two search teams are secure in their cave, but because Zeon is the inner planet, it has created a colossal eclipse of their systems' sun. Tareon will be dark for days.

Back on Zeon in the caves, from deep within the planet comes a low rumble and shuddering that wavers and oscillates and does not seem to stop. Each cave's floor is becoming an undulating morass, like a violent never-ending waterbed. All Zeons have vomited whatever was in their stomachs and soot drops from the top of each cave, slowly covering all in a deepening layer of dust. This is the reason for the straws to breathe through, as all hold onto one another tightly; big eyes of worry peering up through dusty green goggles.

In Cave One up at the ceiling, no one has noticed a crack developing around the upper base of a rocky stalactite, its sharp point facing straight down, and as the planet continues to quake and stretch, the crack grows further around the stalactite's base. The pointed rocky spear hangs down directly above Scepter's leadership party, but who is it aimed at?

The billowing wind outside is now so loud that no one can hear each other. Chronicle can no longer hear Scepter, but since Scepter's arm tightly grasps Chronicle's, if Scepter thinks *Cave Three Lens*, Chronicle changes to it. A check of all cave lenses shows a similar scene: a world on its last ride. Children huddle close to their parents, all looking up at their monitors and lenses. Even some who don't always get along are now embraced in fear.

Chronicle now switches exclusively through all ten cave lenses to see if each group of Nearsiders is still okay. And then it comes: a menacing, increasing ground rumble-wave ending in a crack louder than the closest lightning. With this sudden jolt, large amounts of dust fall on all in Cave One. This cracking occurred only three times during the last pass-by; now it's happening over and over. Zeon's faults are cracking, succumbing to the strength of Tareon's pull. With the fourth bolt, a crack instantly appears in the wall behind all in Cave One and with each additional jolt, the crack grows steadily up toward the ceiling.

The views of the other caves show the same thing, necks craning in one direction or another as each cavern threatens to collapse.

In each cave, a frantic scene begins as chunks of rock break loose from the ceiling and rain down on those huddled below. Each Nearsider quickly rolls left or right to avoid what's falling their way. The heavy stalactites hanging from each cave's ceiling begin dropping like missiles, with some stabbing those below, while other stalactites stab deeply into the cave floor. The rocky formations above have become death spears, a bombardment of raining bayonettes. It's a life-and-death dodge-ball to avoid being killed or crushed. Who will live and who will die?

Suddenly – in Cave One - the weakened stalactite hanging from the ceiling breaks loose and falls, impaling Chronicle's wife Woon in the stomach and killing her instantly.

Through it all, Chronicle is able to stay strangely focused on the monitor, as if he's made for this role, but when he scrolls around to *Cave Four Lens* again, the lens is out and its nothing but static and snow. Seeing this, Scepter yells "Cave Four," but amid the cacophony and rumbling, no one can hear him.

That doesn't necessarily mean Cave Four is gone, maybe the lens has just gone out, but one more cycle through the views, and *Cave Eight Lens* briefly shows a cascade of dust followed by it too going out. Many in all caves would like to close their eyes, but to do so could mean being crushed from above. If death comes, can it please be quick?

On top of all this noise, movement and death comes a strange whistling noise from outside. All in each cave can hear it and in Cave One, Scepter thinks *Major Cave Ten Lens* and Chronicle changes to it. Scepter looks at Kairn, who looks up at his monitor lens and mouths the word "Scolios."

Scolios is Tareon's moon, and this was the second bet between Kairn's stellar sighting colleagues, that Scolios would careen into Zeon. Fully eighty percent of the sighters thought this would happen.

The whistling outside slowly grows like the sound of an incoming aerial bomb. Everyone in each cave peers toward their circular door, and the fast-flickering light around each door jamb suddenly goes dark. "Please be the end?" The whistling increases in shrillness and pitch as it approaches, and eyes close tightly and hands grab whoever is nearby, even those who are already dead. Finally, the whistle then gradually transitions to a horrible roar and there is no impact, as if it's now passed and heading away, and the oscillating light around the door, reappears.

The quakes and cracks continue, and all in Cave One stare up and back as the crack behind them has now grown up to the ceiling. Suddenly, a large chunk of ceiling drops very close to those huddled below. Chronicle's lens scrolls show caves Four, Five, Seven and Eight are all out, and Major Cave Ten is now too dusty to see.

In Cave Ten amid a deepening layer of dust, Kairn has Trillo in one arm and his parents in the other. His parents hold hands with Rayelle's parents, who also hold on to her. Rayelle's other arm is around daughter Evene. All necks crane further down the cave, where chunks of ceiling break off and fall on those huddled below. There is nothing they can do as Zeon's fast rotation and heavy gravity has them pressed to the floor.

And then it happens; a large section of ceiling rock breaks free and falls directly between Rayelle and Kairn, instantly crushing their parents. With their arms, Rayelle and Kairn each reactively roll the other way and embrace their kids. The huge boulder acts as a giant deathly wedge within the family. Where family just was, is now gone.

In Cave One amid the shaking and quaking, a football-size rock breaks loose from the ceiling and drops right between Scepter and his wife Norl, hitting their son Effy in the head. The impact splits the rock in two, but Effy is instantly killed. Scepter and Norl scream in agony and suddenly cuddle up with their lifeless son, but in the rumbling and racket, no one can hear them.

This entombment continues for five days; a shaking, deafening, dusty hell.

One the sixth day, one by one, the racket and shaking gradually lessens. The quakes and cracking subside, the wind retreats below subsonic, the buffeting stops, and the doors stop slamming in their slots. It's still windy outside, but compared with what they've been through, this is a relative calm. All in the caves are now buried under a deep layer of thick dust up to the tops of their breathing straws. They swim out like just-hatched baby turtles and remove their straws, goggles and earmuffs, but not all have lived. Some elderly and children have succumbed, and many are crying.

As others and Scepter – with Comstaff in one hand and the lifeless Effy in the other arm - approach the Cave One door to open it, there are knocks on the other side. They are met by responders from Cave Two, who help remove and roll the battered door to one side. The Cave Two responders yell with the bad news, since all are temporarily deaf.

"Caves Four, Five, Seven and Eight have collapsed, taking all with them! And Major Cave Ten has a partial collapse!"

With that news, all who are able run toward Major Cave to help dig out. Scepter, Norl, Elixor and Chronicle step out of Cave One to view the giant enemy that is now slowly retreating in the sky.

Cradling his dead son and with tears in his eyes, Scepter stabs his Comstaff into the soil and paints their situation bluntly for all who might be able to hear. "This next half-year . . . will be our last."

CHAPTER 2

A Massive Crusade

As the Nearsiders emerge from their underground tomb, goggles and earmuffs quickly come off. Each takes a small drink of water from their backpack and squirts the rest into their eyes to clear them of dust.

After a quick drink, Chronicle returns into Cave One to cuddle up one last time with his dead wife, Woon. He is so old, she is the last of a long line of wives, but with the impending ruin, both thought that they would end up dying together.

Scepter and Norl, looking both at each other and caressing their lifeless son Effy, can barely speak through their anguish.

"I always hoped you two would end up safely on Tareon," admits Scepter.

"After losing our son, I don't want to live through another pass-by, but don't crumble on me. I need you. We need you . . . now more than ever. This next half-year will require important choices. We need your reasoning, your guidance." After a brief pause, "Where should we bury him," asks Norl.

"Since we don't have time for a proper burial, he died in there, and in there he will stay."

As Norl takes Effy's body and heads back into the cave - before following her in - Scepter takes one last look up at the departing Tareon, still huge but retreating in the sky. "Why are we doomed so," he mutters from his weakened dusty frame.

Elixor and many from the other caves converge on Major Cave Ten. Inside, Kairn, Rayelle, Evene and Trillo huddle closely and are crying, reeling over the loss of their grandparents. The boulder that killed them is too heavy to move. Overall, the front half of the cave is not too bad, but the back half has collapsed, burying the Great Elastic and killing tens of thousands.

All who are able head to the back of the cave to help dig out. Some who are buried and squirming are dug out and helped outside; but strangely, the dead and seriously wounded are quickly forgotten and attention is instead turned to freeing the lengthy green Elastic belt.

It takes three days of digging, but the Elastic is freed and all alive gather with it outside of Major Cave to take stock. The huts below Major Cave that Kairn and others once called homes, are gone. Most of those alive are spent and tired and dirty and are still shaking off dust. The Elastic extends out from the cave and snakes many times back over itself. It's a large gathering of those still living, but the totals are humbling. In the sky, Tareon is still very large but gradually spinning away.

"Now, listen up! We are still a large group, but it looks like we've lost roughly half of us," as Scepter starts things off through his Comstaff speaker.

"Approximately 300,000 of us alive, with 300,000 dead; 250,000 dead in Major Cave and 50,000 in the other caves," responds Elixor.

"With only half of us left, time is of the essence. To the valley below Altai for water and a night of rest," commands Scepter.

Rayelle and Kairn's eyes meet with a serious sigh. They know what the coming assault of Altai means for them.

With Scepter's order, the weakened, dirty and what's-left march wearily - each with the Great Elastic over one shoulder - while munching their backpack root vegetables. They are not a pretty sight. Some are missing eyes, replaced by packed-in dust. Others limp or have broken, floppy limbs. It's a long snake-like migration of all remaining Nearsiders, committed in purpose.

Sluggish and feeble, onward they march, past the first large crater with the dangerous soft sand and rocky outcropping at the bottom, past the second crater where – if they had time - they would normally bury their dead, and down the side of the valley to the stream at the foot of the mountainous Altai. The wind is still warm and dry, but at least now, it's minor.

"You've got to say something to Scepter," as Rayelle prods Kairn while they walk, each carrying the Elastic. "We don't have enough people to do this."

"Soon, after a dip in that beautiful stream. These people need it."

At the bottom of the valley lies its river. Although Altai is now snowless, the water in the river proves that Zeon's sizeable ice caps have not totally melted. There is a stone-and-mud bridge crossing the river, but no one wants it. All walk into the water and rejoice in it, for it is a chance to cool and refresh. The water also has one other purpose; to renew the properties of the Great Elastic and prevent it from drying out.

A couple of hours later after a dip and drink of rejuvenation, all gather on the far side, below the slope of Altai. The Elastic is left in the river overnight to preserve its properties. All 300,000 gather around Scepter, Norl, Elixor, Chronicle, Kairn and Rayelle. Kairn takes a visual sighting of the retreating Tareon, which has reduced to the size of a very large moon, and reports the results.

"As we passed, our orbit curled around Tareon slightly, ending up a bit farther from our sun, before breaking off and shooting away, and Tareon did the opposite. It curled around Zeon slightly, getting a bit closer to the sun, before breaking away. This means that our next convergence will be 'bam' - a direct hit. And I estimate that since we've slingshot away from each other at tremendous speed, that this half-year until the next convergence will last only . . . 80 days, and we've already used up five of those."

"First we must see if there *is* a Tareon. Tareon parties One and Two, are you there," echoes Scepter, after extending his Comstaff into the air.

"Hang on a minute. That won't work," responds Elixor, immediately correcting Scepter's expectations of a signal with Tareon.

Elixor knows that his aerial relay antenna balloon high up in the sky was obliterated in the pass-by, and removes from his backpack a long rolled-up tape of the thin Sea Cover material, and calls out to his assistants.

"Garl, Hark, take those loose stones and light a clump of dry grass."

While Garl and Hark do as told, Elixor blows up a balloon of the green material and ties it off, and ties to it a small metal receiver dish. With the clump of dry grass now lit and burning, "Garl, hold this balloon well above the flame until nature does its thing, while I hold the other end of this roll."

Garl holds the balloon with small dish above the burning grass until the heated- and lightened- air within the balloon lifts it and the small dish skyward. Elixor lets the thin roll unfurl upward and stops it before the roll of material runs out. "Scepter, now try calling Tareon again."

"Tareon teams One and Two, are you there," after Scepter again points his Comstaff skyward.

Knowing that a reply from Tareon can take a few moments to arrive, "Elixor, I am always intrigued by your understanding of this electrical stuff. You are going to have to explain it to me again someday," mutters Scepter.

"Tareon reporting," responds Drago's voice over Scepter's Comstaff after a short delay. "We are here and all eight of us are accounted for, sir. The pass-by was a rough ride, but the cave we were in took it well. We're glad Tareon is the larger planet."

"So my brother Nax is okay," asks Scepter.

"I am here, Scepter. What happened, there?"

"We've lost half of us, and all Farsiders are gone. They failed to protect themselves. But the Sea Cover did its job and we've still got the Elastic."

"The Great Elastic," asks a disbelieving Drago. "You're not still going to try to make use of it, are you? With half of the people gone, you don't stand a chance."

Hearing this, Kairn and Rayelle wince at the thought. They know that this affects them, and Rayelle tries to cover Evene's and Trillo's ears.

"Work or not, we have to try," replies Scepter. "I know we should be talking longer, but we are weak and need a good night of rest, and we expect to be talking to you again late tomorrow or the next day, so stay alert, stay smart, and forward with brilliance. Zeon, out."

With the call to Tareon ended, just as Kairn starts to ask "Scepter, I must bring up that . . .," Chronicle points up the valley and suddenly interrupts with "Scepter, what is that?"

All turn and at the upstream end of the valley - just coming into view - is a small army of Farside Zeons, approximately 60,000. They too are dirty and are hobbling and weary. One by one, they reach the river and throw themselves in. Once in the river, each relishes in the replenishing waters.

Scepter and his 300,000 Nearsiders gather along the far shore, curious about meeting their forbidden enemy. It's an enlightening yet awkward meeting, and Scepter allows the Farsiders time to cool and refresh.

Varo – burly even for a Farsider - addresses Scepter from the water. Behind him are his twelve year old twin daughters Jurn and Plur. Varo also sports one silver tooth. "We've wanted to meet you for so long."

"We saw images of your people being blown out of the curled overhangs. How did you survive," asks Scepter.

"Some of us overheard you telling Dorn that the overhangs weren't safe, so we disobeyed and retreated to the caves. We chose survival over what we were told."

"What's your name?"

"Varo, and these are my twin daughters, Jurn and Plur." Looking at Elixor's kite string roll and following it up to the balloon in the sky, "You practice the devil arts," notices Varo.

"Varo, I am Scepter. We will explain more, tomorrow. After your healing bath, you and your others grab shards of our Great Elastic for food and join us at the base of Altai. We've only one night for rest."

Soon thereafter, the Farsiders – chewing small shards of the taffy-like green Elastic - cautiously approach the Nearsider's camp at the foot of Altai. All are wide-eyed at the first sight of each other in centuries.

"Your people are much bigger than us," as Scepter addresses Varo.

"All on our side are forced to work hard physical labor for many generations. It has built us, up. And your kind is much smaller than us."

"No one is slaved over here, but we *do* work together to better ourselves. I suggest we greet and then rest tonight. Tomorrow our pilgrimage will start early, and our peoples will be able to chat along the way."

"You have Silver Eyes," as Varo notices Rayelle and her kids and can't hold back. "We have been told all Silver Eyes are evil and kill them at birth."

"It's a shame you've had such insecure leaders. We find Silver Eyes' abilities, useful" replies Scepter.

One of the Farsiders – Chorn - begins sneezing.

"This one sounds allergic to us," notices Scepter.

"I hope not. I've waited so long for this meeting," replies Chorn.

At the gathering before sunup the next morning, Tareon is still visible as the Great Elastic has been brought from the water and laid out in a wide V-shape, with its center aimed straight up toward Altai's imposing summit. The apex of the V is just below one of the sawed-off ancient great tree stumps, which Scepter and Chronicle stand on. All 360,000 others sit behind the Elastic, even Farsiders. For all serious gatherings, all Nearside Zeons sit except Scepter and Chronicle. Eons ago they walked on all fours, and solemn news often causes them to settle and kneel, humbly.

"Do we still have the vessels containing the tablets," asks Scepter, his voice echoing for all to hear over his Comstaff speaker.

Hearing that, Elixor and his aides Garl and Hark get up and walk to a spot just above the back of the tree stump where two green lids have been threaded into inserts in the ground. They unscrew the lids and pull out two green bucket-sized containers. The containers are similar to earthen time capsule vessels. They open the lids, revealing that each container is full of thousands of tiny white pills.

"Scepter, we have them and the pills are still good," responds Elixor.

"Good," as Scepter reaches into one container and removes two pills. "Start passing these down so everybody gets some. Farsiders, each of you will need two of these little white tablets. One is for tomorrow and the other is for the following day. The air up there at the top of Altai is thin and these will keep you alive. Each person takes two, even children."

Kairn, his brother Arn, Rayelle, Trillo, and Evene sit close together. Farsider Varo sits with his teen daughters Jurn and Plur.

"Rayelle, who do you designate to open the Sea Cover," asks Scepter, his voice echoing for all to hear.

"Sea Cover? You covered your sea," interrupts an astonished Varo.

"Foreman Nord and his daughter Vell" responds Rayelle, who turns to Nord and Vell. "I'm sure you recall the master retainer, with the double joint on the farside of the sea. From here it's quite a walk, so get going."

As Foreman Nord and daughter Vell leave, Scepter changes to the task at hand. "I have overheard talk that what we are about to undertake

30

is suicide, that we no longer have enough people to accomplish this, but while you Farsiders number *less* than those we lost, you are also *bigger* than each of us, so maybe there is a chance. Are you ready to help us?"

"We Farsiders are ready," replies Varo. "But what are we about to do?"

"That which is difficult. It takes the might and will of us all, and success is not guaranteed." Hearing this, Kairn and Rayelle worryingly make eye contact as Scepter continues, "Now, who is next on the ledger?"

Kairn, Rayelle, Evene, Trillo, and Kairn's brother Arn all stand and approach Scepter.

"Our future is in your hands. Are each of you prepared for the sacrifice?"

"We are, Scepter" all five answer.

With that, all 300,000 Nearsiders disperse to take up positions along- and just behind- the V-shaped Great Elastic. They know the routine. The 60,000 Farsiders have no idea what this formality is about and Scepter addresses them.

"Farsiders, this is where we need your help. It takes all who are able to make this work."

As all Farsiders fan out to take up positions among the Nearsiders, Scepter pounds his Comstaff and counts down to all through his speaker, "And three, two, one, hoist!" All Nearsiders lift the lengthy green snake and place it over their shoulders for leverage. Seeing this, the Farsiders also join in.

"Left end to the curled hills on the left base of Altai, right end to the right curled hills," as Scepter issues one final command. "All of those in the middle, up to the summit with us."

"What are we about to do," asks a perplexed and confused Varo.

"If this succeeds, Kairn's family are about to join our two other teams on Tareon."

"You have people on Tareon," shouts Varo. "How do you get them there?" Other Farsiders listening are just as astonished.

Turning to face the great mountain before them, "Walk this way," responds Scepter.

Scepter then shouts one final command through his Comstaff speaker horn, "All together, march!"

And thus begins a massive crusade of all 360,000 remaining up the great peak. It's a united brigade of every Zeon left alive on the planet, and with the Farside dictatorship now dead and gone, this is the first endeavor of unison for both sides in centuries.

In its normal state, the Elastic looks long, but not nearly long enough to span Altai from base to base, but as they march and fan out – with its properties renewed overnight - it seems to forever lengthen as those walking near the ends get further and further apart. Those chosen to launch do not normally carry the Elastic, but since they are missing personnel, Kairn and his family, Scepter and Norl, and even Chronicle join in. This is the importance of the Great Elastic. If any Zeons are to live on, it will be because of this cord and this great mountain. It is their only chance for survival.

Kairn, his brother Arn, Rayelle, Trillo, and Evene walk near each other, doing their part to support the lengthy green snake. Their remaining closeness is important because they will each launch separately, and it is an act so violent that each must be unconscious for the launch. To be awake would be certain death.

"I wish mom and dad had lived to see this; to see us off," Arn admits to Kairn as they walk.

"I don't."

"And why not?"

"Because this will be so dangerous. We will be lucky if we all safely make it."

"I wish I wasn't a silver eye, so I could stay here longer," admits a hesitant Evene to her mother Rayelle.

"Sometimes our rareness can be a curse, but it might be useful when we get to Tareon," as Rayelle realizes they must remain focused on the goal. "And anyway, with what we've just lived through, do you want to be here when our worlds collide?"

"No."

"That's the right thinking," responds Rayelle, but inside, both she and Kairn know the odds of all launching safely are *not* in their favor.

As they walk, Elixor's aides – including Garl and Hark - carry six straight, tall, Launch Sticks. The sticks are a form of the green ooze that has been dried and hardened at Elixor's seaside foundry. They are essentially extra long Comstaffs with added parts. Each stick has a T-bar across the top. Below the T-bar is a mostly-retracted metallic parasol, and under the parasol is a protective metal cone. Below the upper cones are two pairs of rungs; one to hold on to, and another to stand on. Below the lower rungs are another cone and parasol, which are both fully retracted and pointing down. At the bottom, each stick is tapered to a sharp spike.

Elixor – wearing green gloves - carries two small sealed green boxes, and has a green filter mask hanging loosely around his throat. One box emits a small amount of ominous steam.

As they walk, Kairn and Rayelle notice Evene and Trillo are starting to sob. Evene is old enough to remember that some chosen to launch have not lived through this ritual. The only solace in Kairn's mind is that those who don't live through it are unconscious when death occurs.

Continuing the trek, Scepter addresses Varo, who helps carry the Elastic as Varo's daughters Jurn and Plur walk alongside.

"It's a shame that our peoples are only getting to know each other in this final half-year. We've lost much during the centuries of your dictators' rule. Did your mate die in the pass-by?"

"My wife's father was accused of conspiring with others to overthrow Dorn. She and all in her family were rounded up and taken away. We never saw them, again. I try not to dwell on it because it enrages me, so."

Varo can't get his mind off the enormity of the task at hand. "I still can't believe that you can do this; that you can send people to Tareon."

"The benefits of having Altai on our side of the planet, but there are no guarantees," responds Scepter. "We favor mostly women and girls as the best chance for a future on Tareon, and Silver Eyes are preferred in case they find any Tareons. We also try to keep family members together, but we can only accomplish this while Tareon is still close, which is why we need your help and must act quickly."

"How many died creating this Elastic and your Sea Cover?"

"No one. Why do you ask?"

"My leaders would work people until they died, and replace them with others."

"That's because your Dorn dynasty has been heavy-handed with its treatment of others, starting with the smaller tribes overtaken on your side of the planet. On our side we involve all in major decisions. Everyone has a part."

"Hey, how do you know so much about my side of the planet," asks an intrigued Varo.

"Elixor and his aides are adept at making simple electrical items, and we've hidden lenses on your side overlooking your villages. They've enabled us to see what your side has been up to."

"I have heard tales of such electrical stuff, but our leaders deemed it heresy and would banish anyone creating anything new."

"Your leaders spent so much time controlling others and fearing advancement that they ended up being far behind us. Elixor and his aids are constantly coming up with new tools to make our lives easier, and we work that green ooze that comes up from beneath the oceans into all shapes and forms."

By early evening, Zeons on the right end have reached the small curled peaks on Altai's right base. The peaks are curled away from Altai. Tattered older Elastics are still wrapped around the curled peaks and extend up toward Altai's summit. Those carrying the elastic wrap the right end around one of the curled peaks and then knot it just behind and above the peak. With that complete, all on the right flank then work up toward the Elastic's center to help others scaling the mountain's upper reaches. At Altai's opposite left base, the same procedure is repeated. With tattered old Elastics nearby, the left end is wrapped and tied off around one of the smaller curled peaks and all at that end move up and toward the center, assisting others up the great peak.

The summit of Altai is still free of snow as the warm, dry winds of the receding Tareon are still diminishing. Altai is a long-dormant volcano. At the top, a long, straight cavern about 50-feet wide extends down twelve miles deep into the bowels of Zeon. At the bottom, the cavern widens out into a larger chamber. The chamber bottom is covered with the finest sand on Zeon. About half way up the vertical cavern, small holes in the walls once must've emitted dark smoke, which blackened the walls up to the summit, but Zeons have never witnessed such smoke.

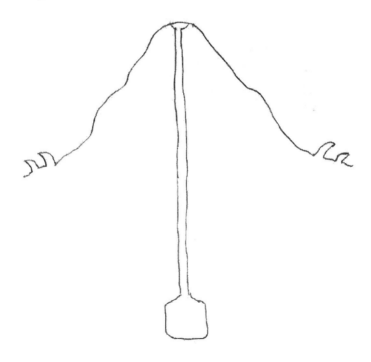

When all have reached the summit at twilight, some are already in the volcano hole, hanging on to the old tattered Elastic vines that stretch down into it. Two tattered old Elastics are routed through hard green pulleys anchored to the top of the volcano wall, and routed back down. Elixor's aides hand the six parasol sticks to those hanging, to send down.

Once the Launch Sticks reach the bottom, others then pull on the old tattered Elastics turning downward into the abyss. They keep pulling and pulling until a large thin cut of great timber emerges, supported by the tattered Elastics under it. They stop pulling when the circular wooden slab is nearly even with the volcano rim.

The great peak's summit is now the center of their universe as all 360,000 populate its crown and upper ridges.

"We will all sleep up here tonight and awake early in the morning," Scepter announces over his Comstaff speaker.

It's a beautiful panorama from up here. All of the smaller curled peaks are in view, as is the distant green-covered sea on the horizon. Though totally treeless, Zeon is still an Eden.

Miles away at the sea's edge, Foreman Nord and his daughter Vell have reached the shore. The Sea Cover is a bit baggy from being stretched, but is still intact. They bed down for the night, as they still have some distance to trek in the morning to reach the master retainer on the far side of their sea.

Almost unnoticeable is a subtle slope to the green retainers along the shore. The master retainer is at the highest point, on the far side of the sea. It's painted purple and is connected to the retainers on either side of it. Not unlike a chain of dominos, cut the master retainer, and all other retainers will begin to release their hold on the Sea Cover.

Two hours before sunup the next morning, all 360,000 atop Altai are awake and active with anticipation. Kairn takes one last sighting of the departing Tareon and calls out Brill, his most trusted stellar sighter.

"Brill, you've seen me do this, but because I'll be down at the bottom, the helm is yours. Are you up to the task?

"I am, sir."

"Very well. You know the timing. Today, the launch windows will be three minutes after sunrise and every 15 minutes thereafter," as Kairn gives his Sighting Scope to Brill.

"Kairn, thank you for teaching me all that you know. I'll miss you. When you get to Tareon, stay alert, stay smart, and forward with brilliance," as Brill's eyes puddle up while taking Kairn's Sighting Scope.

"Forward with brilliance," responds Kairn, which is difficult to admit knowing that Zeon has no future.

As the large throng huddles atop the summit, the following now step onto the circular board supported by old Elastics: Scepter, Norl, Elixor, Chronicle, Garl, Hark, Kairn's family and brother, and at Scepter's invitation, Varo and his two daughters. Elixor still carries his two sealed boxes. Scepter has one last message for the huge throng gathered at the summit, through his Comstaff speaker.

"Now remember, at the sound of each horn, all must be quiet and ready. And at the third light, all must react together. The timing and alignment must both be perfect."

"To my fellow Farsiders," as Varo follows up over Scepter's speaker, "These Nearsiders know what to do, so follow their lead." And if there is nothing else, when ready, lower away," concludes Scepter.

And with that, the flat tree slab disc they stand upon is lowered into the hole. The volcano throat is straight, but there are jagged edges along the way, and the huge slab lightly scrubs the walls on the way down.

It takes awhile, but when the board reaches the distant bottom, all on it step off and the board is left on the floor of the lower chamber.

At the top, the new Elastic is laid out over the volcano opening. Stretched from one end of the great peak to another, it now *looks* tight, but in reality is nowhere near its limit.

On one side of volcano summit hole, Farsider Chorn stands next to the Elastic while thousands of others gather behind him. He looks across to the other side, where thousands of others flank Nearsider Urik, who also stands next to the Elastic. "What do we do now," asks Chorn, looking across the chasm toward Urik.

"Do as I do," responds Urik from the opposite side.

Urik then crawls out onto the green band spanning over the deep hole. Chorn does the same, and as they meet in the center, their increasing weight causes the taffy-like band to sink and stretch further down into the hole. As the others following crawl out onto the Elastic and over Chorn and Urik, deeper and deeper it stretches. The Elastic creaks and groans during this stretching and down at the curled peaks on which it is anchored, is now very taut. From high above the mountaintop the Zeons appear as thousands of tiny ants, an army in unison and purpose. As most of the Zeons crawl down onto the lengthy belt, it strains and creaks even more. When the weights of all 360,000 are on it, the bottom of the Elastic hangs down to within 40-feet of the lower chamber floor. From a putrid green ooze to an incredibly expanding cord – when elongated over the great peak and down into its deep throat - this tightly stretched rubber miracle is now 42 miles long.

It's a busy vertical tunnel as everyone has a position to go to, and Nearsiders instruct Farsiders on where to hang and what to do. Because of their dictatorship, Farsiders have long hoped for a chance to better and advance themselves, and these lucky 60,000 who are left are enamored with- and fully committed to- helping the Nearsiders in this great endeavor.

Next, a sharp stone is used to cut a lengthwise slit into the Elastic at its lowest point where it hangs above the cave floor, and the ends of the slit are quickly sown together to prevent the slit from spreading up the Elastic. The slit is long enough for a Launch Stick semi-retracted parasol to fit through. And finally, one of the tall sticks with parasols is sent up from the floor, inserted up through the slit and turned 90 degrees, locking the T-bar in place so the entire stick hangs from the Elastic. It's a 42-mile long . . . sling shot.

"The Launch Stick is hanging much higher up, this time," Elixor notices, gazing up from the chamber floor.

"We're missing the weight of those who we've lost," responds Scepter.

"These sticks are very specialized," Varo tells Scepter, looking closely at the Launch Sticks.

"They've evolved many times."

"Oh? How so?"

"We have eight people on Tareon."

"Very impressive."

"But to get those eight safely there, twenty others have died."

"My condolences on those you have lost," as Varo realizes that what they are about to attempt is very difficult and fraught with danger.

"Most of our failures were before we got it right. Since then, our success rate in the last two years has been better," responds Scepter.

Eleven miles above the floor and one mile below the summit, Nearsider Urik is the top-most Zeon hanging on his side of the cavern. Across from Urik is Farsider Chorn, who asks "Why are we the top-most Zeons? How come there are no others above us?"

"That's because we're a few thousand people short, which is why we need your peoples' help."

"You mean you don't know if this will work?"

"We never do."

At the bottom, Scepter stabs his Comstaff and calls up to the surface, where sighter Brill has his Comstaff stabbed in the crest dirt.

"Brill, how much time until the first launch window?"

"Fifteen minutes sir," responds Brill, peering toward the horizon where the sun will soon be rising as two other sighters assist him.

"Very well," replies Scepter's voice. "Arn, you are first up," as Scepter turns his attention to those in the lower chamber with him.

Kairn's brother Arn is zipped into a translucent green suit and fitted with a backpack with a clear green tube coming out of the top, which leads to a mouthpiece with a large, pascifier-sized version of the same white pills they took before summiting the mountain. The tube carries small amounts of nutritious slurry, and the tablet is Elixor's greatest invention, a long-lasting lozenge of condensed oxygen. Whereas the small pills they consumed provide one day's worth of air, this large lozenge supplies enough oxygen for weeks. The mouthpiece dangles around Arn's neck, and gloves, a hard green helmet with a reflective green visor, and green goggles are fitted.

Arn climbs up the tattered old Elastic vines and is assisted onto the stick. For a people without trees, Zeons sure climb vines well. He stands on the lower rungs and holds onto the upper ones, positioned under the upper parasol and metal cone just under it. A green Elastic band is tied around his waist, holding him tightly to the stick. His weight causes the stick to sag down to within 25-feet above the cavern floor.

Up at the surface, Brill lays face-down on a hardened green frame which has been laid across the volcano mouth. He is looking down through a green glass monocle, setting the Elastic alignment. Two other Stellar Sighters assist Brill. All others are now in the mountain. Throughout the deep vertical shaft, Nearsiders explain to Farsiders that when alignment is set, no one can move or say anything until jumping off, and all must be totally still. Correct alignment is the most difficult part of the launch. They also explain that when the bright light at the top goes out for the third time, all must jump off onto the tattered old Elastic vines hanging nearby.

At Brill's guidance looking down through the monocle, those at the bottom of the Elastic make small movements east and west. When east-west alignment is set, Brill's Comstaff horn emits a loud "brap" which echoes down the cavern. The same small adjustments are then made for north-south alignment. When north-south alignment is good, a second horn blares. The third horn means all alignments are set. Horns are okay for setting alignment, but for the final launch, light is used because sound travels down the cavern too slowly, and all must jump off the Elastic in unison. Brill steps off of the frame and it is removed, and a green-tinted mirror on a long green stick is extended out over the opening at an angle that will reflect the bright morning sunlight down into the mountain's shaft. As the sun rises, the entire vertical shaft brightens up when sunlight is reflected down into it.

At the bottom, Kairn has climbed up the Launch Stick and faces his borther Arn. "Rayelle will join you on the next launch, the kids will be on the following one, and I'll be on the last launch. We are doing this for mom and dad and for all of those here who won't make it." He concludes with the traditional parting words for anyone about to embark on a difficult endeavor. "Stay alert, stay smart, and forward with brilliance."

"Forward with brilliance," replies Arn with big eyes from within his helmet.

Hearing those words from the floor, "When did your people develop those words of send-off," Varo asks Scepter.

"We came up with *stay alert, stay smart and forward with brilliance* to remind anyone undertaking the unknown to be open, bright, and absorb all possible knowledge for as long as possible."

40

Kairn gets down and the now-goggled and gloved Elixor climbs up to the pointed bottom of the parasol stick. He opens the unsteaming box and embeds the Launch Stick point into the tar resin inside. Tar resin is the strongest poison on Zeon, and may help protect Arn on Tareon.

Next, wearing his green mask, Elixor grabs the steaming box and climbs up to face Arn on the Stick. He briefly opens the lid and Arn gets a whiff of steaming noxious hagweed root, which gently lowers Arn's head and renders him unconscious. Elixor gets down and aides tie Arn's head and hands to the Stick, insert his mouthpiece, lower and shut his visor, and check the protective metal cone just above Arn's head. Just then, a call from Brill's Comstaff echoes down the shaft.

"Thirty seconds to first light."

With that, some Nearsiders hanging along the vertical Elastic quietly emphasize the importance of being perfectly still during the three light sequence. At the bottom, those in the lower chamber back away toward the walls, not wanting to be near the tightly-stretched Elastic. All of Zeon is now quiet and hanging in rapt attention. Their future is now.

Eleven miles up the cavern wall, Farsider Chorn feels the urge to sneeze, but does his best to quell it. His allergies to Nearsiders have *not* subsided.

Heightening the tension, Brill's call is again heard echoing down the cavern, and over Scepter's Comstaff. "Fifteen seconds."

All hanging quietly look up toward the mountaintop. The reason for the three light sequence is so all below can get used to the timing. At the top, Brill briefly twists the stick-and-mirror 90 degrees and just as quickly, turns it back, which briefly allows the morning sunlight to deflect down the mountain shaft.

First light, then out. One mile below, Farsider Chorn still fights against the urge to sneeze.

The quiet tension builds as the mirror's second light comes on and goes out. So far, so good.

The final light comes on and just before it goes out, Farsider Chorn can't hold back and sneezes profusely. The light goes out and all including Chorn jump from the new Elastic onto the tattered old vines beside it. As all jump off the Elastic, a pent up wave of energy makes its way quickly down the long green snake. The Elastic strains and whips until the wave of release reaches the bottom and the stick and unconscious Arn are thrown violently upward. In an instant too quick to notice, Arn suddenly disappears from the bottom chamber. It's a jerk so sudden that no conscious- or untied- being could live through it, and loose sand from the cave floor follows him upward.

At the surface, the mirror stick has quickly been moved aside. The cavern is so deep that the coil and Launch Stick take many seconds to reach the top, T-bar and Arn accelerating all the way, but two-thirds of the way up, the alignment is off and the parasol and Arn's head glance off a hard point along the cave wall. It's just a scrape, but at this velocity, his neck is snapped instantly and he's dead before exiting the mountain. The releasing Elastic billows twelve miles skyward but instead of launching a clean projectile, parasol and Arn tumble lifelessly down range.

In the bottom chamber, pebbles from the side impact rain down. Looking up, all know what this means and Kairn turns and immediately vomits. He knows any brush with the wall is unsurviveable and that he's just lost his only brother. Chronicle steps in toward the center too soon and is struck by one of the larger falling stones, knocking him to the ground. As Norl steps over to console Kairn, she then realizes that Chronicle is in worse shape and tends to him. Rayelle is also sickened by Arn's death, but has the presence to cover up the kids. Her fur and Kairn's fur is now white from nervousness as both they and their kids are overcome with fear, and all at the bottom recoil with dread.

Hanging eleven miles up the cavern wall, "It was all my fault. I wasn't steady enough. I'm not made for this," admits a sobbing Farsider Chorn.

Hanging across from him, Nearsider Urik notices that growing out of the cave wall next to Chorn is a clump of cave moss. "See that clump of cave moss? Grab it and shove in in your mouth."

Feeling guilty and stuffing the clump in his mouth like too much chewing tobacco, Chorn downtroddingly complies.

"There. That'll help you. Keep chewing on it and you'll be fine."

At the bottom, "What happened up there" asks Scepter over his Comstaff speaker.

Hanging eleven miles up, Urik tells everyone to quiet down and shouts down, "We had a sneeze. It's been fixed. It won't happen again."

At the top, Brill asks over his Comstaff, "Was it something I did?"

"Alignment was good," Urik yells up. "We need to be more still."

At the bottom, Rayelle hands the kids over to Kairn and approaches Scepter. "I don't want to go."

"Understandable, but it's either a sure death here on Zeon or a chance at new life on Tareon."

"If we are all to die, I want to die, trying," as she turns toward Kairn and tries to brush away the tears. Kairn hugs her and - with a helpless gaze - lifts his hand, forming their half-circle salute. She matches his salute and those of the kids, wipes away tears, and the good soldier in her takes over as the Elastic has again been brought down close to the floor. As another Launch Stick is hung from the Elastic, she steps into a suit and dons a backpack, climbs up the old vines and onto the stick rungs, and is fitted with a helmet and gloves. The Elastic and stick again sag to within 25-feet of the floor.

"But mom, don't go," shout Evene and Trillo, as they are being zipped into suits on the floor below.

"You know the plan," as Rayelle responds while looking down from the hanging Launch Stick. "You two will launch next and join me after one orbit, and one revolution later, dad will join us."

At the surface, Brill's two assistants have again laid the measuring frame over the hole and turn to Brill, but their attention is distracted by something over Brill's shoulder low and bright in the sky, just above the distant horizon. It is still small, but it's bigger than any distant planet or star, and appears to be coming their way. Brill turns and his knees almost buckle at the sight. Eons ago, Zeons walked on all fours and when humbled enough, they sometimes settle to steady themselves. He taps is Comstaff four times, which is for rare emergencies only.

"Scepter!" His panicked voice is heard by all in the lower chamber.

"What is it, Brill."

"Scolios, it's coming back!"

Stunned, all at the bottom stare at each other. Rayelle too, standing on the rungs of the hanging Launch Stick. After the pass-by, Tareon's moon Scolios swooped out wide of both planets and has swung back around, coming straight in at a low angle.

"How many more launches can we get off," Scepter asks into his Comstaff.

"If we hurry, I'm guessing three," responds Brill from the summit, squinting toward the approaching bright light with a puffy white contrail behind it.

Hearing that estimate down below, Evene crawls up the stick and also stands on the lower rungs, facing her mother, which sags the hanging stick to within 20-feet of the floor. As Evene is fitted with gloves and a helmet, mother and daughters' waists are tied to the stick by a figure-eight half-knot. "Are we too much weight," asks Rayelle down to Elixor and Scepter on the floor.

Before Elixor or Scepter can answer, "Alor, Torq, get down here," as Varo calls up to two other burly Farsiders just a few yards up the Elastic. Varo then turns to Scepter and emphatically declares, "We will pull even further."

"But Evene, I thought you were supposed to launch with me," asks Trillo from the floor.

"If this works and mom and I launch okay, you and Dad can go together on the next launch," responds Evene.

"Brill, what's Scolios's incoming course," as Scepter calls up to the surface.

"It's coming in from kind of low. It's either a direct impact or will sail just across the mountain.

"Good thing the sea is still covered," mutters Scepter. "Oh no, the Sea Cover!" He first looks at Chronicle and his two silver eyes, but realizes the woozy old Silver Eye is not yet alert enough to achieve a mental link, and then looks up to Rayelle, hanging from the Launch Stick. "Rayelle, can you get in touch with Foreman Nord? He's at the Sea Cover!" With their waists now tied together on the stick, Evene knows that separation is needed to link with another and asks, "Mom, are we too close together?"

"Empty your mind and I'll try to achieve a link," replies Rayelle.

Evene's eyes then quickly glaze over and her head dips in a look of total emptiness. With Evene unable to help with a link of her own, down on the floor, Kairn turns quickly to his son, Trillo.

"Son, you know Vell, Foreman Nord's daughter? Can you get in touch with her?"

"Where is she?"

"She's at the sea."

Trillo's eyes now close into a trance-like state, as are Rayelle's. Hanging from the Launch Stick, Rayelle blurts out in Foreman Nord's voice "Vell, hand me the sharpened stone."

Everybody in the lower chamber gasps and realizes that at the far off sea, Nord is about to cut the master retainer and start the chain reaction releasing the Sea Cover.

"Here it is," responds Trillo in Vell's female voice.

Scepter quickly grabs Elixor's box of steaming hagweed root and climbs up to join Rayelle and Evene. While keeping his nose away, he opens the lid and gives them a whiff. Rayelle then falls limp, as does Evene, and Scepter drops the box down to Elixor and points at Trillo. Elixor does the same to Trillo, who faints and is caught by Kairn.

Miles away at the far off Sea Cover, Nord – bending over to cut the master retainer with the sharpened stone - falls unconscious to one side of the retainer, sensing the sedating hagweed aroma that Rayelle inhaled, and Vell falls over next to him, sensing the aroma that Trillo smelled.

Back in the lower chamber, Scepter gets down and Norl commends him on his quick thinking, while Kairn hands Trillo to Varo and climbs up for one final word with his now unconscious wife and daughter as others secure their hands to the stick.

"I love you both, and Trillo and I will join you on the next launch. Stay alert, stay smart, and forward with brilliance." He gets down and their helmets are tied to the stick, mouthpieces are inserted, and the protective metal cone above their heads is checked.

Handing the unconscious Trillo back to Kairn, Varo then climbs up and grabs the lower end of the Launch Stick, a foot or two above the sharp point. "Don't touch the tip or it'll kill you," sternly warns Elixor.

"Alor, Torq, grab my legs and pull down," as Varo calls down to his burly Farsiders.

They climb up and with all three Farsiders hanging from the Launch Stick, the straining Elastic is pulled down to within 12-feet of the floor; maximum pull for a maximum launch.

The thousands hanging along the Elastic quiet down as Brill's horn echoes down from above, signaling first alignment is set. Kairn hugs his unconscious son as the sleeping mother-and-daughter hang ready to launch, and Kairn's fir is still white from fear. They just lost Arn. Will Rayelle and Evene die, also?

The second horn blares and all in the lower chamber back away from the Elastic except for the three burly Farsiders pulling it down.

The third horn blares. Eleven miles up along the cavern wall, Nearsider Urik quietly peers across at allergic Farsider Chorn, who has a clump of cave moss in his mouth and gently nods "okay."

At the top, the stick-and-mirror is placed above the opening. All wait quietly to hear the last call from above. "Fifteen seconds."

"Brill, screw the launch window! Throw the damned lights," roars an impatient Kairn toward Scepter's Comstaff in the lower chamber.

Along the entire twelve mile deep cavern, all heads quietly rotate upward. The mirror is briefly turned and first light quickly illuminates the entire vertical tunnel, before going out.

The entire planet's focus is now together as one. Second light comes and quickly goes out; a world silently at attention.

Finally, the third light comes on and then goes out. Although all jump off in unison, it is really a quick release that takes about ten seconds to reach down to the distant floor. As they jump off onto the nearby tattered old vines, a wave of torque shoots down the Elastic to the floor, quickly building in pent-up strength. The Farsiders at the bottom hold on as long as possible, but the Parasol Stick is instantly ripped from Varo's hands and he and the two holding his legs are briefly pulled up and then fall back down to the cave floor disc. This sudden jerk would normally break the rider's neck, but the rope keeps Rayelle's- and Evene's- unconscious heads tied firmly to the Launch Stick.

All hanging 360,000 remain tight against the walls as the belt suddenly snaps and throngs upward, a rapid vibratory hum and burst of coiled up material whizzing by just inches away, followed by a rush of air behind it. The sidewalls are an accelerating blur as the covered- and sleeping- mother-and-daughter are whisked ever-faster, upward. Their speed keeps increasing until the living missile exits the mountain amid the double sonic boom of the sound barrier being broken. The lengthy green Elastic throngs upward every bit of the twelve miles it was stretched underground and before it slows, the stick and parasol are ejected cleanly through the cut slit like an arrow from a bow.

As the Elastic continues to extend upward and then drops away to the side, all below look skyward, following the small missile. It's not a rocket, so there's no blast of jet fuel; just an arrow with two heartbeats and hope. Using their legs to hold themselves to the old vines, all up and down the cavern break into a short, silent version of the *"departed salute,"* a gentle spiral of arms from down low, upward, which is also used at funerals. Seeing this but formerly forbidden from doing it, the Farsiders hanging also join in.

Onboard the stick, the shiny metal parasol glows red/orange from atmospheric friction as it heats up while speeding upward through Zeon's atmosphere, and the secondary metal cone over their heads also warms at the edges. Rayelle - being heavier - causes a gentle rotation to her being on the lower side, and stick and passengers arc slowly westward. It's a clean launch as both mother and daughter are still unconscious, but on the planet below, there is no time to celebrate.

Those at the surface – as they retrieve the Elastic and send it down the hole - take a quick look at the approaching Scolios as Scepter's voice echoes from below.

"Brill, is there still time for two more launches?"

"No Scepter, only *one*," responds Brill in a dejected tone.

Hearing that down below, Kairn steps forward, still carrying the sleeping Trillo, and helmets are fitted. Scepter looks around the chamber and quickly weighs the situation. Only one good launch left. With Rayelle and Evene gone, Kairn and Trillo *should* be next, but is there a more important option? As the shrill incoming whistle of the approaching Scolios builds above in pitch, looking nervous and wiping sweat from his face, Scepter quickly scans all in the cave chamber and steps toward Kairn and motions Chronicle, Elixor, and Farsider Varo over.

"This is making me sick, but I'm making a decision, and the next launch should be *them*," pointing to Varo's daughters Jurn and Plur.

Jurn and Plur gasp! "What? No," shouts a disbelieving Kairn as Varo asks, "My girls? Scepter, what good is that?"

"If the two just launched make it, that makes ten sent to Tareon, all from our tribe. At the core we are the same, but none of your Farsider people have gone," as tears start streaming from Kairn's eyes. "We may get one more launch after this, but if this is to be the last one, it should be them. There, they will have a chance, a future. Ours is certain death," as Kairn's face is covered with raining tears.

"I don't like your thinking, but I agree," admits Varo with a shrug and a sigh.

Suits and backpacks are quickly fitted over the cowering Jurn and Plur, and Alor and Torq hoist the girls up to the next Launch Stick which has just been hung on the retrieved Elastic. Aides force helmets and gloves onto the girls and tie the girls to the stick. The aides crawl down and Elixor is about to climb up the stick to drug the girls.

"Wait" interrupts Varo, who climbs up with final words with his daughters. "Never forget your mother and I, but you have a chance at a future, and I don't. I love you my inspirations and forward with brilliance." He gets down and Elixor climbs up and gives the squirming girls a brief whiff of steaming hagweed root, which quickly puts them under. Mouthpieces are inserted, their helmets are closed, and the protective metal cone is checked. Poison is applied to the stick lower tip.

Kairn is now a useless wreck and cowering with his unconscious son, distraught at what they thought would be a flight together to the new world. Scepter's wife Norl tries to comfort them as Brill calls down from above.

"Scolios is closing fast," echoes Brill's voice over the Comstaff. Hearing this only makes things worse for Kairn and Trillo, for it is nails in their coffin.

Varo again grabs the lower end of the stick and Alor and Torq grab his legs.

At the surface, Brill is already lying on the alignment frame and blows the first horn. Just then, a strange, warm gust blows across the mountain top, the front bow of Scolios's approaching wave. As the strange incoming whistle they heard while hiding in the caves slowly builds overhead, all focus on getting things done quickly, and the second horn sounds from above. Holding his sleeping son, the teary eyed Kairn finally looks up, hoping somehow for one additional launch.

At the top, the third horn sounds, the alignment frame is removed, and the mirror set in place.

From the surface – bypassing the usual fifteen second warning – Brill skips forward to, "Five seconds."

All hanging look upward and a world is again still. First light, then out.

Hanging most of the way up, Chorn – chewing on his cave moss - feels better about what to do. No problems now.

Second light, then out.

Varo holds his daughters' future in his hands.

Third light, then out.

All jump off and the wave of wound up stress moves quickly down the lengthy snake and builds until the Launch Stick briefly lifts Varo, Alor and Torq, who drop back down to the chamber floor. Jurn and Plur disappear instantly from the lower chamber, accelerate quickly up the long chute, and exit the mountain to a thunderous sonic boom, with the incoming fireball of Scolios looming larger in the background. All are distracted watching the departing girls, forgetting for a moment about the approaching enemy.

Scolios is not a large moon, but Zeon is not a large planet, and Zeons' pull is bringing Scolios in, fast. All atop the mountain quickly gather the Elastic and again send it down.

At the bottom, Varo and Kairn are arguing about who should go next, each now wearing a suit and helmet, but they are too heavy to launch together. Their argument is quickly settled by four chimes from Brill's Comstaff, who yells over his loudspeaker, "Everybody into the hole!"

With the growing shrill whistle overhead sounding as if the incoming Scolios is about to hit, Brill and those near the surface leap down into the volcano throat. Those below see what's happening above and also leap down. A huge meteor, shadow and roar fly across the mountaintop, followed by the loudest ever concussive booms, which don't subside. The booms resonate down the vertical shaft like echoing thunder. Those at the bottom hear the commotion from above and back away toward the lower chamber walls.

Those falling look like flying squirrels gliding down into the deep hole, but as the wake of Scolios passes closely overhead, the suction behind it pulls many falling downward, back up the volcano shaft and out, frying them to a crisp in the friction of the superheated air. It continues as thousands sailing downward are lifted up and sucked out as the ultra-low pressure wake from Scolios stretches for hundreds of miles behind it. The suction is so strong that Zeons eleven miles down the twelve mile shaft are being sucked out. If it were an active volcano, it would be lava, not the living being coughed up and incinerated. Since Brill, Urik and Chorn were farther up, they are among the thousands never seen again, along with the Sighting Scope that Kairn gave Brill.

At the bottom of the shaft, bodies pile up and the roar from wind sucking up floor sand has turned the chamber into a swirling vertical wind-tunnel. Kairn struggles to hold on to Trillo, as does Scepter with his wife Norl.

At the top of the body pile in the swirling wind, Drago's wife Hep struggles to hold onto her daughter Ogard, who is light and in danger of being sucked upward. She frantically reaches up, clutching the upside-down Ogard's arms as her feet and legs are being sucked upward.

"Mom, mom! Don't let me go!"

Amid the windstorm - as others below her struggle to hold Hep's legs to the top of the pile - there is a horrible "snap" as one of her arms breaks, but a burly Farsider next to her quickly grabs Ogard and pulls her downward to the top of the pile where others grab her and Hep. No one is holding the Farsider's legs and he rises upward, never to be seen again; one last gallant act from an enemy before vanishing into the superheated heavens.

A Nearsider with only one eye remaining since the Tareon pass-by, has his lone eye sucked out and up toward the superheated sky. Now completely sightless, his darkness is only momentary, as he too is pulled upward, never to be seen again, and some couples - partners in life - make their last grasps to hold on to each other, rising upward and quickly becoming partners in death.

The wind tunnel and roar continues for a few more minutes as those atop the mostly-dead pile struggle to hold onto each other with eyes closed, because of the swirling, blowing sand.

Eventually, just as the wind and roar starts to lessen, the loudest ever explosion occurs. It's not a quake, it comes from the sky, but it's powerful enough to echo loudly down the cavern.

Finally, the roar subsides and the floating dust slowly settles. A steep, cone-shaped pile of bodies now covers the cave floor. Those at the bottom seeking cover against the lower chamber wall, step in toward the center and look upward. Some in the pile are still alive, but there are not nearly enough to account for those who lined the cavern walls. Thousands are gone, sucked out by Scolios's wake, and most in the pile at the bottom are dead. Thankfully, their weight has kept the Elastics – both old and new - in place, hanging down to the bottom of the chamber.

The dead from the pile are rolled off to the side, off of the round timber board covering a portion of the floor. Varo, Alor, Torq, and three other Farsiders start pulling on the vines routed through the upper pulleys, to hoist some injured up to the surface on the circular wooden slab.

"We'll be back down for the rest of you."

It takes all day and a couple of trips, but there aren't many alive to bring up to the surface. They reach the surface to the following sight: Scolios – leaving a wide, low, puffy white contrail across the sky, passed over just above the mountaintop and - pulled between Zeon's and Tareon's forces - split into two large chunks; one continuing straight out at a low altitude, and the other arcing upward. The loud explosion must've been its severing. On the ground, a wide burned path follows the direction of the low, straight chunk. The dark burned path stretches across Altai, down the slopes and across the valley, and leaves a blackened strip that extends out across the sea to the horizon. In the distance, the Sea Cover has a wide burned skid mark along it and is baggier than ever, but is still in place.

Temporarily deafened and dirty and weak, those at the summit again take a toll of their hell. Their numbers are humbling. From an initial population of over two million Zeons, only seventy are left alive.

CHAPTER 3

Missiles of Hope

PEERING DOWN FROM ATOP THE great volcano, the damage sinks in. Scolios's wake has left more than just the burned streak stretching to the horizon. A wide swath of vegetation on either side of it is also gone. The burned, limp Elastic still stretches to the curled peaks at Altai's base, but no one is visible other than the seventy hoisted up from below. All exposed, and over ninety nine percent of those in the volcano shaft, were pulled up into the atmosphere and vaporized.

"We must make it down to the valley and river to have a chance," Scepter states humbly, not needing to use his Comstaff speaker when so few are left alive.

With that, all seventy help each other to rise. Some of the better ones hoist the injured onto their backs, and all begin the trek down the mountain. Not very far down, Farsider Torq notices the Nearside woman he carries is now quiet, and asks "Alor, is this one still okay?"

"No. Dead," answers Alor.

"Scepter, what is the plan for the dead," asks Torq.

"There's nothing we can do. Gently set her down and we must continue," replies Scepter.

As Torq lays the lifeless woman down, two young boys, Stern and Stip, stop and quietly sob over her body. Their fur is laden with dirt and dust.

"Is this your mother," asks Torq.

"Yes," quietly nod each boy.

"And did your father die during the pass-by or in the mountain?"

"He's on Tareon. His name is Othar," they solemnly admit.

Torq senses the need to get these now-parentless boys past this morbid scene, and kneels down to be on their eye level.

"Never forget your mother and father. Always remember them, but we have to make it down to the river, and your parents wouldn't want you to give up, so gather yourselves up and let's continue onward."

A short time later, Drago's wife Hep - nursing her broken arm - asks for relief and Farsider Alor obliges, lifting her up. This continues as other weak ones succumb and occasionally drop dead. The elder Chronicle is in particularly bad shape, limping and leaning heavily on his Comstaff. In all, eleven more die on the trek down the mountain, reducing their total to fifty nine, alive.

It's long after dark when they - with Scepter carrying his Comstaff and wife Norl - reach the valley river. They drink and soak, most lying face up in the therapeutic and rejuvenating waters. Tareon is still large but retreating in the sky, and the two remnants of Scolios are smaller specks. Far off to the north and south, the prominent ice caps retreated, but continue to feed the rivers, because Altai is still bare of snow.

Most are now in the water sleeping, bodies battered and taking in all possible rejuvenation. Their tepid water has never felt or tasted so good, but Varo is still awake and watching the star-filled panorama slowly scrolling across the nighttime sky. "Hey Kairn, look," he whispers, seeing something coming from the northeast.

Kairn and others look up and see two small lights heading briskly southwest, one slightly leading the other. "Could those be our girls," asks Varo, as he wades closer to Kairn.

"Yes, yes! That's what those who launched before, looked like."

"What is it," asks a tired Trillo.

"The front one, that's mom and your sister."

"How do you know the front one is mom?"

"Because she has always been a leader."

All tear up as they watch, confident that their launched ones - however few - have survived Scolios's wrath, but the streaking lights are quick and within forty five seconds, have dashed across the star-filled sky.

High above, halfway around her first orbit, Rayelle has awakened and loosened the knots holding their gloves and heads to the stick. Gloved, mouth-taped and begoggled, she and Evene suck on Elixor's greatest invention, the condensed oxygen lozenge that keeps them breathing. After their first complete orbit, they came upon the rising second Launch Stick arcing into their path, expecting it to be Kairn and

Trillo, but something's not right as both on the Stick are too small and thin to be Kairn. Looking closer – reddish fur is visible through their thin green suits, meaning it can only be Jurn and Plur. In a major sign of good luck, they were all on the backside of Zeon when Scolios streaked by, and were protected from the conflagration.

All four are coming around again now, and Rayelle and Evene are looking down for a third launch, expecting to see Kairn and Trillo coming up to join them, but as Zeon spins below and Altai comes into view, they see the wide burned scar across its summit, leading down the valley and across the sea to the horizon. Rayelle holds out hope but the longer she waits, inside her goggles are tears. Evene sees her mother's reaction and also starts to cry. With their gloves no longer tied to the stick, they hug, protected only by their parasol and cone of hope, and Jurn and Plur also tear up. There's not much for them to do except go along for the ride, but in the silent vacuum of space, eye contact and *do-as-I-do* will have to do.

Rayelle remembers Kairn telling her that with for every additional orbit of Zeon, speed is increased, which makes the journey to the retreating Tareon, quicker. She decides to make one more loop around Zeon. As more luck would have it, the thinning wake of Scolios pulls them and elongates their orbit into an oblong shape, pulling them out farther from Zeon, before closing in again on the far side, to happen twice per orbit. This greatly multiplies their speed.

Far down below in the valley river, all Zeons have gone to sleep except Kairn and Varo, pulses still racing from the two small reflections of light they saw streak by earlier. Both think their loved ones have now set course to chase down Tareon, but suddenly – out of the same northeast sky and this time twice as fast - the same two lights again streak southwest.

"Son! Son," as Kairn nudges the sleeping Trillo awake, realizing the importance of the moment.

"Huh? What is it?"

"You get one last look."

Kairn, Trillo and Varo solemnly wave, rays of hope exceeded by the finality of separation. "Good bye, my loves."

"Live on, my inspirations," adds Varo.

Once the tears of separation subside, Kairn, Trillo and Varo can finally dream about what Tareon might be.

In the morning along the river bank, Scepter asks if they should make the half day trek to the sea or wait another day. After the hurry of hiding in the caves and the rush to launch before Tareon got too far away, there at last seems to be no sense of urgency.

"We can soak in the river for one more day and heal further before pushing on," offers Alor.

"But between digging out the Elastic, scaling Altai and launching and coming back down, we're down to about 70 days left," adds Kairn.

"Which means our days for enjoying our planet one last time are short" interjects Chronicle. "Though old and weak and missing my wife terribly, I vote for moving on."

The others agree and the remaining few of a once-great people work their way down-river. Occasionally, they see scattered burned remains of others, bodies blown far off the summit of Altai by Scolios, and adults try to keep the kids from checking out the smoldering corpses.

Up ahead a short distance later, Kairn sees a charred, blackened tube lying on the ground, bent and still smoldering. He walks up close and peers down at it before realizing, "Hey, that's my Sighting Scope! It blew all of the way down here?" Since hot smoke still wafts away from it, he tosses some dirt over it and grabs it. "It's warped and no longer usable, but I want to hang onto it."

Continuing on and passing some former settlements, the reed huts they had called homes are long gone. What prized possessions anyone had are but a memory. By mid-afternoon, they reach a gently sloped cove at the seas' edge. Spaced very far apart are three giant stumps of the once great timbers, cut so long ago that no one knows why. The Nearsiders have made subsequent smaller cuts for their storm doors and platforms. The center stump is close to the cove shore.

"We use these great timber stumps for assemblies and ceremonies," Scepter tells Farsider Varo. "Do you have these great timber stumps on your side of the planet?"

"We do. Our leadership used them for a different kind of ceremony; executions – for all to see."

Just beyond the center stump is the sea's edge. The six remaining Farsiders are amazed by the translucent green Sea Cover. Their leadership would've feared building such an endeavor. It's now very baggy from having been stretched *twice*, and the wide burn streak of Scolios's straight track smears it like a darkened runway, but it has done its job.

As they approach the shore, Scepter calls out "Trillo, I believe you helped out on the Sea Cover. Would you kindly lead our friendly Farsiders to the master retainer on the other side?"

"Yes Scepter."

"Can I go too," asks Kairn.

"Uh, can Kairn and Varo remain, and the others go," interrupts Chronicle before Kairn can answer. "I have something to discuss."

Scepter agrees, and Trillo and Farsiders Alor, Torq, Zoy and her teenage son Dwell go along, as do two other teen couples and kids Ogard, Stern and Stip. Stern and Stip are now parentless since their father Othar is on Tareon and their mother died coming down from Altai. Dwell asks if Nearside girl Jin can come along. Since Jin's parents are dead, all agree, and following Trillo, they set off around the sea toward the master retainer. Dwell and Jin have taken to liking each other. Trillo, Ogard, Stern, and Stip are the youngest remaining of the fifty nine left. As they set off, this means there are only adults in the encampment, no kids.

Kairn and Varo – who didn't know each other the week before - are also bonding over their shared sense of loss.

As they sit and dig and nibble worms dug up from the wet beach sand, Scepter starts things off.

"Elixor, we had a tethered relay aloft before the pass-by, to talk to our parties on Tareon. Can you send up another one? It's time to try and establish contact again."

"I'll have to cut off another strip of the Sea Cover material. I'll have it up and working in a day or two," responds Elixor.

"Very good. Also, we left some Comstaffs in the caves. Tomorrow, we'll go in search of them."

Switching to food, "We can nibble on these worms until the Sea Cover is off. There may be young aquatics hatching for us to munch on while other ones grow into a decent meal. We'll have to stay near shore while the vegetation renews, but our normal clouds are reappearing so it looks like we'll get rain soon. We can also open up the green ooze port and start making and chewing on that stuff, again. That's all from me right now. Chronicle, is there something you wanted to say?"

Chronicle has just the situation he wants. The kids are gone and he can get to the heart of the matter.

"Is it worth putting ourselves through all of this hell? Are we not delaying the inevitable, especially since we've launched the last of our kind toward Tareon?"

Scepter sighs at their predicament, as do the others. They don't like it, but all realize that Chronicle is just being honest. "What's your thinking," asks Scepter, unsure of where the conversation is heading.

"Elixor can prepare a broth of tar resin, masked with shrub herbs for silent comfort. It is much preferred to an infernal impact with Tareon."

"Prepare your poison as a last resort," responds a shrugging Scepter, unable to think of any other alternative. "It sounds a less heinous outcome. Varo, are you and your Farsider people adept at reading the old cave symbols?"

"Our caves were used as prisons and most of us have spent many hours deciphering those symbols."

"Good. After talking with our search teams on Tareon, we should spend our remaining weeks learning all we can about our planet's distant past, and why our ancient history is so blank and elusive. I'd like your help on that. And if nobody else has questions, all may now disperse."

The meeting breaks up and Hep, with her broken arm wrapped in a make-shift reed sling, approaches Varo.

"Some of your kind saved me and my daughter in the volcano. When my arm broke, one Farsider in particular grabbed my daughter and pulled her back down. Your people are good people, and I want to thank you."

With her lone good arm, Hep gives the burly red Varo a hug.

"Did your husband die in the volcano," asks Varo.

"He's on Tareon. His name's Drago. He and our other daughter Virn were the first to launch successfully, almost two years ago."

"You must've had hope for joining them, there."

"Ogard and I were the next scheduled to launch, after Kairn's family."

Hours later in the early evening on the far side of the still-covered sea, Trillo leads Alor, Torq, Ogard, Zoy, her son Dwell, Jin and the other kids as they come upon the smoldering bodies of Foreman Nord and his daughter Vell, laying just inches from the Sea Cover Master Retainer. The sharpened rock is next to Nord's hand.

"That was close" observes Trillo, who asks, "Alor, Torq, would you like the honor?"

"What do we do," ask the perplexed Farsiders.

"Cut this purple retainer with that sharp rock."

Alor and Torq do as told and each retainer on either side of the master releases its grip on the Cover, and the process continues to other retainers, like cascading dominos. As this continues, the breezes slowly push the lightweight cover back over itself and slowly across the sea. It'll take a few hours as they walk back around to the encampment, but by morning they will have their ocean back, to be shared by all.

All awake the next morning to another sign of returning normalcy. The large, round, floating leaf pads from the ancient timbers have drifted back toward the cove shore, near their encampment. The pads' alkali/PH content matches the surrounding water, so they never deteriorate. Each pad is strong enough to support a number of Zeons while floating on the water. The pads are used for fishing and also for special ceremonies.

Elixor's foundry tools are still in the caves, but he's already busy, cutting a thin 500-foot strip of the thin Sea Cover and by the second morning, is folding a large piece of the cover material into a small balloon. He carries strange things in his backpack and has pulled out a small curved metal receiving dish, and ties it to the long strip just below the balloon. Next, he anchors the lower end of the long strip under a big boulder. Finally, pulling two flint stones from his backpack, he lights some dry grass and carefully heats the balloon. Before long, the heated air inside is lighter than the air outside, and the balloon and receiving dish rise skyward until the long green fabric is straight, anchored to the ground by the boulder.

"Scepter, there's your antenna relay. Try it when ready," as he gestures up toward the tethered balloon.

"Very well." Scepter points his Comstaff toward the balloon and asks "Tareon Teams One and Two, are you there?" Hearing this, Kairn and Varo – standing in the water picking up small aquatics to eat, head to the shore to be with Scepter and Elixor. Chronicle also approaches, and Elixor listens in, as his brothers Ingot and Spike are on Tareon.

After a bit of a delay, "Tareon Team One here, Drago reporting."

"Tareon Team Two, Othar here. We lived through the pass-by. It lasted days and wasn't easy, but we're all still alive. How many of you are left?"

"Fifty nine," responds Scepter.

"Only fifty nine thousand?"

"No, only fifty nine of us, including seven Farsiders. It turns out that some Farsiders disobeyed their leaders and hid in their caves. They came to our side of the planet and found us just after our last call with you. Tareon took most of us out, and then Scolios came around a second time while we were all exposed up on the mountain."

"So were you able to launch?"

"Two sticks got off."

"Kairn and Rayelle?"

"Negative. Rayelle and Evene on the first, and two Farside girls on the second. There was no time to launch anymore."

"Farside girls? Who made that call?"

"You're talking to him," admits Scepter. "Anyway, we know they got off okay because we saw them streak across the sky the next night, so we know they're heading your way. We hope they make it."

"Kairn must be crushed."

"He is, but he's become friends with Varo, the father of the Farside girls, and we're learning much about each other after so many centuries apart. Oh and, without the Farsiders help, those we launched never would've made it."

Hearing their voices talking to Scepter, Drago's wife Hep and daughter Ogard walk up, as do Othar's sons Stern and Stip. Hep has a broken arm, but tries to keep Othar's sons Stern and Stip close. Stern and Stip in unison blurt out "Hi dad!"

"Are those my boys," responds Othar's voice.

"Yes, but mom didn't make it," respond Stern and Stip. "She was injured and died on the march down the mountain."

"Oh no," as Othar's voice cracks, but then realizes he's got to keep himself together for his boys. "Well, stay close and take care of each other."

Hep and Ogard want their turn, with Drago. "Hi honey. Hi dad."

"You both made it?"

"Ogard's okay, but I've broken my arm, and if it wasn't for a Farsider who died soon after, I would've lost Ogard," responds Hep.

"Listen, we've just erected this new relay and I see you've done the same," as Scepter rejoins the conversation.

"Yes," responds Drago.

"Good. What have you learned about Tareon?'

"It's very advanced, with seven major cities. We've combed through five of the cities. My team is about to check out city number six and Othar's team will check out the last city, but there are no beings, so far. Don't know where they're at, but we'll keep looking."

"Good, but keep a lookout for our travelers first, if they make it. Stay alert, stay smart, and forward with brilliance. Zeon out!"

High above, now thousands of miles arrear, Rayelle/Evene and Jurn/Plur blow rapidly away from Zeon. The extra orbit compounded their speed and slingshot them briskly away to chase down the retreating Tareon. There's not much to do mid-trip - just hang on and enjoy the ride - so they sip minute bits of nourishment and nibble on the oxygen pill. The best they can do is take in their solar system. In the weightlessness of space, there's nothing to get sore.

From space - instead of on land - everything in the cosmos looks brighter, clearer. In toward the center of their system, they see the four inner planets surrounding their healthy sun. To the outer side - beyond Tareon's orbit - are planets seven, eight and nine. About forty percent into their journey, they've slowed just enough to notice the difference, but then the wake and gravity of the larger Tareon starts to reel them in.

Back on Zeon, Trillo and young adults Jin and Dwell have discovered a new cave, and Trillo tells his father Kairn about it. Scepter gathers Varo, Chronicle and Elixor, and Varo invites his fellow Farsiders Alor and Torq.

They set off and soon transition from the cove hills to the sandy zone, with Kairn's charred old stellar sighter tied to his waste. Even though it no longer works, he's not yet ready to part with it. Before long, they walk past the rim of the large burial crater.

"Do you make use of this crater," Varo asks Scepter.

"We bury our dead under the sand at the bottom when we aren't overcome by events. How has your side been celebrating those who have passed?"

"Dorn and his leadership eat them for food. And when the rest of us are hungry enough, I am ashamed to say that we've done the same."

They walk past the rim of the second crater, with the rocky outcropping at the bottom. "And what about this crater," asks Varo.

"This one's hazardous. Kids can walk down it safely but the sand is soft and treacherous. See these large, webbed soles along the rim? They're sand shoes. We adults must wear them to keep from sinking in."

Onward they continue, to more compacted ground and past the entrances of caves One thru Ten. The smell of death still accompanies each opening.

"This brings back bad memories," admits Scepter.

"Did you lose some in here?"

"Thousands, as many of these caves collapsed. And in our hurry to launch, we left many dead in there, including my son."

"I am sorry for your loss."

Hours later, they come upon the two side-by-side caves discovered by the kids and walk into the first one. Its 100-feet deep and half way in, they see symbols and glyphs on the walls. While the kids play with rocks, Scepter, Varo, and Chronicle step up to get a close look at the wall drawings. There is a diagram of their solar system, but it's like the others they've seen – all nine planets, with a good gap between Zeon and Tareon.

"Varo, do your caves have these depictions of our solar system on them," asks Scepter.

"Yes."

"And do they look like this, all nine planets, with a sizeable gap between us and Tareon?"

"They do."

There are also language symbols on the walls, which Scepter scans closely. "Looks like more of the same; mentions of the sea, hunting and fishing, Altai, but nothing new, just like the other caves. Varo, do you see anything unusual?"

"Negative. We see the same symbols on our side of the planet."

"Which proves that long ago, our peoples were common," adds Chronicle. "It's our leadership that has divided us, for so long now."

They exit and enter the adjacent cave. "It's more of the same. There is nothing new here. We'll check out more caves in the days ahead," advises Scepter.

As they return, again passing caves Ten thru One, three Nearsiders approach. "Scepter, we've found six Comstaffs in the caves."

"Good. Varo, Kairn, Elixor, Alor, Torq, all grab one."

As they walk back past the sandy craters toward their seaside encampment, clouds quietly drift overhead. They glance up at Altai and notice its summit covered in puffy grey clouds. Rain - up there for now - but it'll drift their way. Also, the temperature slowly drops, back close to the cool norms of before the passing. Altai will soon be covered in snow and Zeon is for one last time returning to its normal, bucolic self.

As they near the seaside settlement, Chronicle brings up a lighter subject.

"Scepter, there are two young couples remaining who wish to consummate the ceremony of union."

"Three. We would also like to union," spout Farsider boy Dwell and Nearsider girl Jin, stepping forward and unable to contain their anticipation.

Scepter, Varo, Alor and Torq stop and gaze at Dwell and Jin, and also at each other. Farside leaders would've never allowed the union of a "red" with a "brown."

"Your leaders would've stoned you for such talk," as Scepter looks at Dwell. "But it's a new world now, and with what little time we have left, are there any objections?"

None speak up and Scepter finishes with "Very well, then. Three couples for union," but in the back of his mind is thinking of Elixor's poison.

Dwell and Jin are giddy as all return to the seaside camp, and run off to tell the two other young couples.

"We've lost so much, it'll be a humble ceremony, but I can have a fabric harp ready by tomorrow night, and we may get the right weather for it," adds Elixor.

The next night, all gather at the cove encampment. Three of the giant floating leaf pads have been brought in to the shore. Each young couple steps onto a pad, and each pad slowly drifts out into the center of the cove. Each couple has a large circular leaf pad to themselves, a personal gently turning-and-bobbing platform. Off to one side, Elixor has tightly strung thin strips of the Sea Cover between two big boulders, while nearby, assistants Garl and Hark have fashioned hard tubes of the green material into flutes with holes in them. A fourth Nearsider drums a large rock which has been hollowed out.

Scepter and Chronicle stand at the shore. Chronicle has a long green straw and a woven bag with fire grass cuttings in it. Fire grass sparkles at night under the dimmest of light. All others are in a large circle on the gradual slope above Chronicle and Scepter. It's a beautiful night. The slowly scrolling stars on the horizon are reflected on the water, but overhead, clouds have silently gathered. Each giant leaf pad gently bobs and turns on the small ocean waves, as each couple faces one another. With three beats of the rock drum, Scepter starts the festivities. Since losing his infant son, anything dealing with the young and time going forward is difficult, so he's shortened his blessing to not make much mention a future together, since there is none.

"We assemble tonight under the heavens before us to bless these three young couples - Dwell and Jin, Quall and Vail, and Forn and Wee, - in the commitment of union. From separate parents and families, they will embark here forward on a path together, in the time that we have left."

He finishes with three words from the older version of their language. "E-couple, E-join, E-union."

As Elixor and the flute players begin the beautiful union melody, Chronicle blows the fire grass cuttings out his straw and into the air, which rain down slowly flickering over each couple, as each couple then begins the delicate and embracing *Union Waltz*, with their interlocking hands and arms symbolizing and unbroken commitment. All others, hand-to-hand in a large circle above Scepter and Chronicle, begin a group version of the same Waltz. Farsiders - who formerly only performed this only in private - are now free to join in with the Nearsiders.

As those above continue with their choreographed routine, each young couple slows their movement to stand face-to-face on their personal, slowly-turning leaf pad, and quietly close their eyes. As each couple – with eyes closed – then lean together in a trance-like state, a light rain starts to fall. This is what Elixor meant by the proper weather for a union. From the starlit horizon to the flickering fire grass to the slowly turning- and floating- couples in the light rain, it's a beautiful sight. The treeless Eden still shines, when she wants too.

Then, while leaned together on their gently bobbing pads, each couple dips their heads back and out of each male's mouth unfurls a long, slender tongue, which spirals upward to a point. A similarly long tongue from each bride extends upward and spirals around the male's tongue, an interwoven elegant embrace all of the way to the tip.

Next, emerging from each male's throat, glistening clear fluid spirals up each male's tongue to the tip, and down each female's tongue into her throat. And finally, a glowing soft-white ball of future-stock spirals up the male's tongue to the tip, and likewise down the bride's tongue to enter her throat. Subsequent glowing white balls will soon follow over and over as this transfer of semen stock continues throughout the night.

As the formality and ceremony concludes, each couple continues to lean against each other looking upward in this slowly-turning, trance-like state all night long until sunrise the next morning. On the embankment, there are some quiet tears among those breaking up, because this beautiful and intimate ceremony will be the last of its kind ever performed on Zeon.

In space a few days later, Tareon and Zeon are now one-third of their orbits past each other, but Tareon's substantial gravitational pull starts reeling in the two tiny parasols. Rayelle/Evene and Jurn/Plur are all wide-eyed through their goggles, because Tareon is completely different from Zeon. It's a highly evolved world. The seas are deep purple in color, as the water is very rich and oxygenated. The land is mostly thick green forests, something Zeons have never seen, and between each forest are sizeable wild pastures and meadows.

Tareon is also advanced, technologically. There are seven prominent cities, all very large and clearly lit from above, but our four pilots cannot stare long, because they have a maneuver to make.

If our travelers continue facing forward and survive reentry, they will approach Tareon facing upside down and as gravity increases, the blood rushing into their heads will kill them.

The green figure-8 Elastic tying Rayelle's waist to the stick is crossed half-over itself, before also holding Evene to the stick. This allows Rayelle to yaw one way, to her left, and allows Evene to do the same, to her own left. Jurn and Plur are tied to their stick in the same way.

Rayelle starts the maneuver by first looking back at Jurn and Plur, and points to her own eyes, as in "look at me." Next, with her waist tied to the stick, Rayelle yaws the top of her body left, releasing the forward rungs, and grabs the rear rungs. Her hands are now where her feet just were, as she has reversed her direction.

Evene remembers practicing this at home and pivots to her left and again faces her mother. Jurn and Plur watch carefully and quickly copy the same maneuver. Everyone is now feet-down, descending into Tareon's atmosphere.

Next, with her feet, Rayelle kicks a lever which extends the now foot-end parasol from its semi-retracted state, to a fully extended umbrella shape. The metal cone under it also extends at the same time. The two metal skins that protected them at launch will now do so at re-entry. Jurn kicks at her lever, and her lower parasol and cone also deploy outward.

The only advice Teams One and Two told Rayelle about their location was that they were both on the north half of Tareon, and to not land in one of the oceans. While watching her orbit direction and the rotation rate of Tareon below, suddenly, an orbiting metallic device resembling a high-tech version of Elixor's relay antennas zooms across Rayelle's path, slicing right between her Stick and Jurn and Plur's. As it disappears into the distance, another floating dish from different direction also cuts across their path. To her, they are someone's small mechanical moons, but the appearance of a third and much larger dish causes her to start downward prematurely, hoping to end up on the northern half when landing on the other side of the slowly-spinning Tareon. Jurn and Plur quickly follow her lead.

After many days of weightless silence, they notice the beginning of a fast breeze that gets louder and louder, and their helmets are the only protection from what is quickly becoming an enormous roar. They were asleep for the launch and noticed none of this. This time, they get to live through it, *if* they live through it.

The metal edges of their lower parasols begin to turn yellow from heat, then orange, and finally an intense red. The secondary cone under it also turns red, but less-so. The suits, gloves, and helmet/visor are their last line of protection. As the temperatures and heated surfaces increase, they are just inches above being fried. They enjoyed viewing Tareon on the way in, but now they can't bear to look.

As the heat rises and the protective cones get hotter, their burgeoning hell gets worse. The stick they're tied to gets hot, even through their thick gloves, and the lower rungs they stand on start to smolder from the heat. Finally, Evene screams and both she and Rayelle pick their feet up from the scorching lower rungs, and hang only from the upper rungs and waist knot. Without looking, Jurn and Plur instinctively do the same from the intense heat.

With their eyes closed, they gradually notice the darkness of space being replaced by light. And because they've been in space for almost two weeks and have gotten used to the darkness, the light they now sense is quickly becoming very bright; too bright.

Even with the thick helmets on, the wind roar is now deafening. As the intense heat starts to subside, very slowly, Rayelle lets her eyes open, squinting to get used to the Tareon's bright atmosphere, and the reveal below is like no other. From deep cobalt blue to the darkest of purple, the seas are rich with nutrients, minerals, and oxygen. Thick forests of pine-like timbers tower 3000-feet high and meadows are carpeted with wild grasses 100-feet tall. Endless mountains are capped with snow, not just one, like Altai. There is so much to take in, but Rayelle has to look back for Jurn and Plur. It's still windy and noisy, but with the relays aloft that the Tareon teams have launched, their Launch Stick Comstaffs *should* work. Rayelle yells into tiny speaker holes on her Launch Stick, "Turn the crank, just like I do!" The echo of her voice is heard from the holes on Jurn and Plur's Launch Stick.

Rayelle turns the crank above her head and slowly the larger upper parasol opens for the first time on the trip. It's a bit bigger than the lower one, and must be opened slowly or the winds will blow it off. Jurn and Plur follow her lead and start cranking open their upper parasol.

Jurn and Plur are not the only ones who heard Rayelle's command. Far below, Teams One and Two – flying in Transtubes - quietly listen for any voices. Rayelle's voice chimed over their Comstaffs, which lay on the floor of each Transtube.

The Tareon Teams start to tear up that the eight of them are getting new visitors, but their leaders Drago and Othar have no time for feelings. Hearing Rayelle's voice, Drago asks his three others in his tube, "Did you get a fix on that?"

"To the southwest."

"We confirm," comes Othar's voice from the other Transtube.

As Rayelle/Evene and Jurn/Plur float down in their parasol sticks high above, the lower parasols are no longer required, having done their job during launch and the beginning of reentry. Rayelle kicks out a green pin holding the lower cone to the stick. The cone slides down the stick and collects the lower parasol and together, cone and lower parasol break through the T-bar at the bottom and all fall away. What was the T-bar bottom end is now a sharp point. Jurn and Plur follow her lead and do the same and each stick is now ready for landing.

Rayelle remembers being told to avoid landing in the ocean, but approaching over the ocean is good because there are no tall trees in the way. "We'll try for the beach," she yells over the speaker to Jurn and Plur, which is not easy as they have only limited control over their descent. They can kick their lower rungs out and move their bodies to turn left or right, but the turns are slow and minimal, and the beach is a narrow strip between the shore and a tall forest.

As they approach a wide cove, Rayelle and Evene are still a little *ahead* of Jurn and Plur, but Rayelle and Evene are also *lower* than Jurn and Plur, and may not make it to the beach. In addition, there is a prominent pine-like timber on the right point, with lower branches extending out over part of the cove.

"We can't make it to the beach," yells Rayelle. "We'll try for the sandbar!"

A small sandbar in the center of the cove lies a hundred yards before the shore. Rayelle "sticks" the landing on the sandbar. They are lucky, as the waves and tides are low, now. Jurn and Plur come in above the timber branches overhanging the cove and nail a perfect landing on the beach sand. They all wriggle out of the Elastic that has been tying them to the poles and fall to the sand, because they've been weightless for weeks and suddenly feel heavy, even the young girls.

"We're down," Rayelle announces toward the holes in her Comstaff. "But Evene and I came up short of the beach on a sandbar."

"Don't leave the sandbar, and keep your goggles on. We're only a few minutes away," echoes Drago's voice from their Comstaff speaker holes, as all four begin removing their helmets and gloves.

While sitting and waiting to get their leg muscles back, Rayelle looks around the small sandbar. It disappears underwater, but the purple water is too dark to see into. Jurn and Plur – also sitting - look out into the cove from the nearby beach.

Perched quietly on a tree branch overlooking the cove are two IrisCatchers. They are funny little creatures that each look like the case of a tape measure, with rounded tops and a wide flat slit of a mouth along the bottom. They sit quietly with their claws gripping the branch and their narrow end facing down toward the two new visitors on the sandbar below.

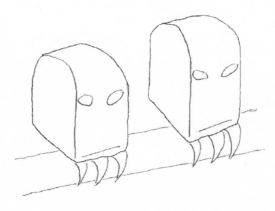

The setting seems good enough until Teams One and Two arrive, but silently to Rayelle and Evene's left, a living appendage rises quietly up out of the water. It looks like a crab's claw, only where the claw would be is a large eye which pivots until it's looking straight at Rayelle and Evene. Then, on their right, another limb/eye rises, and also finds the cowering mother-and-daughter. Rayelle and Evene don't know what to do or which way to go, and Drago's order was to stay out of the water. From the shore, Jurn and Plur are also transfixed, and are the first to notice what happens next. All four quickly jump up on their feet, powered by the adrenaline of fear suddenly rushing through their veins.

Behind Rayelle and Evene, much farther out in the cove, the tip of a long tail silently emerges and rises up. It arches up and forward like an earthlike scorpion tail, and as it slowly sneaks toward Rayelle and Evene, a prominently-fanged mouth starts to open.

"Behind you! Behind you," as Jurn and Plur are now yelling from the shore.

Rayelle and Evene turn to see the mouth opening and viper-like fangs extending, along with a sharply-forked tongue. Since they reversed their direction for reentry, the poison tip is now at the top of their Launch Stick.

"Evene, help me get this out," as Rayelle frantically tries to pull the Launch Stick up from the sandbar to use as a weapon.

While hiding behind the stick, both do their best to loosen the deeply impaled stick. "It's no use! It's stuck!"

They continue to hide behind the skinny Launch Stick as the mouth and protruding fangs approach. The gaping mouth lunges forward and with the first bite, the Comstaff point impales it, sticking out of the top of its mouth. As the mouth crows loudly in anger which echoes throughout the cove, the two eyes snarl with even greater anger. The head then lifts until the stick retracts from its mouth, shakes off the pain, and prepares to come in for another strike.

Weary from the pain of the poison tip, the mouth then turns sideways and with a second bite, breaks the top half of the Launch Stick off and spits it out. "Oh no, we have nothing left to hide behind," as Rayelle and Evene are now totally unprotected.

As the fanged mouth lunges in for another bite, "grab your helmet," as Rayelle and Evene wedge their helmets into the creature's hissing mouth, preventing it from biting down. The mouth then recoils and coughs the helmets out.

With the mouth and fangs of the angered creature opening and coming in for the final kill, one of the huge eyes is suddenly struck from above by a 100-foot long tongue of the tree-mounted IrisCatcher. An animalistic gasp erupts from the mouth approaching the girls and echoes throughout the cove. The other eye is then struck by the other IrisCatcher's tongue. Each IrisCatcher's flat tongue tip expands to a suction cup shape and pulls on each eyeball. The creature's eye arms struggle against the pull of the tongues, but the IrisCatchers grip on their tree branch, holds firm. The tail mouth – now unable to see – lunges blindly forward, guessing where Rayelle and Evene might be. Rayelle and Evene jump left and right, narrowly avoiding the powerful jaws and rancid hot breath of the creature's fanged, slimy mouth. After an intense tug-of-war, each eyeball is ripped from its arm socket and quickly reeled in and fully ingested by each IrisCatcher. The tail mouth falls back down toward the water just as Drago and Team One arrive from above in a Transtube, an airborne vehicle seating up to six in three rows of two.

"Leave your stuff and jump in," as Drago hovers the Tube with the back end near Rayelle and Evene. Othar's Team Two's Transtube emerges from over the tall trees and descends to pick up Jurn and Plur from the beach.

"What in the hell was that," roars Rayelle while taking one of the rear seats.

"You haven't seen anything yet," responds Drago.

The Transtube's front and rear are open, so all six sitting in it can see forward and back. There are also windows on each side. Drago rises in altitude and stops to hover well above the cove, angled nose-down toward the sandbar and creature below. Othar in Team Two's tube does the same.

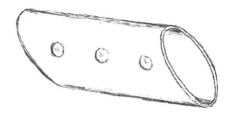

On the blind creature's huge arms, blood from each eye socket has trickled down into the water. Smelling this and coming into the cove from the horizon, a fluttering, frantic school of Sizors swim in. As soon as the fluttering flock reaches the tail mouth - now aimlessly above the water - a giant roar and exhale echoes throughout the cove as the entire sandbar rises up well out of the water. Now the full body is revealed. It's an enormous creature and takes up the entire cove. As it writhes in pain by being chewed to death by the Sizors, it becomes clear that it never was a sandbar, but a head to look like one, a lure to catch unsuspecting prey.

"We call it an Inlet Pod," informs Drago. "It lies in-wait in the shallows. And if we stick around a few more minutes, the IrisCatchers that saved your life will be eaten by another branch with teeth, and that branch will be attacked by another tree. Even the clouds here prey on each other. On Tareon - especially in the water - nothing is safe."

CHAPTER 4

Tareon

THE TRANSTUBES ARE A FAST way of getting around Tareon that Teams One and Two have learned to pilot. Because the Tubes have an open front and rear, air briskly blows through the six seated within, and the Tubes are capable of very high speeds. They are not connected to any tracks and cut the distance between Tareon's seven major cities to mere hours.

In Drago's Team One Tube, the mood is ecstatic. Rayelle and Evene are happy to see others, and remember Drago from before his launch. On Team One are Drago's other daughter Virn, Scepter's brother Nax, and Wren, a sister of Garl and Hark. Although Virn is a couple of years younger than Evene, they remember each other and quickly re-bond. Drago's Launch Stick Comstaff lies between seats along the Transtube floor.

Not nearly as ecstatic, but still good, is the mood in Othar's Team Two tube. The four Nearsiders have never seen Farsiders before and Jurn and Plur only recently met their first Nearsiders. Jurn and Plur also feel like they were whisked away from Zeon without any warning. Othar and Drago had talked and both agreed that whoever picked up the Farside girls would try to make them feel welcome. Others on Team Two include Elixor's brothers Ingot – who is adept and metal working, and Spike – who is a chemist; and Zoree, Garl and Hark's other sister. Othar's Launch Stick Comstaff also lies on the floor, and all on Team One and Two wear Tareon communication bracelets.

Rayelle - still settling into her new surroundings - notices Drago's Launch Stick Comstaff lying on the floor of the Team One Transtube. The parasols and rungs have been removed from it.

"My Comstaff was eaten and we left the other one on the beach."

"It's okay. I've got mine and Othar has his."

"What is this we are flying in," asks Rayelle, staring around the interior of the aerial vehicle.

"There are signs in the cities saying these are called Transtubes," replies Drago.

"And how did you learn to fly it?"

"I crashed the first few I tried out, but it's not hard. Just move these sticks left, right, forward or back, and these petals help turn. You'll learn soon enough. Even the kids have mastered these."

As both Tubes fly inland, Drago points out some of the planet to Rayelle and Evene.

"We are heading toward Worthland, the city my team is checking out. We'll all sleep there tonight and tomorrow, Team Two will head to Northsphere, the city they are investigating. These aren't our names; this is what the Tareons called them. We haven't seen any Tareons yet, but if we do, it's good to have your empathic silver eyes with us. These will be the last two cities to check out. The first five cities were totally deserted."

"If this place is so dangerous, how do you all survive," wonders Rayelle.

"Out here in the forest and jungles our poison-tipped Comstaffs have saved us more than once, but we've learned that the cities are actually the safest places to be, since we haven't seen anyone yet."

"The seas are so purple and the land is so green, and everything grows so big," observes a wide-eyed Rayelle, who can't control her wonder. "It's as if this planet is much older than ours."

"Tareon appears to be a superworld. Everything here is on a gigantic scale, and because this planet is so much bigger than Zeon, the seven major cities are very far apart. It's good that we've found these Transtubes because they greatly shorten the travel time."

The prominent green forests and pastures take some getting used to. Coming from Zeon – which is treeless - everything is quite a shock. The thick forests give way to enormous meadows with swirling wild grasses 30-feet high. As they continue flying, Drago points out small older towns which are now vacant. "We think these older empty settlements peaked a century or two ago."

A few minutes later, the wild pastures and forests give way to an immense expansive quilt of cultivated land to grow food. "These growing belts surround each of the seven major cities."

And then it comes into view: With tall, sleek buildings which connect together as well as to the ground, Worthland is more than modern. All buildings are white, shapely and elegant, as if trying to out-style each other. Some buildings float in the sky and don't touch the ground, which means the Transtubes are the only way to reach them. The tallest building has a stylized "W" atop it.

Flying in closer, Transtubes of differing lengths are on the ground as well as in the air, hovering alongside buildings at various levels, awaiting passengers. There are also longer Transtube trains for moving large numbers of people, but there are no people. The lights are on in the buildings and modern artistic pieces flow water or twirl in the breeze, but no one is visible. There is an eerie emptiness, as if invading somebody else's realm.

"These buildings were a dusty mess after the pass-by, but then the rains came and washed them clean."

Drago and Othar park their Tubes next to the 200th floor of one of the tall buildings. As each Tube comes to a halt high in the air, the building senses their arrival and a surface automatically extends for them to walk in on. Drago and Othar walk in carrying their Comstaffs.

The floor they enter features legless white furniture surrounded by 360-degrees of glass. Everything appears to be hovering above the floor.

"What are these for," asks Rayelle, pointing at horizontal cushions.

"Don't know, but they're soft and they feel good, so we use them for resting. You must be hungry."

Drago has a small clicker in his hand. He waves his hand across one of the windows and clicks it, and a large monitor screen appears. He quickly selects some strange fruit.

"I feel bad about losing my Launch Stick Comstaff," admits Rayelle.

"Not a problem. Comstaffs are needed only to talk to Zeon. To communicate here, all you need are these." Spike and Ingot produce four metallic bracelets for the new arrivals to place around their wrists. "Talk into these . . . and all can hear," as Drago's voice echoes from each one's bracelets. "But the first thing you probably want to do is call home."

"Yes! Yes!"

"The curved panel atop that other tall building is a relay antenna. Point my Comstaff at the relayer and talk, and wait for a response."

"Hello Zeon, this is Rayelle. Can you hear us," Rayelle tentatively asks, while pointing the comstaff as told.

On Zeon, Scepter, Norl, Chronicle, Kairn, and Trillo have followed Farsiders Varo, Alor and Torq to a cave on the Farsiders side of the planet. Scepter and Chronicle carry their Comstaffs, but when Rayelle's voice his heard, Kairn jumps forward and is the first to respond.

"Honey, is that you?"

"Dad, I'm here too," interrupts Evene from Tareon at the sound of her father's voice.

"And I'm here with dad" interjects Trillo from Zeon.

"How was the trip, honey" asks a curious Kairn.

"Other than dodging metallic relay dishes, almost being burned alive and getting eaten by a giant undersea creature, we're alive," answers Rayelle.

Kairn, Trillo, and everyone listening on Zeon, look wide-eyed at each other.

From Varo's distinctive voice comes, "Did my girls make it?"

"We are here father," pipe up Jurn and Plur. "We miss you. Where are you?"

"The Nearsiders have followed us to our side of the planet to see some of our caves."

"We're trying to find out all we can in the time we have left," adds Scepter.

"We saw Scolios streak by a second time when we were on the far side of the planet," adds Rayelle. "When we came around, we could see a burned streak across Altai and out across the sea. How bad was it?"

"It was beyond terrible," responds Scepter. "We were all exposed up on the mountain. There were only seventy of us left alive but eleven died on the march down, so we are now only fifty nine."

"Only fifty nine," asks Rayelle, who can't believe the pitifully low number.

"Like I said, it was beyond terrible."

Rayelle, Evene, Jurn, and Plur worryingly look at each other. Rayelle then asks what she's afraid to ask. "So no one else will be joining us?"

"I'm sorry. You were the last ones to make it off." Not wanting to dwell on the sad stuff, Scepter quickly changes the subject. "So what do you think of Tareon?"

"It makes us look so small, like we haven't done anything with our world," responds Rayelle humbly, while gazing out over the modern, sleek metropolis. "They've built more in one city than we have on our whole planet."

On Zeon, the reaction of all to hearing this is downtrodden. Rayelle's words make them feel inadequate and lazy.

"We try so hard to stay alive and yet, it's not enough," mumbles Kairn.

"How are my boys Stern and Stip holding up," asks Othar, knowing his sons on Zeon are now parentless.

"They're being forced to grow up fast, but they are bonding well with the other young ones and we are keeping them close." Not wanting to dwell on their predicament, Scepter again changes to the task at hand. "Othar, Drago, what's your status?"

"There are seven great cities here," replies Othar. "We've checked out the first five and are about to start on the last two. Each city is sleek, tall and modern, but each also has its own unique look. The structures are different from one city to another and we've come up with an idea. We've noticed that each city has a tall stack emitting a plume of white steam. We are going to search down these stacks tomorrow and try to find the source, to see what powers these cities. These kids might be useful if we get into tight spaces."

Jurn, Plur, Evene and Virn all look at each other.

"But we still haven't seen any beings yet. So far the planet appears deserted," concludes Othar.

"Good work," responds Scepter. "On our end, the Sea Cover is off and grains and aquatics are growing again. Even our cool little breezes have returned. It's almost like normal again, except that there are so few of us left. I have Elixor and his aides rebuilding a monitor to view and a few new lenses, but that's about it from here. Kairn estimates we have about 60 days left until we all crash into each other."

"We're estimating about the same. We'll check back in when we learn more. Stay smart, stay alert, and forward with brilliance," conclude those on Tareon.

"Forward with brilliance, respond those from Zeon."

On Zeon, after ending the call with Tareon, Varo introduces Scepter to this particular Farside cave.

"Scepter, this cave is typical of what we have on this side of our planet. And these are the types of writings we see."

They come upon a wall with glyphs and symbols. The depictions are more dictatorial than those in Nearside caves with scenes of beheadings, human sacrifice, and concubines for the Dorn family hierarchy.

"These views reflect the centuries of fear your leadership has imposed, but these writings and symbols are no older than those on our side, so they don't shed light on any matters concerning our planet and Tareon, but this cave sure has a lot of bones strewn about," notices Scepter.

"Dorn and his family used this and many other caves as prisons to hold his enemies. Most of these bones were men and boys, and females were taken for the pleasure of his leadership."

Hearing this makes Scepter's wife Norl visibly uncomfortable.

Moments later, as they exit the cave, "The outside air is comforting, as there are centuries of pain in there," concludes Scepter.

"We Farsiders endured so much for so long that it became accepted," responds Varo.

On Tareon the next morning, the teams set out in the Transtubes. Rayelle and Evene go with Drago in Team One. Both Tubes fly the short distance to Worthland's smokestack and then Othar's Team Two peels off and heads toward Northsphere, the city his team will be checking out.

"We'll split off here and join up with you on our way back," chimes Othar's voice.

On Team Two's path out of Worthland, Othar passes over seven low, large dwellings overlooking an Infinity Lake. It's all very bucolic and peaceful, except for a concrete chute which juts up from the beach sand in front of the dwellings. The chute is tall and at a slight angle. It has an enclosed flat top and a door at ground level, and looks industrial and out of place against the other sleek structures. He decides to check it out on the way back, but when entering Northsphere, notices another tall, angled structure looking equally out of place amongst similar nice dwellings.

Back above Worthland, Drago guides his Transtube down into his city's smokestack.

"Here we go, down into the mist."

The white smoke is thick, but harmless, only pure white water vapor. He descends staying close to the smoke stack interior walls for better visibility. Down, down they circle, much further down than ground level, and the temperature warms as they get closer to the source. Finally, a service door is visible in the wall. He stops the Transtube and the service door senses it and opens itself, while also extending a platform. All step in and see an elevator, with Drago carrying his Comstaff.

The elevator takes them down even further. The walls are getting warmer, but just before slowing down, cooler. The doors open and they can't believe their eyes. A huge cavern is anchored by an enormous pulsing, throbbing, steam generator, spinning like a powerful turbine.

"You won't believe what we're looking at," as Othar's voice resonates from over their bracelets.

"Let me guess," your city's power center," guesses Drago. "We are looking at the same, for Worthland."

Drago's team walks into what must be a huge control center. They see modern illuminated schematics of the city's power grid, controlling not just electrical power, but water usage, air circulation, flood control, etc.

"We have a lot to check out. We'll meet you at the top of our smokestack in two hours."

"Good. There's something else I want to show you," replies Othar's voice.

A couple of hours later, all exit their subterranean power centers, return to their Transtubes, and soon meet up over Worthland's smokestack. "Follow us," advises Othar, who leads Team One beyond the city's outskirts to the nice structures overlooking the shore of Infinity Lake, a large private body of water not connected to any ocean.

"See the seven nice structures below," points out Othar as they hover over the beautiful lake. "Now look at the hardened shaft jutting out of the sand at an angle. It looks very out of place, and doesn't match the sleek lines of the rest of the city. When we entered Northsphere, we saw a similar angled structure amongst other nice dwellings. There appears to be only one in each city."

"Let's land and take a look," commands Drago's voice.

Both Tubes land on the narrow beach. The setting is particularly beautiful. Infinity Lake seems to reach to the horizon and is large enough to have its own gentle waves, and the narrow sandy beach leads down to it. Overlooking the beach are seven prominent low-slung structures that seem to almost blend in with the short cliffs behind them. Sticking up behind the structures are beautiful pine-like trees. Bisecting this pastoral setting is a square-section concrete structure rising up through the sand, angled about 10-15 degrees from vertical. Compared to the elegant low-lying structures, the tall, angled box is cold-looking and industrial, almost obelisk-like.

"Team Two, check out those dwellings," commands Scepter. "I'm going to try and open this door."

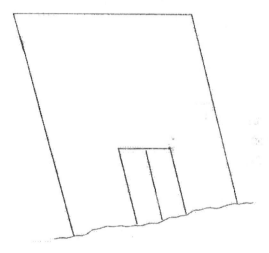

Othar's team checks out the seven sprawling dwellings. Some of the floor-to-ceiling windows are broken from the forces of the pass-by, and there is some dust inside, but they're very modern and sleek, with beautiful views of the lake and watery horizon. On a shiny sleek table, Othar finds a control clicker. It has a stylized Worthland "W" symbol on it, the same "W" they've seen on the tallest building in the city. He waves the clicker near a window and a control monitor appears, displaying settings *"lighting, temperature, humidity, waste, entertainment,* and *food."*

Back out at the base of the tall angled concrete structure, Drago swipes his clicker to open a thick concrete door, poured aggregate two feet thick.

"Wow, this door is so thick. I wonder why," asks Scepter's brother Nax.

Behind it are two shiny metal elevator doors. The edges of these doors are angled to match the slant of the rest of the structure, and the doors are 10-feet tall. Drago swipes his clicker to try and open the elevator inner doors.

"Access denied" flashes on the inner doors.

"Try this one," suggests Othar, returning with the stylized "W" clicker he found in one of the houses.

Drago swipes the "W" clicker and the elevator doors open.

"Do we step in and go down," asks Othar.

"No. Not yet," replies Drago, looking in toward the floor of the elevator car. "There's something unusual about this place. It takes this special W clicker to go in there."

Looking along the door opening, he notices the crack between the elevator car and the structure wall. It's almost wide enough to fit a hand into, and Drago also notices five small beach rocks in the sand, nearby. "Evene, grab those rocks and hand them to Othar."

As Evene retrieves and hands the stones to Othar, "Evene and Virn, your hearing is good. Lie down and listen in this crack as Othar drops the stones, and tell us when they hit bottom."

Evene and Virn do as told and Drago announces "Everybody quiet," and Othar drops the five rocks. The only noise now is the quiet lapping up of small beach waves, behind them.

As everyone waits for the rocks to hit bottom, eyes get even wider at what could be so deep. Finally, after more than two minutes, "There. They hit something" announce Evene and Virn in unison.

All look at each other in puzzlement. "Why is this shaft so incredibly deep? Let's return to the city and see if we can learn more about these structures," orders Drago.

Walking back to their Transtubes, Rayelle stops for one final gaze out toward Infinity Lake's oceanic horizon. "This is the most beautiful place I've ever seen."

They fly back to the 200-story building in Worthland to report on what they've found.

"Scepter, this is Tareon. Do you hear us," asks Drago into his Comstaff.

After a delay, "Zeon here," as Scepter responds from the Nearside seaside encampment. "Have you found anything?"

"Substantially. Under each city is an enormous power center generating more than enough power to supply the city above. It controls everything."

"What's the source?"

"It uses the internal heat of Tareon to spin large power generators called tur-bines, providing heat, cooling, electric power, even flood control and farming for the surrounding area."

"Very good. So they're clearly very advanced. This is why we sent you all to Tareon. When our worlds collide, maybe there is something about Tareon that will enable you to survive. Is there anything else?"

"Just outside our city among sleek dwellings is a strange angled structure. It's on a narrow beach on a lake, and looks very out of place. We don't yet know what it is or where it leads, but we'll try to learn more."

"Good. Keep looking and see what else you can find. Stay alert, stay smart, and forward with brilliance. Zeon, out!"

The next day, while walking Worthland at ground level, Drago notices many of the buildings have a small opening in their exterior walls about six feet above ground level. It's a tight, round opening lined with a shiny moist material. Six feet is pretty high up for Zeons, so Othar stands on Drago's shoulders, as the others steady Drago. Othar reaches in the port with one arm and sensing this, the port activates, grasping tightly around his arm while starting to slowly spin inside. This would hurt except the inner sleeve also warms up and secretes a shiny, oily solution. Othar reacts like he's about to throw up. He pulls his arm out and the port stops, and he asks to be let down.

"It's a strange sensation. I wonder what purpose they have?"

They continue walking and round the corner of a tall sleek building, and see an ominous looking black booth along the sidewalk.

"There's another one," chimes Drago.

"What is it," asks Rayelle.

"These black boxes. We've seen them in the other cities. They must have some civic purpose."

The box is enclosed and about 12-feet high, with no window, and has a door with a prominent locking bar. To one side of the door is an opening, a hole that is shaped like their clickers. The box is dark and heavy, made of thick cast metal, and looks like an extra large privacy booth. On the backside near the bottom, a clear tube exits and turns down into the ground. There are small dark stains on the pavement surrounding where the tube enters the ground, as if some fluid may have previously leaked onto the pavement.

"Have you opened one," asks Rayelle.

"Not yet," replies Drago. "Let's see if my non-special clicker will open it." Drago swipes his clicker and the locking bar retracts and the door unlocks itself and opens.

"It doesn't require the W clicker, so anybody can open one of these."

Immediately upon the door unlocking and opening, a small group of flying black worms flutters up and lands, quietly watching the twelve Zeons from across the street.

All twelve turn and notice the quiet little harmless looking creatures, and Rayelle winces slightly before she turns her attention back to the black booth. Without stepping in, she notices the odor inside the booth. "Hmmm, smell that. Slightly pungent, yet a bit sweet."

Evene also winces at the odor and then notices, "This hole next to the door opening appears shaped to match the shape of your clicker, as if clickers are supposed to be dropped into it before someone steps into the booth."

Inside, the booth is big enough for four Zeons to fit into. A floor drain is at the bottom and there are dark stains around it, similar to the stains on the pavement around the outside pipe.

"It looks like the grill at the bottom is for fluid to drain into," notices Drago as they all look into the booth. "Maybe this booth is for washing or cleaning. Shall I step in?"

Just before Drago starts to put his clicker in the hole and step into the windowless booth, Rayelle grabs his arm and stops him, and looks back toward the worms watching silently across the way.

"Wait! I can't read their thoughts, but I sense that those little creatures are waiting for us to do just that; to step into this thing."

As soon as they step back and Drago swipes to close the door with no one getting in, the black worms take off and fly away, and Rayelle and Evene watch them carefully.

"Yup. They were only interested if one of us stepped in."

Othar looks in another direction and is intrigued by a building across the way. At 250-stories, it's the tallest building in Worthland, and has the same stylized "W" on it as the clicker found in the beach house. "I want to fly up there."

They get in their Transtubes and fly up to the "W" building top floor. An entrance ramp extends and they walk to an ornate entrance door with the stylized "W" on it, but the doors don't open. Drago swipes his clicker but nothing happens.

"Let me try this one," as Othar tries the "W" clicker he found in the lake house. The doors open. "Hang onto that one, it seems special" advises Drago, as they enter the top floor suite.

The suite is very sleek and modern, more-so than the building they were in, and because it's the tallest building in Worthland, it has a commanding view of the city. The look is sleek and minimalist, and everything is of the highest quality material.

Drago's clicker doesn't work anything in the room. Othar's "W" clicker, however, brings up some of the same city system layouts they saw in the underground power center.

At the back center of the room is an elevator island. There are doors on the front, and the eleven other Zeons follow Drago up to it.

"This lift must go down to the street level," assumes Drago.

Drago – still followed by the others - continues walking around to the backside of the elevator box.

"There are doors on the backside, also. It has both a front door and a back door. Othar, wave your W clicker and open these rear doors."

Othar does as told and the rear doors open.

"Now, let's go around to the front side and open those doors."

With the rear doors remaining open, all continue walking around to the front side and Othar waves his W clicker. The front doors open and all that is visible is a fully enclosed elevator car. It's a complete elevator box with a back wall. While the others remain in front, Drago again steps around to the back.

"There is a wall, and no walk-through. They are two completely separate shafts. I wonder if they both go down to the street level. Othar, keep your clicker and you and your team ride down in that front transporter, and my team will ride down in this rear one, and we'll all meet at the bottom. We'll see you in just a moment."

Othar and all in Team Two enter the front elevator and the doors close, and the car starts downward. Drago's team continues walking around the island and they step into the rear elevator. The doors close and they also start down.

Othar's front elevator smoothly picks up speed and in a matter of seconds, has descended the full 250-floors and the doors open revealing a modern, ground-floor lobby.

Drago's rear elevator picks up speed and *continues* picking up speed.

"What's going on here? Why are we still going down? Why won't it stop? It's going much too fast!"

"This thing clearly didn't stop at ground level. We are far below that now," notices Rayelle in their now-darkened box.

Their ride continues for what seems an eternity. After an endlessly-long ride down, the elevator finally slows, stops, and the doors open. They step out into a cavern-like area. The bottom of their elevator shaft juts down from the ceiling rock above it, so the bottom part of the metal shaft box is visible to the floor.

"Hey where are you," asks Othar's voice over the bracelets. "We're at the bottom floor of the building, waiting for you?"

"We're not sure yet, but ride the same transporter up, and come down in the one we came down in, and be prepared; because it goes much, much deeper," warns Drago.

"Wow! We'll see you in a couple . . ."

As Drago's team walks forward, the cavern quickly opens into a deeply buried, completely furnished underground shelter.

"What is this place?"

"We must be many miles deep, much deeper than the city power center."

They walk toward a broader, central area. See-through partitions divide common areas, while solid walls divide personal rooms. The first rooms appear to be bedroom quarters with beds for up to 20 people. "These look like huts, for rest."

The next room has marks on the floor, possibly for exercise or recreation games. "This might be a play area or a place for exercise."

Othar's team arrives in the same elevator and catches up with Drago's team.

Next is a conference room with a large legless table that floats in the air, and chairs with no legs. "This must be a gathering room," guesses Drago.

Evene finds a short spout sticking out of one wall and passes her hand in front of it. "Hey," as a quick dollop of clear fluid comes out. As quickly as she moves her hand away, the flow stops. Licking her palm, "Its water. And good water too, much better than on our planet."

Rayelle rounds a partition corner and gets a look at enormous hangar through thick hardened glass double-doors. "Drago, Othar, look at this!"

All join her at the glass and see through to a football field-sized plant nursery complete with computerized watering and lighting that's still operating. Smaller saplings are in rows near the front, while larger conifers tower further back. The glass panes and access doors protecting the nursery are very thick, and it's clearly *very* sealed off.

"This nursery must be the most important room down here. There's enough food and vegetation to feed a small village, indefinitely."

Elsewhere, Ingot and Spike find a modern, printer-fabricator machine.

"I wonder what this is for?"

On the wall above it are clear vertical tubes of powders in different colors, which feed down into the machine.

"The display is still lit."

"What does it say?"

"It appears to have choices: pictures of food, clothing, and some sort of parts or construction materials. I'm picking food, and since I don't recognize any of these choices, I'll hit *I'm feeling lucky*."

Spike presses a button and the machine hums to life. They jump back for a moment and after realizing that it's not dangerous, slowly approach it as the other ten gather behind them.

"Look, some of the powders are pouring down into the machine."

After a few seconds of noises and sounds like something is being mixed, the machine stops and a door on the far side, opens.

"Wow, what's that smell?"

Ingot reaches down to the open door and pulls out a sizeable bone with hot meat on it, dripping with juices.

"Ummmmmm, there *is* a heaven," as he takes a bite and relishes in its flavor, and passes it around for the others to share.

"This one cabinet makes all of those different things? What a wonderful foundry toy," remarks an impressed Spike.

They continue onward and the final room they walk into is a control room with many overhead monitors showing views from cameras up on the planet surface; views of Worthland, the six other cities, and strangely, views showing the now-distant Zeon.

"Hey, that's our planet! And look here on this table. There are two more "W" clickers."

"Grab them," Responds Drago. "We could use them."

Ingot and Spike notice a display indicating the air content high above on Tareon's surface, reading *Oxygen 25%, Nitrogen 72%, Other 3%*. "Hey Drago, here's our answer on why everything grows so large, the atmosphere is twenty-five percent oxygen, way more than Zeon's fourteen percent."

"Tareon has all the makings of a superworld, both naturally and technologically. We have to head back up to the surface and report on this."

On their way back to the cavern elevator, they notice that just behind it is another concrete elevator box and door, also jutting down from the cave rock. This column shaft and door are angled 10-15 degrees from vertical.

"Hey, look at this lift back here."

"Shall I wave this W clicker," asks Othar, as they approach the angled elevator door.

"No, that might bring it down," counters Drago. "See this small hole in the door? Wave your clicker in front of it."

Othar clicks in front of the hole and the doors open. The elevator car inside is not there, but on the smooth surface of the bottom of the shaft are five stones.

"Evene, Othar, are these the rocks you dropped from lakeside beach above?"

"Yes Drago."

"I'm positive."

"We have to ride back up to the surface and report on this."

They ride the elevator they came down in, back up to the surface, and decide to stay in the elaborate top floor "W" suite since there is no one around to object.

A short time later - while Evene, Jurn, Plur and Virn play a hopscotch-type game at the far end of the suite - "It's time to tell Zeon what we found," proclaims Drago.

Rayelle is off to one side looking at a monitor she has deployed using one of the "W" clickers. She's scrolling through printed records of Worthland, Northsphere, and the five other large cities. There are no pictures of Tareons, but she notices commonalities about the seven major cities.

Drago calls Zeon on his Comstaff, aiming its top dish out of the window.

"This is Drago. Zeon, are you there?"

After a short pause, "Scepter here. We are encamped along the shore. Have you learned anything more?"

"Yes. Under our city, buried very deep underground, is some sort of survival cave. It has monitors for keeping an eye on the surface, accommodations, and even its own farming areas. It looks designed to support 20-to-30 people for long term. They can monitor everything from down there, even looking at Zeon, and it's entirely self-sustaining."

"Interesting. Do you think it would protect you when our planets hit?"

"It's possible. It's buried many miles deep, much deeper than the city power center. The transport lift we rode in seemed to go down forever. The city of Northsphere also has a similar angled elevator, and we're going to backtrack to the other five cities to see if they have them. If each of these cities has a similar cavern, there might be six more shelters like this one. Oh, and Rayelle's been researching records. Rayelle, what have you learned?"

Looking at her monitor, "They are not cities. They're businesses. Something called cor-por-a-tions."

"Businesses," asks Scepter's perplexed voice, as Drago and Othar are equally puzzled.

"A hundred or so years ago, there were many small company-towns. We've flown over the ruins of what's left of them. Over the years, some companies grew and became larger, mostly by buying up other company-towns. This continued and con-sol-i-dated, until there were only seven companies left: Worthland – where we are, Northsphere, Globestead, Kendral, and three others. The farms around each city are to support those living within. These seven companies became *very* large and did *not* trust each other, and grew to be something called con-glom-er-ates."

"Hmm. Very competitive, just like the animal- and plant- life here," adds Othar.

"It sounds similar to our Farsiders, who overran smaller tribes on their side of our planet," responds Scepter. "Any sign of Tareons in your research?"

"None" responds Othar. "It is as if they removed all traces of themselves from both the planet and their records."

"What's going on there," asks Drago, changing the subject to Zeon.

On Zeon, Chronicle and Elixor walk up to Scepter, who has Kairn, Varo, Trillo, and the three young couples listening. Chronicle and Elixor each carry two carved, flat Returners, a thin flat airfoil made from that hardened green ooze. Returners are not unlike boomerangs, and are great fun in Zeon's gentle breezes.

"Children, look what we've got," as Chronicle's voice can be overheard by those on Tareon.

"Returners," yells Trillo, who can't contain his excitement. "Can I have one? I miss the one I had!"

"Sure, and each couple gets one, and Trillo, why don't you go and show the other young ones how they work?"

On Tareon in the W suite, the kids can be heard running off, and Rayelle's attention perks up. She knows Chronicle's tactics, and can tell he's up to something.

As the Tareon team adults gather around, Chronicle's voice asks "Drago, are the kids on your end, listening?"

"They're nearby, but fully occupied," as Drago checks on the kids jumping at the far end of the W suite.

"Good," as Chronicle continues. "Elixor and I have finished a full batch of tar resin, enough for all of us. The only question now is when to take it."

All eight adults in the Tareon suite perk up while trying not to have the nearby kids, notice. All know that tar resin is the deadliest poison on Zeon, as Scepter informs the Tareon teams of what has been going on.

"I've asked Chronicle and Elixor to prepare a batch of tar resin. All of us here on Zeon are doomed, and the only thing we can control is the way we choose to end ourselves. This last pass-by was bad enough." On Zeon, Scepter then turns to address other adult Zeons standing around him, "Are there any thoughts?"

"My wife is gone and my kids may be safe on Tareon, so I say we drink your potion sooner rather than later," suggests Farsider Varo.

"What they're discovering on Tareon sounds interesting," adds Kairn. "I'd like to hear more, but vote for taking the potion before things here get desperate, again."

"We agree" state the others. "Our planet has returned to normal. We want to enjoy it one last time."

"Agreed," concurs Scepter. "We will wait a little longer. Tareon teams, see what else you can find. Stay alert, stay smart, and forward with brilliance. Zeon out!"

Two days later, the Tareon teams are in their Transtubes leaving the previously checked out city of Kendral, talking among each other about the results of their check of the other cities. Rayelle sits next to Drago in Team One's Tube, looking at a map on a monitor she has drawn up.

"Now I see why we missed the angled elevators in these other cities," states Drago. "In Metalville and Sunhaven, the elevators were disguised as though whoever built them, didn't want them noticed."

"And in Fairtown, the elevator came up in someone's enormous house, so it wasn't visible from outside," responds Othar's voice from Team Two.

Rayelle – while looking at the map she has drawn up - "See this empty area about equal distance from these four big cities? Can we head to the right and go in that direction?"

"A hunch," asks Drago.

"No. I'm just wondering if there is anything out there."

"Othar, we are heading to the right toward the large zone between the cities. Follow us."

They veer right and fly toward the expansive empty area. It's a large zone of grass-topped mesas with vertical drops down to verdant valleys, and they fly low over the mesa tops.

As they fly, "So Drago, in all the time you've been here, you haven't seen a single body, dead or alive," asks Rayelle, wondering if her empathic silver eye abilities will ever be put to use.

"Not one. It's the strangest aspect so far. We've seen many animals, but no people. How did the people who built this impressive world hide all traces of themselves?"

"It would be nice if we could find just one being so maybe I could achieve a link, and we could get some answers. I hate not knowing anything. How could an entire race remove every trace of itself? These cities are huge. They clearly required millions of Tareons to build them, and their population must've been substantial."

Awhile later, after flying hundreds of miles into the empty zone, Othar radios, "There's nothing out here. I say we turn back."

Shortly thereafter, they crest the brow of a wide mesa and cross the valley beyond it. Rayelle – sitting up front next to Drago - sees three small reflections of light just above the tree canopy below as they pass over the lush valley.

"What's that? Go back! Go back! Turn and go back!"

The three reflections were positioned one before the other, as if aligned toward something. The Transtube's momentum carries them out across the far valley, but they turn back to check things out and as they swing around, it comes into view.

The wide hill they crested covers a huge horizontal cavern which looks out over the valley below and is not visible from above. The cave is deep, has a flat floor, and appears lit inside. The opening is 150-feet high and 300-feet wide, and runs 3000-feet back into the mountain, and they slowly fly their Transtubes in. It's a well-lit hangar-like structure built inside of the mesa. Their Transtubes look tiny compared to the cavernous interior. They fly in more than half way, land, and get out. There are markings and stripes on the floor, as if for alignment.

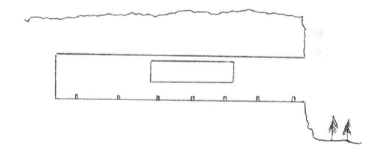

At seven places along the floor - off to one side but aligned with each other - are more of the same black booths that they saw in the cities.

"Hey look, thare are more of those black boxes."

On the backside of each booth, a thick, flexible clear tube emerges that extends along the floor for about 90-feet toward the centerline of the hangar, before coming to an end. Around the tube's open end, small dark stains color the hangar floor.

But the most prominent feature is high up on a side wall, where an immense video screen plays a condensed tape-loop, a video post card for whoever finds it. Drago and Othar land their Tubes near the wall opposite the huge screen, and all take a seat against the base of the wall as they are about to get their first glimpse . . . of the enemy.

CHAPTER 5

Trillo's Returner

TEAMS ONE AND TWO SIT across from the giant video screen, leaning back against the hangar opposite wall as the current tape loop has come to an end and is about to restart. As the images begin, it quickly becomes apparent that there won't be much detail. It's just a quick compilation of history, images, news records, and major happenings on Tareon. For simple foreigners like Zeons, some of it is hard to understand.

It starts with old images of the seas and forests looking much like they do now, but the trees aren't quite as tall. It's followed by images of strange extinct fossils, the creatures of the past. Next are the Tareons. Tareons are about eight feet tall. They are thin, with a head that tapers upward to a point, but males have a small bulb just below the tops of their heads. Eyes are thin vertical slots, close together on the narrowing head. The head widens as it gets lower, out to a skirt-like brim. The body below is tall and lean with long forked hands and feet.

What little fur they have is very short and is initially grey, but over the eons, some Tareons seem to lighten up to almost white in color. Other Tareon tribes are shown warring with each other, mostly for land, but they were smart and learned quickly. As resources were discovered and put to use, some formed into business families, providing one service or another – food, lumber, clothing, etc. These businesses built small towns and all was good and healthy – a competitive healthy, until some businesses grew and purchased other businesses. The bigger each company got, the stronger they got, but they lost connection to their customers and before long, the big companies were only interested in other big companies. The old smaller towns were left behind and the new seven shimmering cities were built, each a headquarters for all who run that city corporation.

In the hangar - while the adults continue watching the video - Evene, Virn, Jurn and Plur go check out the nearest of the seven black booths spaced along the hangar floor. They circle the box wondering what it's for and notice the clear flexible hose coming out the backside and laying along the hangar floor.

Back up on the video screen, there is a short clip of what looks like reproduction. A female hops on the head of a male, sitting over his pointed head and bulb. The encounter is brief and when she leaps off, the top half of his head is gone; it's where his reproductive sac had been. The male falls to the ground, unconscious. His head grows back like a lizard tail, but no longer has a bulb sac, and he can never again provide reproductive stock. From then on, male Tareons are only good for work and labor.

As the video continues, it also becomes clear that females are the ones in charge. A quick glance at statistics shows that only 20 percent of the population is female. This left the female commanders and executives with no shortage of reproductive mates, but the remaining males needed to jettison their head-bound reproductive sacs or they would die prematurely. To remedy this, "pleasure ports" were built into the walls of buildings, just above street level. A tall male is shown bending forward, sticking the top of his head into the wall port. He shakes for a moment and then falls to the ground in a quivering trance. The top of his head is gone, but like a lizard tail, it soon grows back, minus the bulb sac.

"Hey Othar, you stuck your arm in a pleasure port. It's a stimulation device."

At the ominous black booth on the hangar floor, Evene has found the door on the front and swipes a non-special clicker. Unlike the booth in the city, this door does not open, so she runs back to get Othar's clicker, with the stylized "W" on it.

The video also shows that as the cities advanced, Tareons also kept a keen eye on the stars. Small robot scout ships were launched and sent to circle Zeon, to keep an eye on it. Later, as Zeon came closer with each passing, each Tareon city started two great projects. The first was the underground survival shelters built beneath each city, as each company's leadership needed a place for safety. The second project was excavating the large launch complex they are now sitting in, and seven huge winged ships were built, all lined up to fly out of the open end. The launch complex was the *only* endeavor the seven companies agreed to cooperate on, since the leaders of all companies would benefit from it.

At the black booth on the hangar floor, Evene swipes the W clicker and the bar retracts and the heavy thick door opens. Immediately, some small black worms fly into the great hangar and land about 200-feet away, followed by a larger adult flying worm, about 15-feet long. At the first sight of the worms, Rayelle again perks up, watching the worms as carefully as the video on the screen. Evene also watches them closely and then winces slightly at the familiar pungent-yet-sweet odor coming out of the black booth.

Footage from inside the hangar shows white-furred Tareons and their belongings walking up a ramp to board each ship while a long line of grey-furred Tareons step into the nearby black booths, four beings at each time. They enter the booth and a white-furred Tareon with a W clicker closes the door. Seconds later, a quick flash of light around the door jamb indicates something happened within the booth, and then some thick fluid exits out through the clear hose on the backside and goes into the aircraft, to which the other end is connected. The booth door is reopened and four more grey Tareons then step into the box. It happens over and over again, more fluid exiting toward the aircraft while the white-furred Tareons stoically load themselves onto each ship.

On the hangar floor, Evene is now about to drop her clicker in the hole next to the doorway and step into the black booth, when Drago sternly intones "Hey kids, step away from the box!"

"Why?"

"It's dangerous, and get back over here." They close the door and the worms quickly fly away. The kids rejoin the adults, who are still sitting and trying to take in everything on the video.

"Rayelle, there's the reason we haven't found any dead people. Those who did not board the ships all walked into these black boxes, never to be seen again," declares Drago. "And the black boxes in all of the cities must have the same purpose."

On the video screen, the last Tareon to board one of the ships walks toward the camera, in front of the ship with the "W" logo. In a strange female voice, she addresses the camera.

"To whoever may find this, I am Misdar, CEO of Worthland. We are the beings of Tareon, and this is our log. We loved our world and built much, but as our world and the fifth planet Zeon drew closer, we had to leave. We built deep shelters to survive the impact and one day return to the surface, but decided flying to the fourth planet, Loookor, was best. Since Loookor is farther in toward the center of our system, it would be safe. We hope our world somehow survives the impending collision with Zeon, but we have the ability to leave, and are so doing."

She then reaches toward the camera to press a button and the tape loop starts on the giant screen on the wall behind her. Next, she turns and walks back to board the ship behind her. A loading ramp closes and the seven great vessels fly off, each with the logo of the company leadership contained within. And finally, the camera fizzes and smolders as if to self-destruct. It crumbles to the floor and disperses into blowing dust, leaving no trace of itself.

Just after all seven ships have left the hangar, a number of the flying black worms enter, including some larger adults. One adult worm even has a W clicker in its mouth. They gather at the end where the hoses were connected to the ships and start sipping at the dark puddles on the floor through sharp, syphoniing, needle-tongues.

The worm with the W clicker hovers in front of the first booth's door and swings the clicker by, and the door opens and other worms fly in to suckle on the floor stains inside. The adult with the W clicker then proceeds to the six other booths and unlocks the door of each one. Within moments, the worms have sucked up all of the fluid puddles and fly out of the hangar, and the worm with the W clicker flies by and clicks, closing each booth's door, hoping other unsuspecting beings later find their way in.

The twelve Zeons watching the screen are transfixed by what they have seen on the video.

"I need to see it again, to gather more and see what I missed," as Rayelle is the first to speak up.

Othar agrees. It's condensed and not a long video, but they watch it over and over to absorb all they can, and soon realize they will never meet the people whose world they now occupy. It's a marooned, deserted thought, and Tareon now seems bigger and lonelier than ever.

"And I want to look those little creatures up," adds Evene. As the video is again restarting on the huge screen, she swipes up a monitor and searches *animals,* clicking on the picture of one of the flying worms. "They're called 'blood worms.' The Tareons didn't like them, but allowed them because they helped keep each city clean, sucking up all visible blood puddles."

Later, after viewing the video loop three more times, "It's getting late. Let's fly back to the city and report on this in the morning," orders Drago.

On Zeon the following day, Scepter and the others are at the seaside encampment. Elixor and his aides Garl and Hark have reassembled their crude foot-powered tools for cutting and shaping metal. The tools, like everything else, are made from hardened members of that universal green ooze. Aquatics are now sizeable, and some Zeons fish from both the shore and the large floating leaf pads. Even the swirling cool breezes and clouds are normal.

On Tareon high atop the "W" building, Drago prepares to call Zeon on his Comstaff, and Othar has his own Comstaff. Ingot and Spike are off to one side. They have one of the Tareon communication bracelets opened up and are making adjustments to it. The kids are playing near the back of the suite as Drago calls Zeon.

"Hello Zeon? Drago here."

After a pause, "Scepter here. Is there anything new to report?"

"Well, we got our first look at them."

"In the flesh? What are they like," asks an intrigued Scepter.

"Not exactly. We found a large launch complex. It's built into the side of a hill and not visible from above. It's enormous. There's nobody there, but they've left a repeating video log which plays on a screen high on one wall. It's kind of a historical snapshot, a message for whoever finds it."

"What does it show?"

"They're tall and thin, with pointed heads that widen out at the bottom, and thin vertical eyes. There used to be many small towns and tribes with each performing a function or purpose. These small towns became family businesses, but like Rayelle mentioned in the last call, some businesses grew and consolidated until only seven huge cor-por-a-tions were left. As our planets got closer with eash passing, their plan was to build two great infrastructure projects."

"*Two* great projects," asks an astonished Scepter. "Well at least we have one thing in common."

"The first was the building of the deep sustainment shelter we discovered the other day. Each city's leadership built one and planned to take shelter before our worlds collide, but then they changed their minds. The leadership of each city did not trust each other, but they came to an agreement – their first in centuries – to build the launch complex together. Each city's leadership built an enormous ship for their hierarchy and families to fly away on. They were very advanced. They sent small robot craft to orbit our planet and check us out."

"Why didn't they pursue us any further? If they had the technology, why didn't they land here on Zeon?"

"They apparently didn't find us . . . interesting. They knew our world was doomed and we seemed archaic and to have little knowledge or value."

This response again makes Scepter and the other Zeons listening feel humbled and inadequate.

"And here's the weird part," continues Drago. "Not many Tareons got onto each ship. Most others lined up and stepped into a box that seemed to pulverize them down into their bodily fluids. It appears that the waters and blood of many was used as fuel so that those in charge could fly away and escape. Nobody argued with this and all did as they were told."

"How long ago did they leave?"

"Judging by the dates on their timeline, two years ago."

"Damn! That's just before we got the first of you safely over there. If only our earlier launches had been successful, maybe they would've taken some of you with them so that some of us would live on."

"That would not have been likely. The more likely outcome is that they would've made us walk into their death boxes like most of their kind. Everybody's outcome here seemed preordained, something designated at birth. No one objected since if they did, they would be killed anyway. We've found these same death boxes in the cities but didn't know what they were for, but they also explain why we haven't found any dead people. Even in death, Tareons had a usable purpose. It appears that most of the populace was deemed 'expendable' to those in charge."

"That sounds like our Farside leadership, treating all others as easily replaceable. Here comes Kairn. He has just taken another sighting, but he's doing it visually and with measurements since his Sighter was blown away. Kairn, what have you learned?"

"Each of our planets has gone half-way around our orbits. We are now 180-degrees apart, directly opposite from each other. We have about 40 days left until our planets collide."

"Did you hear that?"

"That's what we figure," and after a slight pause, Drago changes the subject. "Are the kids there?"

"Yes, some of the young couples are nearby."

"That's okay. I'll try to make this generic. Have you set a date yet?"

Scepter knows he is asking about Elixor's poison as Chronicle walks up.

"We are thinking about 10 days before impact, just as things start to warm up and get bad again, but we are enjoying listening to your discoveries."

"That would be about 30 days from now."

"Yes, but the truth is that Elixor has the potion just about ready. We could take it at any time now. Elixor and his aids have also rebuilt his seaside foundry and I have them making a new monitor that should link to our tethered relay antenna. I am hoping to connect visually so we can see a bit of what you've discovered. Have you got any monitors there?"

"You draw up a monitor any place you want, here, and every building has a relay dish atop it. Rayelle saved an image of what the Tareons look like. When your monitor is working, we'll try to display it."

In the Tareon W suite, as Scepter begins his next response, his voice also echoes from the bracelet Ingot and Spike have been modifying. Ingot snaps the cover shut and walks the bracelet over to Drago as Rayelle gazes out one of the windows, both at the sky and at the city below.

"Very good," continues Scepter. "I am going to let Kairn, Varo, and the other families talk now."

Amid the multi-echo reverberation from the bracelets, Drago responds, "Hey, we have a small bit of good news. Ingot and Spike have modified one of our Tareon communication bracelets to connect with you on Zeon. We no longer need these stupid Comstaffs."

As Drago and Othar each raise one leg and lift their Comstaffs up with both hands, Rayelle gasps and quickly turns to look at them, and just as she vehemently roars "nooooooooooo," Drago and Othar snap each of their Comstaffs over their bent knees, braking each Staff in half.

"What are you doing," she roars as she falls to the floor and begins sobbing over the broken stick pieces. From the back of the suite, the kids hear her anger and run up to the commotion. Drago and Othar are shocked at the level of her outburst and on Zeon, Kairn and Trillo here it also and their heads snap to attention. She's always been a very focused individual. They've never heard her have an emotional melt-down, before.

"What's all of the fuss? We can get along without them," responds Drago as he and Othar hand their bracelets to Ingot for modification.

"You don't understand. You'll never understand," as she's curled up and crying on the floor, cuddling the broken stick pieces.

On Zeon, Kairn and Trillo are afraid to speak, and look worryingly at each other.

On Tareon the next day, Rayelle, Evene, Jurn and Plur ride the suite's aft elevator down to the deep survival cave. Each of them carries broken pieces of the two Comstaffs. She leads the girls to the doors and windows of the giant nursery forest and presses a green *"open"* button.

Inside the nursery hangar, sprinklers far down the nursery shut off and retract, a buzzer sounds, and air briefly evacuates in preparation for the doors being opened. An automated voice over a PA announces *"Doors unlocking in five, four, three, two, one."*

Within the doors, a huge lock releases with a firm metal clunk, and an *"okay to enter"* light displays. As soon as the doors open, "Ooh, it smells strong in there," winces Evene as the girls recoil from the dominating odor.

"Pungent, yet sweet," notices Rayelle. "This is the same odor from the death boxes up on the surface, but much more intense. I think these plants were recently fertilized. I wonder if blood from the death boxes in the cities was sent down here as plant food."

"Why are we placing these Comstaff pieces down here," asks Evene, as the girls step into the stadium-sized nursery.

"Because they will never rot down here and they may some day be important. Plus, this is the safest possible place."

They find a "Worthland" burlap sack and place the Comstaff pieces inside. Rayelle notices the rows of plants are securely held in place by fences to prevent them from falling during quakes, and places the burlap within the fences, to be held securely in place. "Let's get going. That's a strong odor," as she and the girls then exit and close the automated door.

The next day, Rayelle and the girls are flying out of Worthland in a Transtube.

"Where are we headed," asks Evene.

"Out to where we first landed."

After an hour, the Transtube reaches the cove they landed in. Strange unidentifiable creatures occasionally surface just long enough to create splashes on the water, but the deep purple water hides each creature's true identity. The giant Inlet Pod creature and Launch Stick Comstaff that stuck in it are gone, but Jurn and Plur's Launch Stick is still impaled in the beach sand.

"Look, your Launch Stick staff is still there on the beach."

Rayelle lands the Transtube on the sand not far from the stick. "Wait," quickly belts Rayelle as the girls start to get out. "Put your goggles on."

They all get out with Rayelle carrying a modern, machete-like blade. They rock the Stick back and forth to loosen it and lift it out of the sand,

and Rayelle whacks the parasols and rungs off using the huge machete cleaver.

"Okay, let's go!"

Just before Rayelle steps into the Transtube, she gazes up at the tree branch overhanging the cove and sees three small IrisCatchers calmly looking her way. These are different IrisCatchers from the two that saved their lives.

"Still looking out for us, or do you want to eat our eyes, also?"

They board their Transtube and take off to return to the city.

On Zeon three days later, Elixor calls Scepter over to his seaside foundry.

"Are you bringing me over to demonstrate your monitor," asks Scepter.

"No. Monitors are complex and it needs a couple more days to complete. Smell this," responds Elixor, while stirring a cast metal pot over a reed-fed flame.

"That smells good. What is it?"

"It's our death soup. The ground crops are coming back and I've added some of their natural sweeteners. Even the kids will like it."

"At least *something* is ready," responds a facetious Scepter. "And what else?"

"There's enough tar resin in here that I know it'll work, but to make sure the sedatives are totally painless, I'd like to try it on someone."

"Hmmm. I hate to designate a sacrifice, but Krale has not healed since the volcano and he's getting worse. He's in a lot of pain and is not going to live much longer."

"And I believe he has no family left."

"Chronicle, please join Elixor and I near where Krale lies," as Scepter speaks into his Comstaff.

They walk over to the convalescing Krale who lies quietly on a grassy knoll overlooking the sea, wrapped in woven reeds. "We will check on him now," Scepter tells others attending to Krale. The others leave and Scepter and Elixor kneel down to address Krale as Chronicle walks up. Elixor carries a small green bowl of the soup. Krale's eyes are closed, and dusty grey soot surrounds his mouth and nose.

"Krale, how are you feeling," asks Scepter, while gently caressing Krale's head.

Krale tries to answer but starts by coughing up grey phlegm. "I swallowed too much dust during the passing. I'm dying inside. 'tis slow and painful."

"Do you feel ready to go?"

After coughing some more, "I am ready."

"Elixor has something for that. We will all be taking it soon. Do you want some?"

"Please."

"Are you sure?"

"Please," while still coughing.

"Very well." Scepter lifts Krale's head and Elixor gives Krale a sip and asks, "How does it taste?"

"'tis good. Living has been good. My family has been good. Our planet . . . has been good." Krale then falls into a calm sleep.

Scepter slowly lowers Krale's head and Elixor gently places his open palm on Krale's chest.

"Good work, *chef*" as Scepter commends Elixor. "He liked your brew. Krale told me as we came off of Altai that he wished he had gone when his family did."

"It's interesting hearing from Tareon on how advanced it and the other planets are," admits Elixor. "It sounds like the Tareons are centuries ahead of us in development. I would enjoy seeing their methods and tools."

"Yes, but it's also humbling. We don't have anything approaching their technology and knowledge. If it wasn't for Altai, our Great Elastic, and Tareon coming so close twice a year, we could never get anyone over there. I guess that's why even though other planets checked us out, they found us to be too simple. I guess we're like small insects, not worth much."

Then, calmly, Krale takes one last deep breath. His mouth opens and a final, sedating exhale comes out.

"That's it. He's gone," Elixor quietly declares, sensing that Krale's chest and heart has stopped moving through the palm of his open hand.

"Chronicle, can you get in touch with his essence one last time," askes Scepter.

Chronicle kneels down and wraps one hand around Krale's arm, and Chronicle's silver eyes take on a glazed, far-off look.

"Krale, this is Scepter. Have you any final words?"

"Thank you for ending my agony," as without coughing, Krale's voice is calmly heard from Chronicle's mouth. "I am content now."

As Chronicle releases his grip on the lifeless Krale, "That was nice," as Scepter again commends Elixor. "It was entirely peaceful. If death can be painless, that was it. We should not hesitate to drink your soup when the time is right."

"You know Scepter, we haven't had a proper burial since before the pass-by. Wouldn't this be a good time?"

The next day at the bottom of the sandy burial crater, a hole as been excavated in the sand. Krale's body has been placed in it, fully wrapped in woven reeds. Elixor kneels on one side, just behind a built-up berm of sand. On the other side are Elixor's assistants Garl and Hark, holding flutes. There are thousands of other mounds nearby, the plots of others who have passed on.

At the top of the crater, Kairn, Varo and Trillo are positioned as lookouts. Kairn and Varo stand on the ridge between the burial crater and the adjacent soft sand crater, the one with the rocky outcropping at the bottom. Trillo plays nearby, throwing his Returner up into the wind. There are oversized woven sand shoes along the rim of the soft sand crater. Adults put them on when walking down that crater, to distribute their weight and keep from sinking in.

At the bottom of the burial crater, all 55 other Zeons are joined in a circle around Krale's plot, with Scepter at the head. It's a beautifully normal Zeon day, with soft spiraling breezes and vertical spiral clouds in the sky, as Scepter gives the last words.

"We gather here to say our farewell to our dearly departed Krale. In his final minutes of our final days, he told us he was ready to go. His passing was calm and his suffering is gone, and may he lead the way . . . for all of us."

And with that, Garl and Hark begin playing the beautiful *ode for the departed*, and Elixor begins gently pushing the small sand pile over Krale's body. The 55 circled around begin the departed waltz, a short dance that ends with a gentle spiral of hands starting down low and working their way upward toward the sky. Elixor concludes the covering by drawing a simple elegant spiral in the sand mound covering Krale's body.

Kairn and Varo are positioned as lookouts on the ridge high above, because if a sudden strong gust of wind should approach, those within the burial crater must be told so they have a few seconds to prepare. While Kairn and Varo talk, Trillo plays with his Returner, tossing it up into the circular breezes which bring it back his way. On the third throw, a strong gust of wind blows it far down into the adjacent soft sand crater, where it settles to ground on the far side of the rocky outcropping at the bottom.

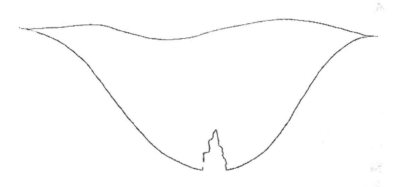

"I'll be right back" as he takes off down into the crater in pursuit of the Returner. Trillo is quite comfortable in this crater and has spent countless hours playing in it.

"Wind gust! Cover up," as Kairn yells down into the adjacent burial crater.

"Okay son, but watch your step" as Kairn then replies to the fleeting Trillo, knowing his son is still light enough to not sink into the soft sand.

"So, why did your people put up with Dorn and his family dictators for so long," Kairn asks Varo.

"His family had so many informers amidst our ranks, whenever an overthrow plot was in the works, he would find out, and many more were put to death. He rewarded his informers well for good information and that kept them loyal."

As they talk, Trillo rounds the base of the 30-foot high outcropping at the crater bottom and sees his Returner leaning against the backside, on the sand where it meets the base of the vertical rock face. He reaches down to pick the Returner up and a small bit of sand under it sinks away, revealing a miniscule sink hole.

"Hmm. What the . . .?"

After picking up the Returner, using one foot, he touches the edge of the small hole and the sand under both of his feet quickly gives way as the hole grows just large enough to swallow his thin body. He falls in just under the rocky formation above as the Returner lands harmlessly to one side of the hole.

Up at the crater rim, Kairn doesn't notice that Trillo has disappeared behind the outcropping at the bottom and *not* reemerged. Finally, "Trillo, now is not the time for hide and seek! Son? Son?"

After there is no response, Kairn quickly steps over and slips his feet into the oversized sand shoes and runs down into the crater. Varo does the same and quickly follows Kairn down. "Son, where are you," as Kairn rounds the outcropping at the bottom.

Kairn comes upon the small hole, now just big enough for a body the size of Trillo's to fit through, and the Returner lies just off to one side.

"Son, are you down there" asks Kairn, poking his head down into the the darkened hole.

"I'm here" responds a frightened Trillo in a quivering tone, about 10-feet down from the opening. "I've come to a stop on some steps along a solid rock wall."

"Don't move! We'll get you out!"

Kairn digs the hole out wider and reveals the first of many steep buried steps headed down under the outcropping. He and Varo step down into the hole and crouch down, stopping just above the frightened Trillo.

"It's dark down here, and musty, like it's been closed off for a long time," observes Kairn.

"I hear that your side has illuminators. Have you got yours," asks Varo.

"Yes" responds Kairn, pulling out a short, brightly lit rod and pointing it downward. Another of Elixor's inventions – when exposed to sunlight for a few hours - illuminators stay brightly lit for six-to-eight hours. He points it downward between the outcropping - which tapers outward steeply - and the wall the stairs descend along. "This place is deep. It's also dangerous and we're not prepared for this. We'd better go tell the others."

On the rim high above the burial crater, the 55 mourners could not find Kairn and Varo and are walking down toward the seaside encampment when Kairn, Varo, and Trillo run up from behind.

"Scepter, we've found a new cave," proclaims a panting Kairn.

"Where?"

"At the bottom of the soft sand crater."

"Under the sand? That's a strange place for a cave."

"No, it's more like . . . under the outcropping."

"How is that possible? Does it look very promising?"

"It looks and smells . . . different. Very different. I think we opened it for the first time in a long time."

"Should we go and check it out?"

"Yes, but not tonight. Can we weave more sand shoes and charge more illuminators? It's very dark in there."

"Yes. I'll have them ready in two days," responds Elixor.

Two mornings later in the soft sand crater, a party of eleven gets an early start as most have not been sleeping well, and the thought of something new is the biggest discovery in weeks. At the base of the rocky outcropping, each steps out of their sand shoes and down into the hole, which has been dug out wider so that adults and Comstaffs can fit through. Once in, they carefully descend the steep chiseled stairs along the cave wall. The party consists of Scepter, Chronicle, Kairn, Varo, Torq, Alor, Garl, Hark, Elixor, and two others. All are carrying illuminator sticks, and Chronicle, Varo and Kairn each walk with Comstaffs.

"It has a certain smell . . . and feel," notices Varo, while descending down the steep stone stairs.

"It's humid, very damp and musty," responds Scepter. "Be careful, Chronicle. It's very steep."

They reach the cave floor and walk on soft sand between jagged boulders. They pass small pools of trapped fresh water and some of the rock walls have a shiny glistening texture, as if their veins are filled with rich metals. Some 150-feet past the pools, they come upon markings etched into the left wall, which perks the explorers up.

"These are just what we are hoping to see," notices Varo. "Scepter, what do you make of these characters?"

"This is strange. I don't recognize any of these symbols. They look completely different. You all continue ahead. I'll work on these markings."

"I'll rest and stay here with you," adds Chronicle. "Maybe together, we can decipher these."

The nine others continue onward. The cave goes deeper and progressively gets narrower. Before long, they are too far ahead to yell back to Scepter and must use their Comstaffs, and after descending two more miles, they come upon two rock-carved carts. Each cart is rectangular with an open top, and large enough for six Zeons to stand in. Under each cart are two round balls, which roll in a half-round channel excavated into the cave floor. The balls and channel are shiny and slick, as if coated with grease.

"Look at these carts. I wonder what they were used for," asks Varo.

"Probably for mining or removing rocks, and they seem to roll in this floor channel," responds Elixor.

The nine continue walking, following the floor channel in the ground, which parallels their path. Before long, they see other spur channels merging with their floor channel, some from the left and some from the right, and some channels have more carts in them. This continues for a couple more miles as they are now very deep underground.

"Varo, are there any caves this deep on your side of the planet," asks Kairn.

"Nothing even close to this deep. This one seems quite unlike the other caves I've seen."

Rounding a gradual bend, "Look, there is a boulder blocking the floor channel," observes Kairn. "I don't think it's supposed to be there. The channel is supposed to be clear. Let's see if we can roll the boulder out."

The nine explorers then push the boulder out and back across the channel until it gathers enough speed to roll up out of the curved track and off to the far side.

"Did you notice the bottom of the boulder was curved to match the curve in the channel," observes Elixor. "I don't think it was there by accident. I think it was put there to block the channel and prevent the carts from getting past this point."

"Stop talking like that," responds an insecure Kairn.

"I'm just saying."

Strangly, there are no carts beyond the boulder they removed, and as they continue further, Elixor notices an unusual commonality among the boulders they are passing.

"Look at the far side of all of these boulders: the side facing the direction we are heading. They're all scorched with blackness on that side, as if they were once subjected to intense heat from the direction up ahead."

"What could cause all of that heat," replies Varo.

"Whatever caused this, the heat was incredible," adds Elixor while looking back. "The boulders well behind us have all been scorched."

"And look at the cave walls ahead. They're also turning black. There must have been something very hot up ahead," adds Garl.

"This cave seems so unlike all of the others we've found. I wonder what else we'll find," adds Kairn.

After a couple of more miles, the cave has narrowed to about 20-feet high by 40-feet wide, with the slick floor channel still alongside the path. Finally, approaching a solid wall at the end, they see it: A large horizontal slot in the rock face in front of them. The opening is about 10-feet tall, and the top and bottom edges are perfectly parallel with each other. Each end is a perfect half-circle arc connecting the top and bottom edges. The slot is about 30-feet wide and looks like the shape of a stretched, elongated running track.

At the sight of the darkened slot opening, all in the search party are silent until, "Scepter, this is the search party," as Kairn sheepishly calls into his Comstaff.

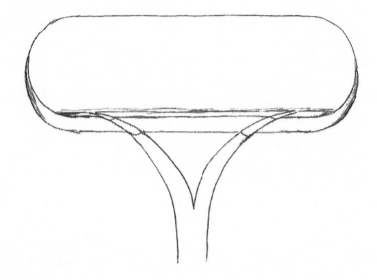

Back at the entrance cave wall symbols, Scepter and Chronicle pour closely over the wall symbols as Kairn's voice echoes over their Comstaffs, which have been stabbed in the floor sand.

"We are listening. What have you found," responds Scepter.

"The cave goes very deep. We are miles beyond you. As it narrows, we passed carts that we believe were for removing rock. Each cart rolls in a slick channel. There are many spurs and carts off to the side. The cave ends at a thick wall which has a wide horizontal slot opening into some sort of a large tunnel. And Scepter?"

"Yes?"

"This hole is not natural. The edges are too perfect. Someone cut this slot."

Back at the wall symbols, Scepter and Chronicle turn and stare wide-eyed at each other. "Go on."

"The cart channel in the floor splits just before the slot opening, one split turning left into the slot tunnel, and the other, to the right. We didn't want to proceed any further until we called you. It's getting late and our illuminators are losing strength. We are turning and heading back toward you. It looks like we're going to be down here all day tomorrow and we have to prepare for it. More illuminators are needed and more support people must be in place. We're heading back your way, now."

Back at the wall symbols - noticing that one etched symbol appears at different locations - Scepter responds, "Good. There it is again, up there and over here. We're looking forward to seeing you and will continue studying these symbols."

An hour later, the nine who explored up ahead are rejoining Scepter and Chronicle, who have stepped back and are leaning against a rock while gazing at- and still pondering- the symbols.

"Scepter, we'll have to prepare this entrance cave as a staging area tomorrow," advises the approaching Kairn, followed by the others. "This is a strange cave and as it goes much deeper, who knows what we'll find." Turning to the symbols Scepter and Chronicle have been studying, "What have you learned from all of these symbols?"

"Very little," replies Scepter. "Most of them are completely foreign, but a few bear resemblance to an older version of some characters in the other caves."

"Is there anything you can make out?"

Stepping toward the wall with the symbols, "Only one symbol I see over and over in a number of places: here, here and here."

"And what does it say?"

"Well, the characters within it spell out the name . . . 'Zhama.'"

Hearing that name, Chronicle turns and frantically runs back toward the cave exit and seeing one of the small water pools, throws himself in, trying to drown and kill himself. Scepter takes off after him, tackles him from behind, and pulls his gasping head up out of the water. Chronicle is shaking and totally terrified, and is quickly going into shock. No one has ever seen the old one react or run like this, and the nine others run up from behind.

"What is it, Chronicle? What made you run like that?"

"Let me go! Let me go," shouts a scared and terrified Chronicle, coughing up water from trying to drown himself. "I know what I'm doing!"

"No you don't! You've lost all control!"

"That name! Something about that name!"

"What is it, Chronicle? You've lived forever! What could make you want to kill yourself?"

"That name! That name! Something about that name!"

"What about that name? What is it? What is Zhama?"

"Something so old, I do not know; only what comes with it. What it represents."

"What does it portend? What do you feel? What do you sense?"

With a horrid look of utter terror in his silver eyes, "Fear. Destruction. Total annihilation. Something not survivable."

CHAPTER 6

Inward

A LL NINE OTHERS HEARING CHRONICLE'S words are rapt with fear. He's always been a pillar of knowledge and calmness.

"He's lived forever. If *he's* scared, what does that mean for the rest of us," warns a worried Hark.

They gather up the thunderstruck Chronicle - now in shock - and one by one, climb the stone staircase assisting Chronicle as they go, and crawl out the hole at the base of the rocky outcropping. Scepter returns to the wall symbols to retrieve his Comstaff and Chronicle's Comstaff. "What secrets do you hide," he mutters, taking one last glance up at the wall symbols, and he and the others exit the cave just after the sun has set behind the crater rim.

In the evening at the seaside encampment, they huddle about what equipment is needed for the next search of the cave. Nearby, on the same hill Krale laid on, Chronicle is laying, wrapped in leaves. Lit by reed-burning torches and the early evening's emerging stars, Elixor has calmed him with an herbal mix. Chronicle's Comstaff stands impaled nearby as Scepter walks up.

"How's he doing?"

"I've had to flood him with herbs so he'll sleep soundly now, but it took a bushel. I've never seen him so wound up."

"Good. He should be safe for awhile. Join me and the others."

The nine who ventured into the cave are surrounded by the 48 others. Scepter steps up on the seaside tree stump and tells all what they've found.

"Now listen up, everyone. Our young Mr. Trillo discovered a new cave opening under the rocky outcropping in the soft sand crater. We've gone in a few miles, but we hope to push in further. Elixor, we'll take illuminators in with us, but we'll need more charging outside of the cave

113

entrance, and we'll also need backpacks and goggles. The air down there is thick and musty so we may need some of your oxygen tablets. Can you and your aides be ready in two day's from now?"

"Yes, Scepter."

"Good. We'll need attendants standing watch at the hole, and we'll set up a small base camp on the floor opposite the cave symbols. Are there any questions?"

"Scepter, what do the cave symbols say?"

"They are older symbols of a language that we've never seen before, but the one symbol I could make out said something called 'Zhama.' The sound of it is what sent Chronicle into shock."

Hearing this, all others recoil and look at each other.

"We only went a few miles down, but we saw evidence of mining equipment," offers Kairn. "We also saw signs of something else."

"Signs of what?"

"A horizontal slot cut so perfect, it's not natural," adds Varo. "Someone had to have cut it, and it's cut through the hardest, thickest granite you've ever seen. We're not the first ones to go down there."

"Any sign of bodies? Any skeletons or bones?"

"None."

Just then, from Tareon, Drago's voice comes over Scepter's Comstaff.

In the top floor W suite on Tareon, Rayelle firmly clutches the Launch Stick Comstaff retrieved from their cove landing site, but Drago and Othar talk into their bracelets, "Hello Zeon? This is Drago."

On Zeon, "Scepter here. We're all gathered around and listening. What have you found?"

"We've combed through a couple more of Tareon's caves, but have found nothing new. More depictions of our solar system looking much the same; all nine planets with good separation between Zeon and Tareon, and Rayelle's been researching more records. It turns out; the Tareons occasionally talked to the inhabitants of planets seven, eight and nine. The beings on those planets are also very advanced. It's looking like much of this system is very far ahead of us."

"Hmm. Your reports keep reminding us how little we know," replies Scepter.

"What's new, there," asks Othar.

"We too have found a new cave, under the soft sand crater. It's deep and very strange, and the cave paintings mentioned something that scared Chronicle so bad that he went into shock. Elixor had to give him a bunch of herbs to calm him down. Something called . . . 'Zhama.' It looks like some mining was once done down there, and two days from now, we'll go in deeper and find out more. It's late and we need some sleep before tomorrow's preparations. Stay alert, stay smart, and forward with brilliance. Zeon, out!"

Later that night on Tareon, the twelve in the W building top floor suite are asleep on cushions and pillows, which they have placed about the suite floor. Rayelle has her Comstaff nearby, but Drago quietly takes it, and he and Othar sneak out, riding down the forward elevator to street level. They find a Transtube and fly out to the beach houses on Infinity Lake, and land.

"Hello Zeon? This is Drago," in a quiet voice, even though they are a few miles from the city center. "Can you hear us?"

On Zeon it is also night time, and some on Zeon also can't sleep. Their heads spin with thoughts of what could scare Chronicle, so.

Kairn lies on his back on the seaside ancient great tree stump, looking up at the heavens. Trillo lies with his head on Kairn's chest, also looking up at the stars, which again arc slowly across the clear sky from west to east.

"Hello Zeon? This is Drago. Can you hear us," as Drago's voice comes quietly over their Comstaff, as if this is a private matter.

"Drago, this is Kairn," who also replies quietly. "Trillo is here with me, most of the others are asleep. Listen, how is Rayelle doing?"

"That's why we are calling. It's just Othar and me. We're a few miles from her where we could talk to you by ourselves. I'm sure you heard her outburst the other day. Ingot and Spike modified these bracelets so we can talk to you there on Zeon, and something about us no longer needing our Comstaffs really set her off. Have you ever seen or heard her react like that?"

"No, she's always been focused on whatever task is at hand. That's how she got picked to manage the Sea Cover and Great Elastic projects."

"Kairn, this is Othar. Have you ever known her to keep things in; to not share things that are bothering her?"

"She's not shy. She's never afraid to say what's on her mind. How's she been since that outburst?"

"She got over it quick enough and went out to their landing site and retrieved their other Launch Staff, so now she has a Staff of her own and carries it everywhere. She even sleeps with it, but we sneaked it away before calling you."

"One thing I've learned about Silver Eyes is that besides being able to connect with others, they're also very adept at blocking out their own thoughts, so if you try to get Evene and her ability to help you with that, it may not help. Keep calling in every few days so she can hear our voices, and if she comes unglued again, let me know and I'll ask her what's up."

The call ends and Drago and Othar fly back into the city and ride up into the W suite, and quietly place the Comstaff next to the sleeping Rayelle.

The next day on Tareon, the teams are at the top of the W building. Drago, Othar and Rayelle study a topographical map of Tareon on a monitor. Othar notices a button on the screen margin marked '*deploy*,' and asks "Rayelle, what happens if you click over '*deploy?*'"

Rayelle runs her clicker over the screen button and a sudden beam of energy creates a large 3D globe of Tareon in their office, a few feet in front of the monitor. With jutting mountains and sunken valleys, every feature is highlighted in detailed physical relief, as are the seven brightly lit cities.

"Wow, that button is magic," exclaims Othar. "Out of nowhere, there is suddenly a model of this planet!"

Intrigued by their new model, Elixor's brothers Ingot and Spike walk over and together, all five pour over the detailed globe of Tareon.

"The detail here is most impressive. Their cartography is very advanced."

"What's this deep fisher down here in the south, very far from the cities?"

"It's a canyon; a very deep one, and it appears to be the deepest one on the planet."

"And what would happen if we can find a cave very far down in that canyon?" By looking lower down in this planet's crust, wouldn't we be going back further in time?"

"That's an interesting thought. If we can find an older cave, maybe it'll provide some answers for more of this planet's history, and how our planets have come together. It's so far from these cities, it'll take a good four days to fly out there and back, so we'll have to prepare for this trip."

On Zeon two mornings later, eight of the nine forward explorers from the previous trip - plus Scepter, are opposite the cave paintings, equipping to head down the same path as two days earlier. They don backpacks, green goggles, gloves, and illuminator sticks. Scepter and Farsider Alor have Comstaffs. As they start down the path, sunlight from the cave entrance above is blocked by the shadow of someone else coming in. It's Chronicle and his Comstaff, with Elixor following closely behind. Chronicle has slept in, and is still getting over the effects of Elixor's powerful sedatives.

"You all get started and I'll catch up," as Scepter sends the others ahead.

Looking both tired and worn by all his emotion two days before, Chronicle descends to the floor and joins Scepter in front of the glyphs.

"Are you okay to be down here?"

"I think so. It was the suddenness of hearing something so old, so lost for such a long time, but I think I've accepted it now."

"Good. Did a couple nights of sleep bring back any more memories?"

"No. This is something much, much older than even I. It's not coming from memory, but from the traits of those before me, and is engrained in the very fibers of my soul. Something very far back, but yet known to be frightful, and I wanted to come down here to see these symbols again and to take one more look at something."

As Chronicle turns and looks back up to where the cave wall, opening, and the outcropping sticking up from the cave floor come together, Elixor reassures Scepter. "Don't worry. I'll be with him here. And if he loses it again, I've got plenty more knockout hemp."

Chronicle - craning his head upward - points out the convergence of cave wall and outcropping from the floor, to Scepter. "Now see how the slope of the outcropping and the wall come together at the top?"

"Yes."

"And notice how – below ground, the outcropping is sloped very conical, too smooth to be a jagged natural?"

"Yes."

"Someone tried to keep people out, to keep this cave shut. We were never supposed to find this place."

"Great," replies a sarcastic Scepter. "The others up ahead will be thrilled to hear that. We'll be back later for new illuminators."

After descending and seeing the floor channel and mining carts for the first time, Scepter catches up with the eight others who are waiting at the horizontal slot. The darkened slot is ominous looking and the first thing they notice is the thickness of the hard granite surrounding the opening.

"Look at the thick wall, like it's needed for great strength," notices Alor.

They step closer and peer through the slot and look into a huge tunnel. The tunnel goes both to the left and to the right, is much taller than the top of the slot, and is perfectly round; a tunnel cut through solid rock. It's a giant round tube cut deep within the planet. The channel the carts are in, splits and bends to the left and to the right, and merges into the floor channel of the enormous tube tunnel. The cart channel adds a little more depth, and might also be for drainage of water or some other fluid. The black tunnel walls look shiny, as if they are wet or slick.

Peering into the huge tunnel, Scepter asks what first comes to mind. "Alright, who goes to the left and who goes to the right?"

"Torq and I will take a crew in the left direction," voices Farsider Alor, who carries a Comstaff.

"And I'll take a crew to the right," responds Scepter.

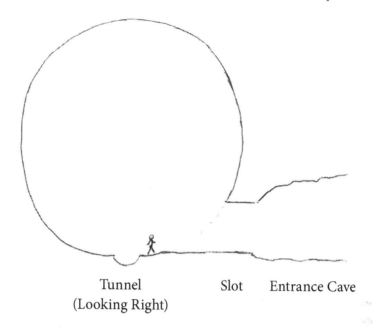

Tunnel   Slot   Entrance Cave
(Looking Right)

Varo takes a step into the giant tunnel and immediately slips and falls. "Hey, the floor is slick and so are the walls. What is this stuff?"

"It's the natural grease lubricants of the planet," replies Kairn. "Some of it comes up with that green ooze we knead."

"Either we walk and have bad footing or we ride in those carts we passed," explains Scepter of their options.

All vote for the carts and quickly run back to retrieve two of them. Alor, Torq, Garl and one other hop in one cart. With one or two easy pushes on the greased channel, it easily rolls forward to where the channel merges with the tunnel floor channel. Scepter, Kairn, Varo, Hark and one other board another cart and do the same, but how to make them go, once in the tunnel?

"With the slick walls and floor, how do we make them go?"

Scepter looks down and studies the cart. On the outside of the front end, a wooden cover can be removed to reveal a metal plate. Scepter pulls the cover off and the cart starts to slowly move forward along the channel track as if guided by an invisible force, and as his cart veers into the tunnel right direction, he yells back to Alor's cart. "Remove the cover on the front, to go!" Alor does as told and his cart veers into the tunnel left direction.

"Use the Comstaffs to stay in touch," yells Scepter with one last command as the two carts disperse in opposite directions.

Still trying to make sense of their simple oar cart, "Hark, is there another cover and metal plate on the back end of this cart," asks Scepter toward the rear.

"Yes, Scepter. This rear cover and plate must be for going back to the entrance slot." While still looking back, Hark points out something else to the others in his cart.

"Scepter, look toward the rear. There is a gentle arc to this tunnel. As we go forward, there is a gradual bend to the left."

It's only noticeable over a long distance, but the light from the slot opening they are moving away from will soon go out of sight as the inner wall of the gentle bend will soon get in the way. In the left direction in Alor's cart, they are noticing a similar opposite gentle arc, to the right.

The carts are not fast, about the same as a brisk walk, but they seem the best way to travel. The explorers' illuminator sticks light the way ahead, but no farther than the subtle arc of the bend ahead. The huge tunnel is perfectly round and a daunting 50-feet in diameter. The entire wall surface is coated in thick shiny grease, and the walls are as black as coal.

"This thing is enormous," remarks Kairn, as their first reaction is to marvel at size of the 50-foot round tunnel. "And look at the small ridges in the walls. It was cut by one manual stroke after another."

"And it's cut through some of the hardest granite on the planet. It must've taken years to dig this tunnel," adds Varo.

"Is it just me, or is this cart gradually speeding up," asks Kairn as they continue rolling ahead.

"I think you're right" replies Varo. Scepter slides the wooden cover to partially obstruct the front end metal plate, and the cart slows back to its original pace. As the cart slowly proceeds onward, Scepter touches his Comstaff tip to the tunnel floor and advises "Torq, Alor, if your cart speeds up, cover the forward plate to slow down."

A couple of miles later in Alor's left direction cart, "My illuminator is getting weak," observes Torq.

Hearing that, "We've also lost one," responds Scepter's voice from the other cart.

In Alor's left direction cart, they soon come upon a fork in their tunnel. From the left, another equally large tunnel blends into theirs, pointing back in the direction they came from, with a floor channel that merges with theirs.

"Scepter, we've come upon a junction merging from the outer side. We're going to follow it."

A short time later, after diverting into the left spur and navigating another gentle curve, they enter a large, very tall chamber. Suddenly, the top half of their tunnel ends, leaving them navigating an open-topped trough. The cavern is enormous and very tall. The channel gently arcs toward a large, very tall box structure with sides, but no front or back. Inside the box structure are huge broken pieces, possibly forms for shaping something; something very large.

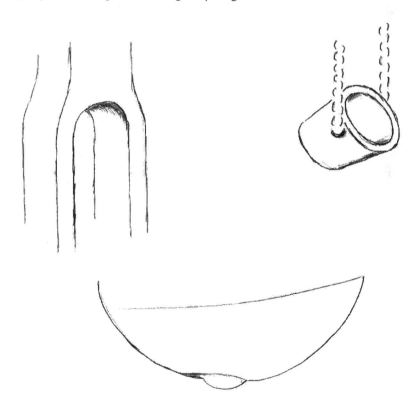

Above, giant chains hang down from a cave ceiling so high that they vanish up into the dark. To the right - suspended on more giant chains - is an enormous stone bucket. A second stone bucket lies broken on the floor, as if it fell from its chains and crashed onto the cave floor. All surfaces facing their entry point are scorched black, as if they were once subjected to horrendous heat. Everything in the cavern is on a gigantic scale. There is a weak, ominous, ancient breeze, and it's also very warm, and may at one time have been much, much hotter. Alor covers the front plate and their cart comes to a stop.

"Oh my, this cave is huge!"

"What have you found," asks Scepter's voice over their Comstaff.

"Smell this place," notices Garl from the back of their cart. "Coke, sulfur, salts – and it's still warm. If I didn't know better, I'd say we're in the mother of all foundries. Someplace metal was worked . . . on a grand scale."

All in Scepter's cart hear this, as do Elixor and Chronicle in the outer entrance cave.

"If there was heat, there must've been smoke," responds Scepter's voice. "Garl, from our starting point and your route and distance, do you think you could be under Altai?"

Garl turns his body 180-degrees to the right, 90-degrees to the left, and then left again, as if retracing their direction. "I believe so."

"Good. Could the small holes in Altai's wall be where the smoke was released?"

"It's possible. The route up to open air would be much shorter."

"Good. You've just answered one of our unknowns."

"Scepter, the top half of this outer spur has opened into some kind of a very tall foundry cave," adds Alor, describing the scene. "Everything in here is enormous."

"And look at the boulders," adds Garl. "They are scorched toward this big tunnel, as if they too were burned like those in the entrance cave."

"I don't scare easiy but this place gives me the creeps," adds a nervous Torq. "Uncover the back plate and let's back out of here."

They back out of the cavern to where their tunnel meets the main tunnel, and resume going forward in the left direction.

As Scepter's cart continues further in the right direction, Scepter doesn't notice that the metal necklace around his neck quietly lifts by itself and sticks forward, almost as if to point the way ahead. Seeing this, the others in his cart are transfixed by it. Varo – who sports a metal tooth - briefly chuckles, but his metal tooth flies out of his mouth, flying forward into the dark. A little further - with Scepter's necklace now pulling tautly against the back of his neck - the metal relayer dish atop his Comstaff also flies off, forward and around the bend ahead, all by itself.

"What is going on? Alor, are you losing metal items from you or your cart?"

"Negative, just the light getting dimmer as our illuminators weaken."

They've now both gone twenty miles in the opposite directions from the entrance cave's original opening, making them 40 miles apart.

Then, in Scepter's right direction cart, something totally foreign slowly emerges from around the bend up ahead. It's large and a scene of apparent destruction. On both the inner- and outer- wall directly across from it, it looks as if something very large which previously blocked the path ahead has been broken through. Initially speechless, they approach slowly and stop their cart.

"Whatever it was that blocked the way has been completely busted through."

It's almost as tall as the tunnel, starting from one yard above the floor up to about one yard below the ceiling, and is 45-feet thick, yet it has been completely busted through and because of its large diameter, most of the busted obstruction is well above their heads.

Along both sides, shards of fibric remnants stick out into the tunnel path, all broken through by some powerful force which continued further ahead in their tunnel. Scepter stops the cart and they all get out.

Kairn reaches to break off a shard sticking out from the outboard side. It sticks out wider than the outboard opening, and he breaks it off and smells it.

"It's damp and has grain, and has the musty smell of the rest of the cave. You know what this is! It's a piece of a great timber! This is one of the ancient great timbers! It's not growing because there's no sunlight, but how did it get down here?"

Scepter breaks off other shards sticking out wider than the outboard side opening – reaching some higher shards with his Comstaff - and suddenly, the entire outboard side log slowly rumbles further outboard, away from their tunnel. They all jump back from the sudden movement and have to steady themselves on the greasy floor. The crossing tunnel the timber lays in is also coated with black grease, and slowly, the giant timber rumbles further away, revealing that its tunnel is very long. Some 150-feet away, it finally comes to a stop, hitting the outboard end of its tunnel.

"Don't pull anymore of these timber pieces," Kairn warns Scepter.

They walk across and look at the inboard side of their tunnel. On this side, they notice huge metal teeth extending in from the tree tunnel wall, looking like claws that grabbed the timber to hold it in position, as if to stop it from being extended further across their tunnel. Scepter shines his illuminator between the bark outer surface and the timber tube wall. Running away from the grabbing teeth are two clear, bright blue flexible hoses which might have fluid in them. Because of the small gap between the timber and its wall, he can't tell where the tubes lead, only somewhere further inward, toward the center of their planet.

"These teeth appear to hold this side of the timber in position," notes Scepter, as his party also peers inward. "If I remove some shards, this piece of the timber should stay in place."

The others step back, out of the path of the huge tree trunk, and Scepter breaks off a number of shards.

"There, see? Nothing! Only the outboard side will move away. Let's hop back in the cart and continue forward."

They hop back in and Scepter uncovers the cart's front plate, and resume going forward in the right direction. They start up and roll slowly past the timber destruction, and just a few yards past the broken timber, Scepter's cart passes a small horizontal opening on the inboard side of the tunnel. It's down low and is just big enough for one person to crawl through. Because it's so low and the granite is so thick, they can't see where it leads, only further in toward the center of their planet, and they slowly roll by.

"We'll check that small opening out, later," advises Scepter, who calls out to Alor in the left direction cart.

"Alor, we just came upon one of the great ancient timbers. It was positioned across our path but had been completely broken through by something. If you come upon one, be careful on the outboard side. The pieces extending out from it hold the outer trunk in place. If you remove them, the trunk will move, although away from you. And just past the great timber was a small hole, low on the inboard wall, just big enough for one to crawl through. You may see something like it."

Each cart's crew is now completely wide-eyed. They can't believe what might come next.

In Scepter's cart, about a hundred yards past the first shattered great timber, they come upon another one. It's just as thick in diameter and broken entirely though by some awesome force. They slow while passing the destructive scene and just past it, they see a similar small opening, low on the inboard side.

A hundred yards further, there's a third broken timber, and a hundred yards further, yet another, each with the low hole after it. After they've past their sixth giant broken timber, Alor's voice is heard from the opposite direction.

"Scepter, we've come upon our first timber."

"Is it broken through," Scepter quickly asks.

"Negative. It's completely intact, at least from this side, and we just passed one of those small openings, low on the inboard side." Hearing this, Scepter slows his right direction cart.

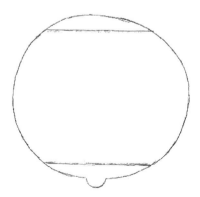

"Is there a space at the top and bottom of the timber?"

"Yes. We will have to crawl under and continue on foot."

"Very well. On the inboard side, notice the teeth that grab the timber, and the blue tubes that run away from the teeth. We're passing our seventh broken timber now and are continuing forward."

Alor's left direction crew gets out of their cart and all crawl under the giant log across their path. The floor channel seems to work well for crawling under obstructions, and is just wide enough for Zeons to lie in. Once past the giant timber, Alor and crew continue walking gingerly on the greasy tunnel floor.

As they proceed, Torq notices small white granules in the black grease. He reaches down, picks up a small granule, wipes it against his fur to clean it, and takes a bite.

"It's hard, with a bit of salt and calcium. It's bone! Scepter!"

"Yes, Torq."

"There are pulverized white pebbles embedded in the grease along the floor. I tasted one. They're bone fragments."

"Are you sure," replies Scepter, looking down and noticing similar fragments in his own direction.

"When you've served time in the prison caves on my side of the planet, you never forget what bone tastes like," replies Torq.

As Alor's left direction crew continues walking forward, their view ahead suddenly gets darker. "Scepter, we've lost another illuminator."

"We've just lost another also," responds Scepter. Scepter stops his cart and calls back to the entrance cave. "Elixor, can you hear us?"

"Yes, Scepter."

"Send others into the tunnel with new illuminators, and give them each a Comstaff. They can use the mining carts. Uncovering the plates on the carts makes them go. Tell them to catch up to us."

"Two groups of three are departing in each direction, now."

"Good." Switching to his own predicament with his outstretched necklace in front of him, Scepter mumbles, "That's it! I'm done fighting this!"

He takes the necklace off, but before he can place it in the cart, it flies forward out of his hand and down the tunnel and around the bend ahead, into the dark. "Shhh," as he emplores others in his cart to be quiet. All in his cart suddenly quiet down and listen.

After about forty seconds, there is a small metallic impact which echoes back past them. They all wince and gulp and look wide-eyed at each other.

"It hit something."

Scepter resumes proceding forward with the cart. "How many broken timbers is that, now?"

"Ten."

As they continue forward, Kairn is starting to look uncomfortable, almost pained. "Scepter, my stomach is starting to feel unsettled."

"We've got one in our party feeling the same way," responds Alor's voice. "And we've just crawled under our second obstructing timber, but we're down to one illuminator. Backups, where are you?"

"Alor, we are about to crawl under the first timber in your direction. We'll be with you shortly," responds Druett, the leader of Alor's back up party.

In Scepter's right direction cart, Varo is also feeling queasy, and the tunnel is starting to warm up. Their fur is now flattened and wet as all are sweating profusely. "Scepter, we're passing the first broken timbers now. We'll be with you soon," echoes Horum, leader of the backups heading in Scepter's direction.

"Good. We're down to our last illuminator," and to those in his cart, "How many broken timbers is that now?"

"Fourteen, and this next one will make fifteen."

The timbers are each equally spaced 100 yards apart, and the gentle bend of the tunnel means that each next timber does not come into view until after passing the one before it. Just past their fifteenth broken timber, Scepter's last illuminator flickers and goes out. The tunnel is now totally black, and he slows his cart to a stop. The cart balls rolling in the floor channel come to a halt, resulting in an eerie, quiet blackness.

"What do we do now? We can't see anything."

"I'm going to proceed ahead at a slow creep. The timbers seem to be equally spaced, so we know how far it is to the next one," responds Scepter.

The cart balls resume rolling as they are again crawling slowly in the dark now totally blind, and all are sweating profusely and starting to breathe heavily. As they roll slowly forward, there's a sudden 'splat' off to one side of the cart.

"I just threw up," admits Kairn.

After a few more yards, there is another 'splat' over the side, as Varo also throws up.

"I may be the next to heave if we go much further," adds Scepter.

Now maybe 70 yards past the fifteenth broken timber, "Scepter, stop the cart," urges a weakened, panting Kairn.

As the cart again stops, "Listen, up ahead."

Its pitch black, and all quiet down. Some yards ahead, there is the slight sound of a breeze blowing, as if through a small opening. It's not loud, but it sounds serious, almost as if to portend something . . . menacing.

"Backups, where are those lights," Scepter again asks.

"Just passing the 14th timber," responds Horum. "We'll be with you in a minute."

In the left direction in Alor's cart, just after crawling under the fourth intact timber, their last illuminator starts to flicker and weaken.

"Let's step down and walk in the floor channel, so when it goes dark, we can't fall in." Twenty yards later, that last light goes out.

"We'll continue to walk ahead slowly in the dark. Hold onto each other so we keep in contact. We know the distance to the next timber." Alor then notices, "Hey Scepter, the floor channel we're walking in is getting warmer in temperature."

There are "splats" off to the side as Garl soon throws up, followed by Torq, as all are starting to pant for more air. "What could be doing this? It's getting so sick and hot in here."

About 70 yards past the fourth intact timber, Alor blindly decides "Let's stop walking here and lean against the floor channel edge, for support."

All in Alor's stop and quiet down.

"Listen! Just ahead, that light breeze. It sounds like wind blowing through a small opening. What could it be?" There had been no light breeze in the miles covered so far. "Backups!"

"We're crawling under the fourth intact timber now," responds Druett, leading Alor's three backups. We're just a minute away."

Alor – panting from hyperventilation – again calls into his Comstaff. "Hey Scepter, are you guys feeling drained, weakened and heavy?"

"Yes, we can't go much farther," responds an also-panting Scepter. "We're about spent. I'd like to take my oxygen pill, but if I do, my stomach would instantly throw it up."

Each group is stopped miles apart, alone in the dark and panting; not from lack of oxygen, but from the suffocating blackness, which robs each person's eyes and mind of visible reference points.

Then, in the left direction, about ten seconds later, Alor's party turns and looks back, hearing the footsteps and seeing the sweeping lights of their three approaching reinforcements.

In the right direction in Scepter's cart, they too look back and see the sweeping lights of their approaching backups' cart.

As the backups approach each search party, their lights sweep back and forth to illuminate the greasy tunnel floor.

As Horum's cart approaches, all in Scepter's cart look back. "It's about time" intones Scepter. As he concludes with "Are we glad to see you," Horum and his party swing their lights up to where their beams illuminate the tunnel just beyond Scepter's stopped party. The sight just a few yards past Scepter's cart stops the three backups, cold. Horum fumbles to quickly stop his cart, and all in his cart teeter and kneel in humbleness.

In Alor's left direction, a similar occurrence happens. Druett's party walks up from behind, lighting the greasy tunnel floor with their lights. Alor's crew is leaning against the floor channel edge and greets them with "Finally, some light." As Druett's party shines their lights up and past Alor's crew, the sight just beyond causes Druett's crew to stop, stagger, and kneel, with one even dropping his illuminator.

Alor's and Scepter's crews notice their backups reactions, and all turn to look forward and behold the altar . . . of their cathedral.

CHAPTER 7

A Solemn Somber Truth

IN ALOR'S LEFT DIRECTION WALKING crew, all turn and look forward expecting to see another intact timber lying horizontally across their path, but this fifth timber is instead buckled into a vertical V-shape, with the center of the V pushed violently closer to them, as if something on the far side has deeply struck and nearly busted-through the enormous timber. The V-edge - running up and down - is a morass of extending huge timber splinters, crossing each other and sticking out left and right. The timber resembles a giant broken femur bone, pushed jaggedly toward their party. They look toward the top and bottom of the timber to see what impacted the other side, but the chaotic debris fills the tunnel, obstructing too much to see. The huge timber emits creaks and groans as though it's straining against great force.

"What could cause all of this," asks a panting Alor as faces contort to understand and make sense of what they are seeing.

In Scepter's right direction cart, all turn and behold a giant ball of solid iron, every bit as huge as the 50-foot diameter tunnel. The enormous ball is cold, hard and black and covered with grease, and has embedded itself *deeply* into the sixteenth timber. Although all are sickened and breathing heavily, they approach slowly. Their timber also creaks and groans as though high stresses are being imparted through the weakened giant tree fibers. It's a scene of colossal destruction on an epic scale.

"Scepter, our fifth timber is not intact" as Alor's frightened voice chimes over Scepter's Comstaff. "It has been busted nearly through by some force on the other side. What could it be?"

"We are looking at a giant ball of the great ferrous ore, every bit as big as the huge tunnel. It must've crashed through the other timbers and stopped here in our sixteenth timber, and its intense magnetism must also be what's sickening us," replies Scepter.

Because the cart they are standing in provides a little more height, Scepter rolls forward slowly, up close to the monstrous black sphere. The diameter is so big that the bulbous underbelly protrudes out toward their approach, and the ball's mid section towers far above their heads. Scepter's and Horum's crews stop their carts and get out.

"Look at the size of this monster! How could it have gotten here?" Recalling the cave that Alor's crew diverted into earlier, Scepter surmises, "If that was a foundry cave in the other's direction, maybe this ball was forged there and rolled into this tunnel. Alor, Torq, if you are looking at the back side of this impact, I wonder if you're on the other side of this destruction. Tap on your timber."

Scepter reaches out and lays one gloved hand on the huge greasy black ball.

In the left direction, Torq – with his Comstaff - thumps his buckled timber a number of times. "Scepter, did you feel anything?"

"Nothing, which makes sense because even though we've travelled many miles in opposite directions, we haven't gone far enough around to fully encircle the planet, but it also means that there are at least two of these monsters?" Their eyes bulge even wider in disbelief at the thought of more than one of these enormous magnetic balls hidden deep within their planet.

"Even though the damage here is severe, it looks like we may be able to crawl under in the floor channel and see the other side," notices Scepter, leaning over eyeing the bottom of the huge ball. "Alor, see if your floor channel is clear."

"We have to break off a bunch of splinters and shards, but it looks like we can get through."

After clearing the debris, all seven in Alor's party – now including the three backups - crawl under the hemorrhaging timber, just inches below the million ton ball and one by one, rise to stand on the forward side. They now get the front-side view that Scepter's crew has been seeing.

In the right direction, Scepter's now eight-strong crew also crawls under their ball and ruptured timber and rise on the timber-buckled side. They get their first look at the tangled backside that Alor's crew has been seeing. While breathing heavily, Scepter states what they've found.

"So every timber beyond this is intact, and every timber leading up to this is broken through." He then addresses the three backups who just joined them in the tunnel. "These giant ferrous balls raced through here at unimaginable speed and crashed through each great timber until finally stopping here. What forces could cause all of this? And just beyond every timber is one of these small holes, low on the inboard side, but it's been a long day and we'll have to check them out later. Backups, we are weak and tired. You and your lights are fresh. Continue on and see how many intact timbers lie ahead and return to the entrance cave and tell us your findings. If Alor counted four intact timbers on his side, maybe there aren't many further, up ahead. We'll take a couple of these illuminators and take one cart back."

"Scepter, our backups will count the broken timbers ahead and return," echoes Alor's voice from the opposite direction. "We'll meet you back at the entry cave."

"Good. Elixor, we are returning toward your entrance point," as Scepter sums things up. "Is Chronicle still with you?"

Back in the entrance cave - while Elixor is responding - Chronicle is drawing in the cave floor dirt using the tip of his Comstaff. "We've been listening to your every word. I've been asking Chronicle if any of this sounds familiar. He says it's nothing recognizable and is all too old for him, but that we are dealing with something very dangerous and powerful."

"Whatever it is, he's underestimating it. These things are beyond enormous. We are tired and sickened and will return to you in a couple of hours."

While Scepter's three replacements walk further ahead, he and his crew crawl back under the imposing ball and return to the front side.

"Varo, here's your tooth, and here's my relay dish and necklace," as he scans the front of the huge iron ball one last time. They get in the rear cart and Scepter uncovers the rear plate, and the cart moves back in the direction they came from, at a slightly faster pace than their entry speed.

In the left direction, "You might have a long walk ahead," Alor tells his three replacements. "Count the number of broken timbers ahead. We'll see you back at the entrance cave, or maybe late tomorrow. We need a good nights' sleep."

Alor's three replacements start walking ahead as he and his crewmembers crawl back under the giant ball and timber. Soon after Alor's crew have crawled under the fourth and final intact timber and boarded the rear cart, his backups call.

"Alor, there is another horizontal slot on the outboard side with channels that blend in. We've found another cart."

"Good, that will speed up your travel. We'll gather late tomorrow after we've all had a good night's sleep. We are weak now."

Althoughed weakened and getting weaker, as Alor- and Scepter's-groups leave to return to the entrance cave, all eyes stare firmly back at these massive ancient behemoths buried deep within their planet.

A couple of hours later, Scepter's cart and Alor's cart are finally nearing the entrance cave at about the same time, and all are lying semiconscious atop each other in their carts. All are exhausted and gasping heavily, as if they are hyperventilating.

Elixor is ready at the juncture with a couple of aides in the tunnel and more in the entrance cave to greet the weary bunch.

"Jump in and steer," Elixor yells to his assistants. They guide the carts into the spurs in the entrance cave, and he follows up with "Cover the front plate, to stop."

Each cart comes to a rest and the other Zeons help escort the spent crews out. Elixor has positioned illuminators in the entrance cave, to better light it.

"They need air. Take them up the stairs and outside." Chronicle is no longer around, having left for sleep after hearing that the parties were turning back. As the others escort the weakened ones up the stone staircase, no one notices the diagram Chronicle scribbled in the dirt floor opposite the cave markings, based on what the search crews found, of a large circle – representing Zeon - with two smaller circles forming the tunnel inside it, and at two points 180 degrees apart, two circles representing the giant magnetic iron balls.

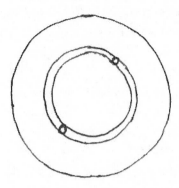

It's nearly midnight and has been a long day when they sit up against the base of the rocky outcropping next to the crater cave entrance. The slowly-panning stars and cool Zeon breezes are just what they need. All are given water and offered bits of aquatics. They take the water, but refuse the food. They are weak and hungry, but their stomachs are still recovering.

"Can we just sleep here tonight?"

Elixor quickly reasons it is much easier than trying to carry the weary wanderers up out of the crater. A couple of hours later, the six backups also emerge, also looking sickened, but not as weak as those who spent the whole day deep within their planet.

The next morning at the base of the outcropping and after awakening late, "Were there any calls from Tareon yesterday," as Kairn asks Elixor what happened while they were down underground the day before.

"Yes. I told them we were checking out the new cave. They were on their way to a deep canyon, two days from their city. They were hopeful of finding older caves there."

Scepter lays out rules to Elixor for the sand crater cave hole. "Have someone stand guard over this hole day and night. No kids without an adult and no one past the entrance cave. It's not safe beyond that point."

"Yes sir."

"What are those," asks an intrigued Scepter, noticing Elixor placing shiny metallic rocks into his woven reed backpack.

"Metallic rocks I broke off from the entrance cave walls. They have the conductive metals I use for making electrical items like lenses and monitors.

"That reminds me, meet me early this evening by the seashore near your foundry. I need to learn more about how things work."

Late in the afternoon at the seaside encampment, Scepter, Chronicle, Alor, Torq, and Kairn meet with Horum, Druett and the four other backups who explored onward in the tunnel the night before.

"Druett, so up ahead of your embedded iron ball, there were how many broken timbers?"

"Fifteen, Scepter."

"That's the same broken number as on our side," as Scepter looks at Horum. "And each side had four intact timbers past the one that stopped the iron balls?"

"Yes sir. The sixteenth timber on each side of the planet stopped each ball," responds Druett. Timbers 17, 18, 19 and 20 are intact on each side," adds Horum.

"And as far as we know, each of our teams was half way around from the entrance cave and there are only two of these monstrous things?"

"Twenty and twenty is forty," as Chronicle joins in, gesturing toward the great timber stump nearby. "The total number of great stumps on our planet is forty. The total number of timbers buried deep below matches the number of stumps."

"Yes, but how did they get down there," asks a confounded Scepter.

Early that evening at the seaside encampment, the 43 other Zeons listen raptly to the 15 total who ventured down into the monstrous tunnel the day before. Kairn, Varo, Alor, Torq, Horum, and Druett each have their own captive, wide-eyed audience. They have been eating well and look fairly rejuvenated from their long underground sojourn the day before.

Off to one side, Chronicle has used the bottom of his Comstaff to scribe in the wet sand. He has again drawn the circles-within-a-circle of Zeon he drew in the entrance cave the day before, and has also drawn the Zhama symbol. He squints, trying to recall all in his lengthy memory and to understand how the planets work.

It's a beautifully normal Zeon early evening. Just offshore, the giant ancient leaf pads slowly rotate on the water, and on the embankment slopes, gentle spiraling breezes create soft waves through the wild grasses. In the sky, the thin vertical spiral clouds which are unique to Zeon are highlighted by the just-setting sun.

At the seaside foundry, Hark turns the rocks Exilor brought up on a foot-driven lathe, which strips aluminum and copper strands from each rock and rolls them onto a nearby spool, while two other completed spools are nearby.

Scepter – holding his Comstaff - nibbles on a root vegetable while pondering how the planet's electronics and magnetism work. Elixor once explained it to him, but he needs a refresher.

"Hey Kairn, we have something for you," volunteers Elixor, as he and Garl approach Scepter and call Kairn over.

Kairn approaches and Garl whips out a new stellar Sighting Scope, made of a hardened tube of that universal green ooze with green glass lenses sharpened underwater to a fine accuracy.

"Wow, a new Sighter! Thanks. This old one was roasted by Scolios, and I'm ready to part with it."

Kairn happily tosses his charred old black Sighter into the sea, grabs the new one, and steps up on the nearby great sawed-off tree stump. He lies on his back and looks upward to find Tareon as it is early evening and the first stars are just reappearing.

"It might take you awhile to find Tareon," Scepter tells Kairn. "It's still well out there, although it's no doubt getting closer again."

"I'll find it," confidently replies Kairn. "I've spent my life watching its pulse."

"Elixor, explain to me again how our planet works" asks Scepter, as Garl returns to the nearby foundry. "You've told me before, but I need to hear it again."

Using a green stick, Elixor answers by drawing a circle in the wet sand. "Most all planets – like ours - are essentially a rotating magnet. All we know is that our planet has a dense central core, a positive pole and a negative pole, and between them a magnetic field. The magnetic field is always there, but we don't see it. Expeditions toward the north – as far as they went - have reported brilliant northern lights which make the field above our poles, visible. The fields of our planet and Tareon are what disrupt each other each time the planets converge. It must be quite a light show and would be great to watch, if only we didn't have to hide in the caves. Our planet's rotation is what maintains our orbit around our sun. The same goes for Tareon and all other planets.

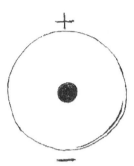

"And this . . . electrical stuff, where you make things happen through wires, how does that work?"

"We learned from lightning that certain metals buried in our soil will conduct electricity and transmit a signal. The metal in those rocks I brought up yesterday is now being sliced down to thin strands of wire. When I lay wire out in a lens or a monitor and put an aerial relay on it, if I send a signal to that relay - we can see what the lens sees - or show what's in the signal, on the monitor."

"So our planet is simply one huge spinning magnet?"

"Yes, and the bigger the planet, the stronger the magnet, which is why when passing each other, we take on more damage than Tareon. It exerts more torque and pull on us, than we do, on it."

"You've used that word 'torque' before."

"Torque is the result from the spinning and magnetic field. Torque is what makes the world go round."

Recalling their tunnel trek the day before, "The first things we encountered in the tunnel were the giant broken timbers. I broke off some shards from the outboard side of one, and that section slowly rumbled away from us, down its greasy crossing tunnel."

"That's an easy one. When you swing your kid around, his legs and lower body try to pull away from you, right?"

Hearing of his deceased young son Effy, Scepter quickly acquires a blank, far-off stare, and Elixor realizes too late that he's picked a horrible analogy for a childless father.

"Oh no! I'm terribly sorry! Please forgive me for that poorly chosen example. I'm sure you miss your son, dearly."

"Apology accepted," as Scepter sighs humbly, ". . . For you've just brought back some fond memories, and yes, when I swung him around, his legs would try to pull away from me."

"That's because objects want to fly away from a spinning center. When you broke off pieces sticking out wider than the timber tunnel, our planet's rotation sent the outer timber sliding away on the grease until it hit the end of its crossing tunnel. Less secure scum might give this tendency a fancy name like 'centrifugal force.' We just call it *objects moving away from a spinning center.*"

"So, our planet's rotation maintains our orbit around our sun?"

"Yes, but our orbit is not perfectly round, because each time we have passed the larger Tareon, it has drawn us closer and closer to its own orbit path, and the next convergence will be 'bam:' A direct hit!"

"So our planet is a spinning magnetic ball, and buried deep within it are these two giant other magnets, which if freed up, will again try to race around our planet's core?"

"Yes" sheeplishly answers a stunned Elixor, suddenly unsure of where the conversation is heading, while settling on his legs to stabilize himself.

At the nearby foundry, both Hark and Garl listen up. They know how magnets work and can sense that Scepter may be onto something pivotal.

"The 16th timber on each side – the one that stopped each huge ball - creaks and moans," as Scepter continues with Elixor. "Each timber is straining to keep those giant magnetic balls from busting through. If broken away from the backside, each ball will start up, and if they speed up – and if no timbers are in the way - won't they impart some sort of . . . *torque* on our planet?"

"Yes," as Elixor starts to teeter unsteadily from the major implications.

Laying face-up on the nearby tree stump, Kairn lowers his new Sighting Scope and also listens in.

"This thing we've discovered is not natural" admits Scepter, who settles on his hind legs also, to steady himself. "It's a mechanized monster on an immense scale. Somebody built it . . . to do something colossal, and if the timbers move outboard driven by nothing more than our planet's own natural forces, what if this whole monstrous machine is designed to run off our planet's natural forces?"

Scepter gazes out and looks at the giant leaf pads gently turning on the water, and notices their slow rotation. To the side embankment he sees one of a little "dust devil" breezes spinning dirt up into its wake. A look upward shows the thin vertical spiral clouds spinning in the twilight sky. Elixor does the same and the implications are overwhelming both of them. Their eyes flash back and forth rapidly as if becoming enlightened to an answer right in front of them, or more directly, right under their feet, and the possibilities are quite literally, earthshaking.

Just then, on the shore embankment, one more dust devil spins up, but unlike the usual gentle ones, this one keeps accelerating into a tightly wound frenzy.

"If we free up the magnets and our planet's own forces make them go, what's to stop them" asks Scepter as he and Elixor are fixated on the twister's increasingly tight spin.

"They will just keep . . . accelerating, moving faster and faster," responds Elixor. "Two giant magnets free to . . . chase each other."

"That's the key," mutters Scepter with one last squint. "Revolution, acceleration, circulation," and finally "Could it be?" and – breathing heavily and being overcome with a sudden revelation - both he and Elixor faint and fall unconscious onto the wet beach sand.

Kairn quickly runs over to the knocked-out Scepter, while Hark and Garl attend to Elixor. They shake the unconscious ones and sprinkle drops of water on them.

"Scepter, wake up!"

"Elixor, come too!"

Scepter and Elixor awaken and shake the droplets off, and each quickly rolls over to look at the embankment dust devil that enlightened them. It's still quickly rotating, but is starting to slow.

At this point it's just a guess, but focused on the dust devil's swirling rotation, Scepter and Elixor in unison mutter, "Thank you."

"Scepter, what is it," asks Kairn. "What overcame you?"

With the deepest seriousness, "Call a meeting for tomorrow morning. Everyone must be there, even the parties on Tareon."

Late that night, Kairn - next to Trillo - has trouble sleeping; partly because of Scepter's words, and party because of his wonderful new Sighting Scope. He has found Tareon and is letting Trillo look at it.

"It now looks bigger than the other stars. Is it on its way back," asks Trillo.

"Yes and tomorrow - with its steady growth overnight - we won't even need this Scope to see it."

By the seaside foundry, Elixor also cannot sleep. He understands the implications of Scepter's earlier questioning and lies on his back watching the billion star sky slowly move from west to east as it does every night, because of Zeon's rotation.

Scepter is wide awake drawing in the sand just in front of the seaside great timber stump where he conducts speeches. He draws with the tip of his Comstaff while holding an illuminator in his other hand.

The next day on Tareon, the two search parties fly over open mesas in their two Transtubes. Drago pilots Team One with Rayelle next to him, while her Comstaff lies along the floor between their seats. Othar and his team follow in the other Transtube.

"It's taken two days of flying to come out here. I hope this canyon is worth the effort," echoes Othar's voice over their bracelets.

Finally, they crest a wide mesa and emerge over what they're looking for: A great canyon three miles deep which they had seen on Tareon's distant maps.

"Oh my, look at that!"

"Wow, it's huge! And deep!"

All in both Transtubes suddenly sit up and are wide-eyed at this massive and deep gash in Tareon's crust.

The enormous canyon is very deep and wide, but its tall walls gradually narrow in the upstream direction. Drago and Othar fly down lower and lower into the majestic gorge until they are not far above the treetops covering the canyon floor. A healthy river cuts a path through the forest floor canopy.

"What are we looking for," asks Rayelle.

"Any cave that is down low in the canyon walls," replies Drago. "The lower the cave is, the better. All of these layers in the canyon walls have built up over millions of years, and if we can find a cave deeper down in Tareon's crust, we should be going back further in time."

They proceed upriver looking to the sides along the canyon walls. After a short time on her side, Rayelle briefly glimpses a deep shadow in the rock wall partially obstructed by taller treetops in front of it.

"I think I saw something! Turn back along this side."

Drago swings a U-turn to the right and Othar follows. They fly in the opposite direction at a slower pace, just above the forest canopy. They slow even more when approaching a taller tree where the canyon wall starts upward.

"There, just behind that tree," points Rayelle. "See that shadow?"

The cave opening is just wide enough for the two Transtubes to land on its threshold. The Transtubes have been fitted with relay antennas to transmit signals to and from Zeon, and all twelve now wear the modified communication bracelets, but Rayelle gets out clutching her Comstaff.

"Watch your step, kids. Don't disturb anything," advises Drago.

It's not a deep cave, maybe 30 yards deep. The kids – Jurn, Plur, Evene and Virn - run in first and soon find boulders and small pools of water on the left side. The pools harbor strange little creatures.

As the adults follow the kids in and also look to the left, four squawks from Scepter's Comstaff blast from each Transtube relay, their bracelets, and Rayelle's Comstaff.

"Whoa, four chimes." I've never heard of that before. We'd better listen in," implores Othar.

Once into the cave, Scepter's voice echoes over their bracelets and Rayelle's Comstaff. "Tareon teams, are you there?"

"We are and hear you clearly," responds Drago.

At first glance, the cave does not look remarkable, but it *is* what they're looking for.

They walk a few yards in and gaze up at the left wall. There are depictions of strange creatures no longer seen on Tareon: large eight-winged horseflies, giant two-headed snails, and saber-toothed birds.

"Wow, look at these strange little aquatics in the water," notices Evene.

"And these depictions on the wall are very different. This cave must be older," notes Othar.

On Zeon it is also mid morning, and Scepter has all remaining 58 Zeons gathered in front of the encampment great timber stump. What looks like a small, rotating purple-and-green moon in the sky is Tareon, a blatant reminder of doom's approaching return. Scepter starts by removing a reed cover over the diagram below which he drew overnight. It shows Zeon with a 90-degree slice cut out of it. In the face of each slice and well under the crust, a hole leads back into Zeon's interior, representing the tunnel they discovered two days before. The holes in each cut line up with each other, making clear that the giant tunnel surrounds the planet like a worm hole dug all of the way around.

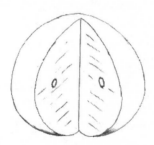

"Tareon teams, I know you can't see the diagram I've drawn, but three days ago in the soft sand crater, our Mr. Trillo and his Returner discovered a new cave entrance underneath the rocky outcropping," as Scepter begins his introduction. "Our long search two days ago uncovered the diagram I've drawn here of a tunnel deep within our world which encircles our entire planet. And within that tunnel - at two places along the way - are giant orbs of the great ferrous ore, iron; each 50-feet high, and weighing who knows how many millions of tons. Each giant ball is about 180-degrees apart and came to a stop in the 16th of 20 giant buried timbers which have been extended across the tunnel path."

On Tareon - listening while looking up at the cavern left wall glyphs - the two teams start to stare at each other. They can't believe what they are hearing. Their simple home planet has never been known for anything special, and they are as entranced as those on Zeon who are looking at Scepter's diagram in front of the tree stump. One by one, the Tareon team adults turn and look up at their cave's right wall, and each reacts silently and in the same way. Their heads and eyes scan a large depiction and squint and wince that something is wrong, and then sit and become saddened, humbled by a solemn, somber truth.

On Zeon, Scepter continues: "When the first parties to Tareon sent word that it was very advanced, we sent others in the hope that somehow – when our worlds collide - those on Tareon may be able to survive this impending collision. And also – since Tareon is more advanced - maybe there was an answer, an explanation for how our planets have come so close. I don't yet understand how everything works, but I'm here to tell you all . . . that Tareon did not come to Zeon. We . . . came to it."

CHAPTER 8

Miners

JUST THEN – IN A dejected tone to Scepter's revelation - Drago's voice comes over the Comstaff from Tareon. "Scepter, we can confirm your guess."

"How so," asks a shocked and surprised Scepter, as aghast as the rest of his crowd.

"We are in a much older cave on Tareon, at the bottom of a deep canyon. And we're looking at an older depiction of our solar system."

"And?"

"And there are only *eight* planets. Zeon . . . isn't here. There's a big gap between the fourth planet, Loookor, and Tareon."

"There's our proof," as on Zeon, Scepter quickly fires a steely look toward Elixor and continues with his presentation, now knowing that his hunch is correct.

"Deep within the bowels of our humble planet is a machine. A machine so simple, it moans and groans to roll again. A machine so great and powerful . . . it can move a world.

All listening – on both planets - get bigger-eyed than ever. Those on Tareon become unsteady and have to sit, staring at each other in disbelief as Scepter continues.

"The two giant balls within our earth are enormous magnets. Our own planet's magnetic field and polarity, makes them go. Chip away and cut the great timbers that halted them, and these magnets will roll anew. Eons ago, our planet was somewhere else. Where or how far, we do not know, and only these great timber stumps remain. The writings in the entrance cave are so old that even Chronicle cannot decipher them, but one thing we've made out is . . . they called this machine 'Zhama.' Who here . . . would like to re-start Zhama?"

After the crowd again rustles and then quiets down, "How much time do we have?"

Scepter looks at Kairn, who quickly glances up at the steadily-growing Tareon and answers "20 days, and that's to impact. If this machine is to deflect our world, it'll have to start up well before that."

"Next question."

"We have nothing else to live for. What other options do we have?"

"I was looking forward to drinking our soup," offers Garl, who realizes too late that the kids are present.

"Soup," asks Trillo, as the three young couples, Ogard, and Stern and Stip also listen up.

Kairn tries to cover Trillo's ears, but it's too late and the damage has been done.

Listening on Tareon, Drago tries to cover Virn's ears, and Rayelle attempts the same to Jurn and Plur, but Evene pushes her mother's arms away and asks, "Soup?"

On Zeon, Scepter drops his shoulders and admits, "We were going to have to tell them, sometime. Kids, we've brewed up a broth that we would consume before Tareon crashes into us. No pain, no terror, no quakes, no noise. Just sleep."

The girls on Tareon fire a worried look at the adults, sensing that those remaining on Zeon are talking about killing themselves.

"But now we may have a purpose; an endeavor," continues Scepter. "There is still certain calamity and we may not live through it, but it's something to do with the rest of our lives in what days that we have left. This will not be easy. It will be a monumental task to cut away the eight intact timbers, plus the two holding the giant orbs. We will have to work day and night and the conditions down there are sickening. Do we still have the cable saws we used to cut slabs off of these giant stumps?"

"They are in the accessible part of Major Cave, and I have enough metal to make a few more," responds Elixor.

"Good. We only need to make one cut through each timber on the inboard side, and the outer section will then slide outboard to the end of its crossing tunnel. Don't touch the 16th timbers, the ones that stopped each ball. We'll handle them, last. We'll need all able-bodied adults rotating in the tunnels to get this done in time."

"I'm small. Can I go into the tunnel," ask Othar's sons Stern and Stip, in unison.

145

"Stern and Stip, since your father Othar is on Tareon, no. Those of you who have loved ones on Tareon need to be able to talk to them again, and I have another task for you young ones. Elixor, can you make a couple of lenses, and how is that monitor coming?"

"Lenses are easy and the monitor is almost ready, and I've got a new idea. By attaching illuminators directly to our goggles, it will free up our hands to do the cutting in the dark."

"Good. We'll need all possible short cuts to get this done in time. Oh, now look at that," as Scepter's humbled eyes glimpse the distant summit of Altai. "The snows are again disappearing from our great mountain, and the air is starting to get warm and dry for one last time. It's going to be a race to dig Zhama out, so Elixor, you'd better keep our sleeping potion nearby."

The next day in the entrance cave - with goggles housing illuminators - a party of 12 set out in the ore carts. Six head left, lead by Farsiders Alor and Torq, with Alor carrying a Comstaff. Six others head right, lead by Varo and Kairn, with Kairn clutching a Comstaff. Because they both have family on Tareon, Scepter did not want Kairn and Varo in the tunnel, but they convinced him that they would not do any cutting.

Dragging from the rear of each cart is a thin, sharp, 100-foot-long metal cable. The cables have simple green hand grips at each end. Each Zeon also carries a backpack and many pairs of woven gloves.

A short while later in the left direction, Alor's crew rolls up to the first intact timber, timber number 20. Three in his crew stay on the near side while three others crawl under to the far side, and one end of the cable is thrown over the huge timber. Those on the other side grab it and together, they shimmy it over to the inboard wall of the tunnel. With gloves on, one pulls toward himself and then the other does the same, toward himself. The cable is thin and very sharp, and the back and forth motion quickly cuts through the greasy damp bark, but the progress slows entering the core of the wood. They've done this a number of times on the giant stumps above ground, but those were dried stumps which cut easier. After a couple of minutes, two other crew members take over and continue cutting, while the two who just finished bend over and pant in the musty, damp air. This happens over and over to refresh each other. Its laborious work and most of these men have lost all family members, but the discovery of these giant magnets has provided hope and purpose in these last days of their planet's last half-year.

In the right direction, Kairn and Varo's crew have carted to the embedded ball-and-timber and crawled under, to walk and reach the intact 17th timber. Varo is with two others on one side, while Kairn is with two others on the opposite side. After awhile and seeing their others are becoming spent, Kairn and Varo break their vow to Scepter and begin sawing, taking rotations with their comrades.

While this goes on deep underground, Scepter, Elixor and Garl are by the seaside foundry where they've gathered young ones Dwell, Jin, Trillo, Ogard, Stern and Stip. Each kid wears a backpack. Elixor has a dowel-shaped clear green glass lens in hand. Garl holds a hand-crank green drill with a crude metal bit in it, and they stand near a sandstone seaside boulder. As warm breezes begin blowing through the grasses, watching over all is a now-sizeable purple-and-green Tareon, a spinning, growing Cyclops in the sky.

"Kids, see this glass lens with a wire hanging out," instructs Elixor. "You drill a hole in rock and press the lens in with the wire in the back, but make sure the end of the wire is sticking out."

"You take this drill, lean your weight into it, and crank," adds Garl, while drilling a hole into the boulder. "When you've drilled a hole deep enough, press the lens in."

Dwell takes the drill and practices drilling a hole in the boulder. Garl produces two more drills and hands them to the other kids. "You will work in teams of two."

"Where do you want the lenses put," Elixor asks Scepter.

"Kids, put one on Altai, but you don't have to go very far up, just high enough to look out over the curled peaks. Put one looking out over the sea, a couple in the old caves, one overlooking each crater, and you can go into the entrance cave below the crater, but no further."

Elixor gives the kids more lenses and they run off, Trillo pairing up with Ogard, Stern with Stip, and Dwell with Jin.

Back underground in the left tunnel, six hours after Alor and Torq's crew started cutting, a replacement crew of six shows up, including one female. The new crew also brings a fresh, sharpened cable. Blackened and covered with wood chips, Varo and Alor's crew returns to the entrance cave and meet up with Kairn and Varo's crew, who were also similarly replaced. Together, the two weary crews climb the stone staircase to get some air.

Outside at the base of crater outcropping, the two other young couples take their worn cables to be sharpened at the seaside foundry. Scepter and Norl – in sand shoes - meet these miners at the base of the outcropping. Their faces are covered with dark soot and wood shavings, and Scepter can tell from their heavy breathing that Kairn and Varo have cutting down below.

"Kairn and Varo, I told you not to overdo yourselves," as Tareon looms larger in the sky above Scepter's shoulder. "Don't you want to talk to your loved ones on Tareon again?"

"We're sorry sir, but we couldn't just watch the others work so hard."

"How is it looking down there?"

"At the end of this first full day, we will be half-way through the first timber on each side."

"So, two days to get through each timber and we've got four intact timbers on each side. That's eight days if we can maintain our tempo, but our planet's rotation is beginning to speed up and with the days getting shorter and shorter, it could seem more like 10-to-12 days, which doesn't give us any time to spare."

Two mornings later, Alor and Torq's crew of five again heads left with a sharpened cable to take over for the current crew. As Alor's crew carts up to see the progress, at first glance the news is good. The overnight crew has just finished cutting through the first timber, timber number 20 on the left side, and it rumbles outboard on its own, slowly receding into its greasy crossing tunnel, but the reward has come at a price as four bodies lay dead on the tunnel floor.

"Why didn't you get help?"

"And stop cutting?"

Alor doesn't have an answer for that. "Load the bodies and get some rest, and we'll start on the next timber. No, wait! You can leave the bodies here. If we free this thing up, it'll just run over them. Go take care of yourselves."

The spent crew wearily carts away and Alor and Torq repeat the previous log's routine. They cart forward to the 19th timber and again throw the cable over and begin cutting on the inboard side.

In the right tunnel, after carting to the embedded ball-and-timber and crawling under, Kairn and Varo's crew of six arrive at the 17th timber to a similar scene. The first intact log is rumbling out of the way, but there are four dead.

"We did our job, but we are weak," pant the two who are alive, wheezing heavily to take in all possible oxygen. "Please don't make us carry the dead."

"Your effort is gallant. Tend to yourselves."

Kairn, Varo and their crew continue on ahead and begin cutting the 18th timber. In the fifth hour of their six hour shift, two succumb to heat and exhaustion and die, and Kairn and Varo then make a morbid improvement. By draping a dead body over each end of the cable, each corpse's weight makes the cable cut more with each stroke. At the end of their six hour shift, they are halfway through the 18th timber when another crew of six walks up to replace them. This crew has two females.

Varo, Kairn, and their two others return topside to the cool air, again blackened, greasy and sweaty. Alor, Torq, and one other of their crew are also panting and resting. Each time they emerge, Tareon has grown larger in the sky.

"We lost three," reveals Torq.

"We lost two," admits Kairn.

They are not even trekking to the sea for rest, now. They sleep at the foot of the crater's rocky outcropping within yards from the entrance hole.

Two mornings later, Alor and Torq again head into the left direction with a crew that includes Hark and two others, for a total of five. They take over for a crew of six that includes young couple Quall and Vail, who are hard to identify because of the black soot. Four of their six are dead, but the 19th timber is slowly gliding outboard.

"The smell of death is everywhere down here," as the female Vail cannot hide her disgust.

"One more shift and you'll no longer smell it," bluntly responds Alor.

As the spent Quall and Vail limp back to the aft cart and leave, Alor and Torq cart forward to the 18th timber, throw their cable over, and shimmy it to the inboard edge. There's no talking now. Everyone knows the routine.

In the right direction, Kairn, Varo, Garl and two others walk up to the 18th timber, but the timber is still attached and not yet cut through. Two lay dead, one on each side of the log. The other two are also dead, but each still has their gloved hands wrapped firmly around the cable handles. The cable is 99.9 percent through the giant log.

"Oh no," Kairn observes, as Varo crawls under and grabs the other end of the cable. With one last pull of the cable, the timber is cut and starts sliding off to the outboard side.

"So close, when they died."

"Cutting these giant logs is killing us. I hope the end is worth all of this effort."

Kairn, Varo, Garl and the two others then cart forward and start on the 19th timber.

Six hours later, a crew of four - including two women - arrives to take over. Kairn, Varo and Garl are alive, but their two others are dead.

Kairn, Varo and Garl return topside to the crater outcropping and meet Alor, Torq, and Hark.

"We lost two."

"Same, here. If we all end up dieing first, the kids will have to finish the cutting."

Two days later, Alor, Torq and Hark again head left, with one female. As they cart up to the 18th timber, two are dead as the timber rumbles away into its crossing tunnel, while the two standing are shaking, arms trembling from the repetitive motion of sawing for hours without rest. In a state of shock, they silently watch the outer log rumble off to the outboard side. With a blank, zombie-like stare, each then suddenly drops to the floor. Alor and Torq reach down and touch the necks of the two who've just collapsed.

"It's no use."

"They're both dead."

Alor and his crew hop in the forward cart and roll on to timber #17, and begin the process of cutting.

"This is the last fully intact timber on this side," Alor reminds those in his crew. This *should* be good news, but there is no response from the others, as each giant log brings great pain and slaving hardship.

In the right direction, Kairn and Varo take a team that includes young couple Forn and Wee and Elixor's aide Garl, for a crew of five. They crawl under the embedded 16th timber-and-ball and proceed onward on foot. Timber 17 is clear and number 18 was cleared two days before. As they approach timber 19, it too is now out of the way, but two dead bodies lay nearby. One lonely figure is lieing, resting against the tunnel wall.

"Where are the others in this party?"

"They continued onward to the 20th and last timber."

Hearing this, Kairn and Varo's team continue forward to the 20th timber. Sitting spent and alone along the inner wall are two blackened figures, and they can't tell who until they get up close.

"Scepter? Norl?"

Scepter was consumed by the guilt of sending others into the tunnel, and Norl would not let him go in alone. After dispensing the 19th timber, they had deliriously productive thoughts of starting on number 20. Kairn and Varo give them water while Forn and Wee rub their legs.

"Scepter, Norl, why did you come down here?"

"I had to do my share. We're losing too many people each day," mumbles the disheveled Scepter.

"And if he comes, I come," adds a weakened, woozy Norl.

"Forn, Wee, assist them back under the ball to the cart and return here; and Varo, Garl, and I will get started on this timber."

When Scepter and Norl reach the surface, they look as spent and blackened as the others. Chronicle comes down into the crater to greet them and tears up at their sight.

"You both look like you're ready to drink our death soup."

"We can't now that so many have died down there. We have to see this task, through." Norl is too tired to remind Scepter how much his people need his leadership, but this might be his finest hour.

At the warm breezy seaside foundry, since his aides Garl and Hark are down below, Elixor sharpens the lengthy cable saws with the help of youngsters Trillo, Ogard, Stern and Stip. They use raspy metal stones to sharpen each cable. Even Chronicle and Hep – with her one good arm - will take turns. The pain and misery each endures is visible and affects all remaining.

That afternoon in the left tunnel, Alor, Torq, and Hark are half-way through the last intact timber when the afternoon crew of Elixor, young couple Quall and Vail, and two others show up. Elixor finds his friends Druett and Horum, dead. He tears up and starts to fall apart, when Alor grabs him sternly and warns, "We have to work through it! It's the only way!" The new crew takes over while Alor, Torq, and Hark head back.

In the right direction, Kairn, Varo, Forn, Wee and Garl are half way through the final intact timber, when Scepter, Norl, Zoy, her son Dwell and Jin show up. The blackened and panting Kairn has words of advice for the new crew.

"Don't overdo it. We're going to get through it." But even with Kairn's confidence, Zoy will die tonight.

Kairn, Varo, Garl, Forn and Wee meet Alor, Torq and Hark topside as youngsters Trillo, Ogard, Stern and Stip are there to meet them. "We'll take your cables and sharpen them," offers Trillo.

"Don't need to" responds a blackened and panting Kairn. "We're on the last stretch, now."

The kids are happy to hear that and pour cool water over the blackened miners. Scepter's Comstaff leans nearby against the outcropping and from it echoes Rayelle's voice. "Hello Zeon, are you there?"

"Mom, is that you," responds Trillo while pouring water over the blackened miners.

"Where have you all been? I've called the last couple of days."

Kairn realizes that for once Scepter and his Comstaff are separated and that he can talk freely - albeit with the kids present. "We've been down below, digging out the blocking timbers. After tonight, there's only one to free up on each side, the one with the giant ball in it."

"How's it been?"

Rayelle has to wait for a response because Kairn breaks down and tears start to release. "It's been hard. We've lost so many."

On Rayelle's end in the Tareon "W" tower, Drago and Othar hear Kairn crumble, and listen closer. Kairn knows that the kids might also be listening, but is too tired to care.

"Drago, Othar, your kids are here. All the kids have been a big help. Chronicle and Hep – with her broken arm - are the only adults we've kept out of the tunnel, but even they have helped. Rayelle, we love you. I'm going to let the others talk now. I need rest."

"Dad, are you there" ask Jurn and Plur's voices, as Kairn rolls over to rest.

"Yes, my inspirations," responds a weary Varo.

As the late afternoon shadows grow long, all disconnected take turns catching up. They are separated families, worlds apart. Othar and his sons Stern and Stip bring each other up to date, and Drago and his daughter Virn connect with daughter Ogard and wife Hep.

Just before nodding off to sleep, as the early evening stars reappear, Kairn glimpses a blatant reminder through his tears of why they put themselves through hell, as the sizeable purple-and-green crosshairs of Tareon now block a large swath of the evening sky.

Early the next morning but without fanfare, the last intact timber on each side is cut through and slides steadily outboard, driven by nothing more than Zeon's natural rotation. Scepter will call a seaside meeting for later that evening so all have time to rest.

In total, thirty seven Zeons have died during the cutting of the eight great intact timbers. The following Zeons are still alive: Chronicle, Scepter, Norl, Kairn, Trillo, Alor, Torq, Varo, Elixor, Hep, Ogard, Hark, Garl, Stern, Stip, and the three young couples. From a population of two million Zeons, there are twenty one left.

That total humbled by this one: as of tomorrow, there will be six days until impact.

CHAPTER 9

Beyond the Tunnel

A T SUNSET THE NEXT EVENING, most are soaking in the water at the seaside encampment to replenish strength and nurse aching muscles. Only Hark and Garl - at the shore foundry - and Chronicle, are not in the water. Hep, with her arm still in a sling, floats near Varo. Since their total has dwindled to only twenty one left alive, the cove now looks bigger and emptier than ever. Overlooking all is the elephant in the sky as Tareon has grown two hundred percent larger since the day before, and the dry, warm unnatural breezes of convergence are beginning to blow.

On the shore, using his Comstaff tip, Chronicle has again drawn the circles-within-a-circle in the wet sand. Scepter's Comstaff stands impaled in the shallow water with its protective cover off and metallic dish pointing skyward. The Tareon teams are listening on the other end in their suite high atop the Worthland "W" building. It might be the last time they all talk.

"Where are we at now, on the surface" asks Scepter, who is too tired to care who hears what.

"The kids have placed lenses on Altai, overlooking this sea, the cave openings and the craters; and we've repaired the monitor from cave one and have it ready," responds Elixor.

"Good, and down below we now have all intact timbers cleared and only the ball-embedded 16th timber to cut away on each side, which may not take long. If my hunch is correct and our planet's field and rotation make those giant magnets roll, after chipping away only so much broken timber, those giant balls will crush the remainder, along with the souls of our dead ones. What do we have to chip away at the embedded timbers?"

"We've made these axes," answers Garl from the foundry shore. "We've made handles from the wood found below and mounted these sharpened stones on them. We have four of them."

"Good. We'll need two axes chopping at each ball."

"Kairn and I have made a good team. We'll each take an axe," offers Varo.

Hep immediately looks at Varo with all the hope in the world. She doesn't speak but her eyes say it all: "Please don't go."

"Varo and Kairn, you two have bonded and performed well, but your loved ones on Tareon hope to hear your voices again and this is a suicide task," as Scepter unwittingly comes to Hep's rescue. "Whoever frees up those giant iron balls will be crushed by them."

With Scepter's thinking, Rayelle, Evene, Jurn and Plur - listening on Tareon - breathe a sigh of relief. With each planet now filling the other's sky, they all hope to talk to Kairn and Varo again.

While Scepter was talking, Farsiders Alor and Torq walked out of the water to the foundry edge and each grabbed an axe.

"Scepter, our families are gone and Alor and I are prepared to start the unknown so that each of you may live on."

"Are you sure, Torq?"

"It is our purpose. Our destiny."

"Your commitment to our endeavor is admirable. We need two more sacrificial souls, then."

On the shore, Hark and Garl each grab an axe. "Scepter, Garl and I are also without kin, and would be honored to free up one of the giant magnets."

On Tareon - hearing Hark's voice - "Wait a minute, you two are our brothers. Aren't *we* worth living for," interrupt Wren and Zoree.

"We meant here on Zeon. Sisters, you two are now adults, as are Garl and I. You are old enough to account for your actions, as are we. Garl and I made good progress chopping through the timbers and are determined for those here to proceed onward without us."

"Hark and I will start tearing these tools down and take them to the caves," adds Garl from the shore.

Before Elixor can respond, "There won't be a next time," bluntly responds Kairn.

Just then, the first blustery dry gusts from Tareon blow across their brows and whip up dust above the shore. The wind gusts are a clear reminder that their hour is late.

"Kairn is right. This is a one-way mission," offers Chronicle, still staring at his circles on the shore. "Everything new we've discovered is down there, and to stay up here is certain death."

The kids gasp at his bluntness, as do those listening on Tareon. "Sorry kids, but in the face of pain we must retreat or take the silent way out."

"Elixor, do you have our poisonous porridge, ready," asks Scepter.

"It is and I will bring it with us."

"Very well. We will head underground in the morning. Tareon teams, I'll let the others talk now, but I just want to say that this impending collision and fusion of our worlds may destroy all of us, but you've found deep, sustainable bunkers and may somehow survive it. We do not yet know what this ancient machine within our world can do, but we intend to end our lives, finding out. We can't get relay signals underground, so to my brother Nax and all of those there on Tareon, this may be the last time we talk and if it is, then stay alert, stay smart, and forward with brilliance."

"Forward with brilliance," respond those listening on Tareon.

Others wade toward Scepter's impaled Comstaff and start talking with those on Tareon. As Norl wades closer to Scepter, he peers up toward Tareon, which Kairn, Trillo, and Varo are already doing. The warm dry breezes marking the approaching apocalypse are steadily increasing, quickly drying their fur above the water.

The next morning, all twenty one on Zeon have been awakened before daybreak by the now-whipping warm winds. They load-up at the rocky outcropping in the soft sand crater, adjacent to the cave hole. Tareon is bigger than ever, having grown another 100 percent overnight. Also, sunup is approaching sooner, meaning each planet's rotation is again speeding up. Each day will be hours shorter than the previous day.

Mounted on Elixor's back is the monitor from Cave One, and behind it, his backpack. Elixor carefully loads Chronicle's backpack, which emits a small amount of eerie steam. "In here is a sealed pouch of our herbal closure. It's our only painless way out so don't let it rupture."

Kairn is taking one last naked eye look up at the now-menacing Tareon while Scepter makes one last call as the others crawl down into the cave hole.

"Tareon teams, are you there? It's getting warm and windy here. We're about to go under and try to free up this monster. We will likely never reemerge. Good luck to us all."

The Tareon teams are in the top of the Worthland "W" building, with Zeon filling the midday sky. As warm breezes begin blowing debris throughout the city below, Othar and Rayelle scan floating monitors for articles from Tareon's past, trying to learn all they can.

"It's getting warm here also," as Drago responds to Scepter's voice. "We are preparing on this end. Before long, we will be in the deeply-buried survival shelter. We wish we were all together during these final hours."

All on Drago's end add, "We love you all and forward with brilliance."

Kairn, Elixor, Scepter and Norl respond, "Forward with brilliance."

On Zeon next to the crater hole, Elixor wears a hip-side woven pouch. After removing his gold tooth, he grabs handfuls of loose sand from the outcropping and fills the pouch on his hip, and follows the others down into the hole.

Mindful of the giant magnets below, Scepter removes the small metal antenna dish from atop his Comstaff and also his metal necklace, and hands them to Norl, who places them in his backpack and then steps down into the hole.

"You know Scepter, if we hadn't discovered this monster down below, we would already have consumed that soup," notes Kairn, just before stepping down into the hole one final time.

One by one, all twenty one Zeons crawl into the cave hole and descend the stone staircase. Alor, Garl, Chronicle and Scepter each carry Comstaffs. For the young kids, it's their first time into the entrance cave. As they reach the floor and pass the carvings and writings, Chronicle and Scepter take one last look up at the markings, a language too old to be deciphered. Alor, Torq, Garl, and Hark each carry an axe.

Downward they continue until reaching some of the mining carts. Garl and Hark get in the lead cart and Alor and Torq get in the second cart. The seventeen others get into three other carts, Scepter driving cart three, Kairn cart four, and Elixor cart five. They roll downward and soon come upon the wide horizontal slot that marks the outer edge of the magnets' huge crossing tunnel. The kids gasp at the sight of the darkened slot and what it portends. All stop their carts just before the floor channel splits both left and right, into the large crossing tunnel.

"Hey kids, are any of you still carrying lenses," asks Scepter.

"I have three in my backpack," responds Drago's daughter Ogard. "And I'm still carrying the drill," adds Trillo.

"Good. Jump out and put one facing this slot in front of us. If we're lucky enough to bring our monitor up later, maybe we'll be able to see what this looks like when Zhama gets going."

Trillo and Ogard quickly jump from their carts. Trillo finds a boulder surface which faces toward the ominous slot and promptly drills a hole in the soft sandstone boulder. Ogard screws in a lens and the kids each hop back into their carts.

"Hark and I will go to the right and free up the backside of that ball," intones Garl from the lead cart. "Alor and Torq will lead the rest of you to the left."

"We should signal each other before we commence chopping, to try and free the balls up about the same time," responds Torq.

"Agreed," concludes Garl.

"What's that smell," asks Trillo as Garl and Hark veer to the right.

"That's the smell of death," responds a blunt Scepter. "You're going to see many of our comrades' dead bodies down here. It's going to get warm, stinky and sticky down here and you may start to feel sick."

Alor and Torq lead the others in the left direction. An hour or two later, Alor stops at the outer spur that leads to the giant underground foundry and remembers that this is the first time Scepter, Kairn and Varo have been in the left direction.

"Scepter, this spur isn't long. Check it out and come back here and push on to catch up with Torq and myself."

Alor continues down the long arcing tunnel while Scepter leads the other carts into the left fork. After a short distance and gentle bend, the top half of the tunnel opens up and they enter the colossal foundry cave. To the right they see the giant stone bucket suspended from enormous chains, while the other bucket lies broken on the floor below other hanging chains. Ahead of them is the imposing blast furnace with broken forms inside. All in the carts are silent and cannot believe what they are seeing.

"Wow, this place is enormous."

"This must be where the giant magnets were forged," notes Elixor. "They must've slaved here for years pouring molten iron to form the giant magnetic balls."

"Scepter, even here there are many bone fragments," as Varo notices pulverized white bone fragments embedded in the greasy trough.

"If this works and we can restart Zhama, thousands more did a lot more work than we have," adds an impressed Elixor.

"How could we have known so little about our world for so long," mutters a confounded Scepter. "Hey kids, jump out and put another lens in place."

Trillo and Ogard leap from their carts and find recessed steps leading up out of the tunnel trough. They climb the steps, find a boulder, and promptly drill and install a lens looking toward the giant furnace and hanging overhead bucket.

"This place is creepy. Can we back out of here," asks Trillo as soon as they reenter their carts.

In the last cart, Elixor uncovers the back plate and starts back in the direction they came from, and Kairn and Scepter soon follow. A short time later, they all reach the main tunnel and again start forward to catch up to Alor and Torq in the left direction.

After covering a good distance, Scepter's cart leads the others past the small hole, low on the inboard side and then timber number 20, and the maggot-ridden bodies of the four who died cutting it. He doesn't slow very much and wants to get the kids past the somber, putrid scene. The kids are scared and covering their noses, because of the strong stench.

"How did they die," asks a squinting Trillo from the rotting odors.

"Cutting these giant timbers," responds Kairn. "Nearly all of us did." Kairn then shines his illuminator down the outer, crossing timber tunnel so the kids can see the large piece that has slid outward. As they slowly pass each dead body, Elixor tosses a bit of sand from his pouch toward each corpse. If he can't bury them, at least it's some dust of the planet they all come from.

"Am I going to see my dead mother Zoy along here," asks Farsider boy Dwell.

"No, your mother died in the other direction," responds Kairn. "Her effort was noble and courageous. She worked every bit as hard as the rest of us."

In the tunnel right direction, Garl and Hark have reached the menacing giant iron ball and crawl underneath in the floor channel, to get on the backside of the embedded timber.

Garl leans his Comstaff against the tunnel wall and he and Hark climb up the ruptured wooden fibers to reach the top of the broken timber. "We're in position," Garl yells toward the Comstaff. "Let us know when you are."

Back in the left direction, Scepter leads his carts past timbers 19, 18, and 17, all with a similar scene, four-to-six dead bodies near each sawed timber.

"I'm feeling sick," remarks Trillo. The other kids don't look good, either. As they approach timber 16, all get a look at the backside of the embedded timber and its huge morass of fibric destruction.

"Wow, what could cause all of that?"

With their Comstaff leaning off to one side, Alor and Torq have climbed high up onto the broken timbers as if to start chopping from top down, and Alor responds to Garl's voice over the Comstaff.

"Garl, we too are in position."

Scepter's cart and the other carts pull up and stop.

"Now hold on everyone," orders Scepter while exiting his cart. "We've got to assess this. Watch your step everyone, the floor is covered with grease."

In the right direction - with their own Comstaff leaning against the wall - Garl and Hark can hear Scepter's voice.

In the left direction - with all now out of their carts - Scepter sizes up the situation.

"Hey kids, if you want to see what we're up against, crawl under and look at the front side of this broken timber, but don't have any metal on and come right back. And Trillo, if you're carrying that metal drill bit in your backpack, take it off and leave it with us."

Trillo removes his backpack and - sickened but curious - Trillo, Ogard, Stern and Stip get down into the floor channel and crawl under the carnage to arise on the front side of the enormous iron ball. The huge sphere bulges out and towers far above their heads.

"Wow. I can't believe it. This thing is beyond huge!"

"It must weigh millions of tons."

"And there's another one just like it? I can't even see the top of it. I wonder how old they are."

"It's scary and I feel sick. I'm going back."

As the kids again crawl under and return to the backside of the timber, Scepter continues to the four axe men. "Once you start chopping - at the first sign of timber weakness - each of you will have to let the other team know. These two magnets are opposite each other, 180-degrees apart, and something tells me they're supposed to stay that way."

"Yes, Scepter. What will you all do?"

Scepter peers toward the inboard edge of the timber, toward the teeth in the inboard wall that stopped each timber and held them in place, and the two strange blue hoses that run inward from them.

"These inboard side teeth closed and grabbed to stop each timber in the correct position. And these bright blue hoses running inward from them are very interesting."

Scepter takes a few paces back toward the small horizontal hole, low on the inboard wall.

"And each timber has one of these small holes just past it, low on the inboard side, as if each of these was some sort of . . . escape route. I think it's time we crawl through this small hole and head inward toward the center of our world."

Since there is no other alternative and everyone is now feeling queasy, one by one, each crawls through the opening, which is just high enough to allow one Zeon with a backpack, through. It's a good thing the hole is wider than it is tall, because the monitor on Elixor's back barely fits through. With his Comstaff, Scepter crawls through last and turns around to poke his head, shoulders and Comstaff top one last time into the enormous magnet tunnel.

Scepter knows it is the last time he will address these four sacrificial axemen, alive. "Men of Zeon, we owe you our lives – and that goes for you too - Hark and Garl. Are there any last words?"

"Scepter, may what you live to see . . . be worth our lives," as from the other direction, Garl's voice comes over Scepter's and Alor's Comstaffs.

"Scepter, we wish we had your leadership of respect and honor on our side of the planet," adds Farsider Alor.

"Your people are not the evil we were told," adds Torq. "These final days of bonding, pain, and common endeavor have been worthy."

"Agreed," responds Scepter. "The ambition and commitment of you four will move us onward, if there *is* an onward, and so when you are ready, forward with brilliance."

"Forward with brilliance" respond all four.

Without hesitation, both teams start chopping away and the upper portions of their weakened timbers. Each chopping impact echoes away down the long, dark tunnel. When your family is gone, you do what you can.

All seventeen who crawled through the small opening now see the remainder of the giant timber running inward toward the center of their world. The inboard side opens into a long cavern, with the huge timber extending into the distance like an oversized torpedo tube.

They get a better look at the teeth which extended from the tree tunnel perimeter to stop the trunk from gliding further outboard, and the two bright blue hoses that run away from the teeth, also inboard along the trunk. The hoses are clear, firm, and may contain fluid, possibly water. There is a path running inboard along the trunk and clear blue hoses. The hoses extend along the floor like two endless snakes, but the huge timber is about one yard above the floor. What could be holding it up?

"There's only one way to go, so let's follow it," advises Scepter.

The chopping echo dissipates behind them as they advance along the inner cavern, and because of the timber's impressive length, it must've once extended hundreds of yards into the sky.

As a tremor of Tareon's impending closeness shudders through the planet, "Look at how long it is? They must've stood impressively tall, when alive."

"It seems to run forever."

"I wonder what it was like when they were above ground? Our planet must've been very different."

Finally, after hundreds of yards, they approach the far end of the timber, which has been sawed off cleanly.

"Scepter, the end of the timber is approaching."

Passing the cut end, they see a large metal eyelet which has been drilled deeply into the cut base. A thick steel rod fits over the eyelet and is held by a giant bolt and nut. The rod continues inboard, as do the two clear blue fluid-filled hoses. Because of the large tree diameter, the eyelet and rod are well above their heads, while the hoses run along the cavern floor.

They follow the rod and hoses forward almost another mile. Finally, they see a larger chamber emerging. Up ahead, eight blue hoses from the right and 30 hoses from the left appear to be converging with the two they've been following, toward a common point. Overhead, a similar convergence looks to be happening with the large rod. Four rods from the right and 15 from the left appear to be merging with the one they are following, and on the opposite side, 20 more rods converge, coming from the far right side of the planet.

The blue hoses – a total of 40 now - end side-by-side at a long, low coffin-like structure. On the opposite side, 40 more blue hoses also connect to it. It looks like a giant centipede, only instead of where legs are sticking out, blue hoses are connected.

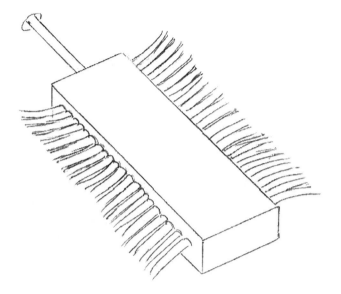

"Those hoses on the opposite side must be coming from the right direction timbers," surmises Kairn.

"They all come from here," responds Elixor. "It's some sort of . . . manifold, sending fluid toward every timber. These tubes deployed the teeth that stopped the timbers from sliding further out into their tunnels. There's fluid in these clear blue hoses and they are still hard, holding pressure after all of these millennia."

"Everything down here deep in the planet seems to be protected, hidden from destruction and decay," adds Varo.

"Well it won't be much longer if our world collides with Tareon," responds Scepter.

Overhead, each rod ends at a large crank arm, extending down from the dark, tall cave ceiling. There are 40 crank arms hanging down, all arranged in a very large circle, to allow room for each crank to swing back and forth.

"There seems to be a mechanism or linkage overhead that connects to each timber. The thought and engineering put into this is incredible," remarks Elixor.

"It seems that much of our small planet has been . . . hollowed out. Most of these spaces are natural caverns, but others have been dug out for one purpose or another," observes Kairn.

"This hollowness might be why our planet transmits sound so well over long distances," notices Elixor. "We can probably thank these caverns for why our Comstaffs work."

"Let's step over these hoses to the left and work our way up to the far end of the manifold," advises Scepter while looking ahead.

One by one, Scepter and his followers step over the blue tubes to work their way to the far end of the manifold, stepping in gaps between each hose. As the first few in their group step over the last pair of hoses, a tremor rocks the cavern and a chunk of ceiling breaks loose and falls, crushing Othar's sons Stern and Stip. The boulder comes to rest atop some of the hard blue hoses, and from underneath the boulder, there are horrible screams from each trapped boy.

"Oh no! Stern? Stip? Are you there? Can you hear us?"

"I fell in between the hoses, but the boulder has crushed my hand. Please help! It hurts. I can't move!"

"Me too. I think my hand is broken," adds the other child.

The others back-track, and all gather around the huge rock.

"Give us a minute. We'll figure this out," as Scepter tries to calm the injured kids.

"Hurry! I'm hurting!"

"Everybody, let's try to push this thing off further away from the manifold. Maybe it will roll down the hoses," commands Scepter.

All seventeen others step up on the manifold side of the boulder and try pushing it away. They grunt and groan and lean in, but it doesn't move.

"It's no use! It weighs too much. There aren't enough of us."

"Let me try," as Scepter plunges the tip of his Comstaff under the bottom of the boulder and tries to pry the huge rock upward. As he pushes up on the top end of his staff, it emits popping sounds like it's about to split, so he backs off.

"It's no use. This thing is too heavy."

Just then, another tremor rumbles through the cavern. The rods and cranks overhead swing and sway, and the boulder rocks a little, causing horrible cracking sounds from the bones of each boy's hands, and Stern and Stip scream even louder.

"We've got to do something!"

"Norl, with this monitor on my back, I cannot reach my back pack," directs Elixor. "Would you reach in and pull out the two hemp-covered items? But don't unrap them unless you want to cut yourself."

Norl retrieves the two rolled-up soft-bound items and hands them to Elixor. "What are those," asks Scepter.

As Elixor carefully unfurls the first of the two rolls, a thin, shiny sharp wire is visible, with a green handle at each end. "They are miniature cable saws. Much smaller versions of the ones we used to cut the timbers."

"And what are these for?"

"To amputate their arms," as Elixor carefully unraps the second one.

The boys and others gasp at Elixor's thinking. "If it's the only way to free them and proceed onward, we must be prepared to deal with it."

As Elixor hands the cable saws to Kairn and Scepter, he then reaches into his side pouch and removes a small roll of the old Sea Cover material and two red pills.

"These boys are in great pain already, but an amputation without a sedative is horrific," adds Scepter.

"Not if they take these red pills first, but one of these will knock each of them out and we'll have to carry them from this point on," replies Elixor.

"Both boys are nervous. What if they resist taking the pills and can't swallow them," asks Kairn.

"Stick the far end of these straws down their throats, place a pill in the straw, and blow. There is no way they can reject it," as Elixor pulls out two of the old breathing straws.

As another tremor rumbles through – again rocking the boulder and making the boys scream louder – Elixor bites off two segments from the Sea Cover roll and advises, "Tie these around their arms just below the shoulder, to stop the blood flow."

While this is happening, no one has noticed that Varo has quietly stepped away to one side and appears to be meditating, as if to recall a long lost memory.

"Will these wires cut through their arms quickly," Scepter asks Elixor, while looking at the sharp cable saws.

"Loop each wire one time around each boy's arm and pull the ends in opposite directions, and the wire will cut cleanly through bone in one stroke, but give them the pill first. It takes a minute or two to knock them out."

Underneath the boulder and confined by the hoses, the boys' anguished faces imagine waking to life without an arm. With their father Othar unreachable on Tareon and their mother's death coming down from Altai, they've been forced to grow up quickly, and neither feels ready for this grotesque severing of flesh and bone.

As others bend down to force a pill into each boy's mouth, Varo – now with a menacing brow and intense stare of total rage – roars "Vellane," which echoes throughout the cavern.

All others in the party freeze at Varo's roar, and at the left tunnel ball - hearing Varo's roar over his Comstaff - Alor stops chopping and responds, "I don't know what's going on up there but when he does that, you'd better give him space."

Hearing Alor's advice over the Comstaff, the others in Scepter's party each take a step back, even those who were about to place the pills in each boy's mouth. Varo steps to the forefront and his maniacal stare quickly scans the large boulder. He lies down on his back in between two of the hoses the boulder rests on and plants his feet up on the underside of the boulder.

"What is he doing?"

"I don't know, but something tells me we have to be prepared," as all others take up positions on either side of the boulder.

One more tremor rolls though and the boulder again rocks in movement, and horrible cracking sounds are heard from below as though bones are being crushed, with each kid yelling blood-curdling screams.

While this is going on, Varo's mind goes mentally elsewhere and the anger in his menaced face intensifies. His eyes of hatred are open, but he doesn't see the boulder in front of him as he is now in another place and time. And finally - while again roaring "Vellane" throughout the cavern - Varo presses his feet up into the boulder underside to perform a leg press, locks his knees, and raises the boulder a few inches.

Both boys scream in agony as the others quickly pull them out. Varo unlocks his legs and the boulder again falls back onto the firm blue hoses just before another tremor rolls through.

"Are you alright? Oh, their arms are broken," observes Norl.

In pain and crying, each boy uses their good arm to support a smashed forearm and hand that would otherwise be dangling.

"Step over the remaining hoses before another tremor causes more boulders to fall," Elixor quickly advises.

All follow his lead and in no time, all seventeen have reached the far end of the manifold. "Untie the tourniquets and re-tie them around their necks as slings to support their broken arms," adds Elixor.

As Norl and Kairn secure the slings in place, Elixor pulls out two small yellow pills and places one toward each boy's mouth.

"Here, chew on these. These ones won't knock you out, but they will take away some of the pain."

"That was quite a feat of strength, and who is Vellane," Scepter asks Varo, who is rejoining the group.

"Vellane was my mate."

"And how do you produce so much force?"

"I go back to the day she was taken from me and think of something that stirs great hatred."

"Oh? And what would that be?"

"My old leader."

Just then, another tremor rolls through, a clear sign of the two planets' impending nearness. "Scepter, time is getting shorter. We must keep pushing onward. This long manifold rod disappears beyond that wall ahead," as Elixor refocuses everyone.

At the far end of the manifold, a long round metal rod sticks out and disappears through a hole in the cave wall. The wall has an opening to the left and right of where the rod goes through.

"Something is behind that wall. It looks like both openings lead to a common back-side. Let's see where this left opening leads."

At the left tunnel ball, Alor and Torq have chopped away the top 20 percent of the mangled timbers when suddenly there is a loud, deep timber "crack!" The sound echoes away down the tunnel. Alor talks toward his leaned-up Comstaff, to Garl and Hark on the opposite side of the planet.

"Garl."

"Yes?"

"We've just heard our first loud pop of the timber giving way."

"Keep chopping, but be careful."

In the central cavern, Scepter's party hears this over their Comstaff. Just then, a quake wave rumbles through the planet, another reminder of Tareon's approach. In the right tunnel, Garl and Hark's timber creaks, moans and pops loudly from the stresses of the shifting planet.

"It must be the stresses of Tareon getting closer, and I'm starting to feel heavier. Our planet must be spinning faster," surmises Hark.

Both sides resume chopping, but at a slower rate. Garl and Hark's timber continues to creak and moan.

Scepter's party continues onward through the opening in the cave wall where the piston rod goes through, and they enter a smaller cave of a floor strewn with boulders. In the center of the chamber, between boulders, is a rock bowl filled with underground water and sitting in it, looking up at the wall they just rounded, is the slowly-rotting corpse of a lone figure.

"What is that?"

Some tear up at the sight of an individual who is so different, but they wipe the tears away as a sense of wonderment soon takes over. They've searched their planet for centuries, looking for signs of anyone else, anyone different. Who or what is this long-dead stoic figure sitting upright in the small pool?

"And Scepter, look up here."

The figure stares up at the backside of the wall they just rounded. High up on the wall is an illuminated screen showing a large circular ring. At two areas on the ring, 180-degrees apart, are two groups of 20 crossing lines, representing the buried tree trunks, and a red light shines at the 16th tree on each side, representing the embedded giant iron balls.

"It's some sort of . . . control center. See the screen? It monitors the movement of the magnets within the tunnel."

"And it's still lit up and operating after all of these centuries."

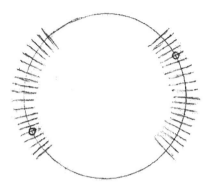

Just below the illuminated screen is something long and horizontal which appears to be covered up by hinged doors.

As they approach the lone rotting figure mostly submerged in the small pool, they are transfixed by it. They've never seen a being that didn't look exactly like modern-day Zeons. His peeling hands are just above the water on wide, stone armrests which have 20 switches on each side. Sticking up between his legs and just above the water is a long lever, not unlike an old train brake. Between the figure and the control board, a sizeable pendulum hangs on a chain from a darkened high ceiling, with the pendulum's sharp metal point aimed straight down.

Even though the figure is sitting and mostly underwater, the differences from current Zeons are obvious. The figure is taller, but thin, with no fur on the remaining cream-colored leathery skin. The face is long with a jutting chin, an open mouth, and eyes that peer up toward the light board with a lonely purpose as if nothing else matters except keeping an eye on the two giant magnets. After his death eons ago, his hair continued to grow and is now impossibly long, floating out away from his head on the surface of the water. Similarly long are his finger nails, which also continued to grow.

Only one aspect connects him in any way with a few current Zeons: his two bright silver eyes.

CHAPTER 10

Mice in a Wheel

ALL SEVENTEEN CRANE THEIR NECKS for a look at the figure, but Scepter, Kairn, Varo, Chronicle, and Elixor look particularly closely; their lone connection to Zeon's distant past.

"Chronicle, it has eyes like yours, and your one eye, Trillo," as they first notice the bright silver eyes.

All stare wide-eyed at the figure. The kids climb up on boulders to get a better look, even Stern and Stip, using their lone good arms.

"Look at the skin, it's been on forever, but looks like it's starting to decay. See the slowly receding flesh," notes Kairn, looking closely at the skin on the hands.

"It may be the air from our opening the entrance cave," responds Elixor. "He was fine, sealed up in this musty pool and thick air."

All are momentarily jostled by another tremor wave reverberating through Zeon's structure, which creates small waves in the stoic figure's bath.

"Scepter, our timber is weakening," as Alor's voice is heard yelling nervously from the left direction timber.

The figure is so old that other than the silver eyes, it has no resemblance to Chronicle or modern day Zeons.

"Chronicle, do you think there's enough flesh remaining to link into his being," asks Scepter. "Do you think you can make a connection?"

"He's been here forever, but if there are enough bodily enzymes left, it's worth a try. This is what we've searched so long for," responds Chronicle.

Scapter takes Chronicle's Comstaff and Elixor takes Chronicle's backpack – the one with the poisonous soup - and Chronicle steps up and settles down into the small pool, next to the slowly-rotting figure. Chronicle now faces up toward the same control board as the figure, places one hand over the figure's hand, closes his own eyes, and after a brief pause asks, "Who are we?"

After a short delay and some verbal noises that sound like different translation attempts, a deep baritone from the distant past comes from Chronicle's mouth, and resonates throughout the cavern.

"We are the Acids of Yore. Where are we?"

"We are in the control center for Zhama," responds Scepter.

"Oh yes. It's been so long, so very long. How did you get in here?"

"Through a sealed hole at the bottom of one of the giant craters."

After a short pause, "These giant craters: Are there eight of them on the planet, with two adjacent to each other?"

"Yes."

"They are not impact craters. They are where we quarried the ferrous ore. This planet has never been hit."

"Why did you build Zhama?"

"We were number three of in a system of five and long range observations said we would collide with planet four."

"How long did it take to build Zhama, and why that name?"

"Thirty years. Thousands died. We finished with one month to spare. It was named by the designer who drew it up. So where are we now? Where did Nozeon come to rest?"

"Nozeon, asks a perplexed Scepter. "In the Milky Way, in the Taurus region."

"Milky Way? Taurus region? These terms are so far from where we came, I do not recognize them. What is the situation now?"

"We are number five in a system of nine and are coming close to planet six."

"How long until impact?"

Scepter looks at Kairn, who answers "Four days, but the way our days are getting shorter, it may seem like only two days, to us."

"You're screwed," bellows Yore's baritone. "It takes two days for Zhama to spool up!"

"And we have to cross Tareon's path," adds Kairn.

"What," asks a confused Scepter.

"By my observations, we are lined up to hit Tareon, but on its inner half," as Kairn gestures with his hands. "Our planet has to fully cross Tareon's path to get outside of Tareon's orbit and be safe."

"Is the sixth planet larger," booms Yore's voice with another question.

"Thirty five percent larger," responds Scepter.

"There is no time to spare! You must free up the magnets!"

"The magnets were stopped by the 16th timber on each side," replies Scepter.

"Oh yes, now I remember. Timbers 17 through 20 are intact. Would you like to retract them?"

With an astonished and suddenly-worried face, "The timbers are moveable" asks Scepter.

"Press the bottom four switches on these armrests, and timbers 17 thru 20 will retract into their tunnels."

Scepter quietly steps away, totally sickened. He realizes that everyone who died digging out the first eight timbers, needn't have, and Norl does her best to console him.

"It's not your fault. You couldn't have known."

"If only we had ventured inward, sooner."

Suddenly, another tremor wave rumbles through the cavern structure.

At the left embedded ball, the timber starts cracking as the giant ball starts breaking through. The weakened interlocking timber fibers along the V-edge start separating and pulling apart like a ruptured gate being forced open. "Scepter," yells Alor, who leaps down to the tunnel floor, but one of his legs breaks, the bone snapping like a twig. Torq jumps down and tries to drag Alor toward the low escape hole, but loses his footing on the slick grease.

"Save yourself! Go on without me!"

Scepter's followers and Garl's crew both hear this over their Comstaffs. The weakened timbers are heard popping and cracking under the intense strain.

In the right direction tunnel, Garl's timber also cracks and weakens. "Ours is going, too," as his panicked voice is also heard over Scepter's Comstaff.

In the left tunnel, the wounded Alor tries to push Torq toward the escape hole, but Torq won't go alone. They've known each other since childhood, a bond forged through prisons and hardships, but with every step he takes, Torq's feet slip and lose traction on the greasy tunnel floor. Over and over he again tries to step, crawl, or roll toward the small escape hole, but the pull of Alor's crippled body causes Torq's feet and hands to slide mercilessly in vain. Torq reaches for the leaned-up Comstaff to try and pry the tip into the floor, but the tip also slips and slides away. With the fibers ripping apart above as Torq refuses to leave his life-long friend alone, the grease that helps each ball roll has become their own slippery quicksand, and Torq gallantly almost has the injured Alor to the escape hole when the giant ball breaks through the remaining timber fibers and quickly crushes Alor and Torq just a few feet short of the hole. Four horrible screams along with crunches of both Comstaffs going out are heard over Scepter's Comstaff. Alor and Torq's bodies are flattened into pancaked pelts by their giant rolling ball, and heat from their warm bodily fluids fizzles on the dark tunnel floor. The stone carts parked in the left floor channel are no match for the giant orb and are also instantly crushed, as are the bodies of all who died; stone and bone pulverized into the smallest of bits, as small as the bone fragments found earlier. Rolling over everything in its path, each giant ball doesn't even deflect upward, and a grinding rumble deeper than the bowels of hell follows their movement, causing vibrations that shudder through the planet's entire framework. These monsters are beyond heavy.

In the control center cave, Scepter and all in his party peer up at the illuminating ring on the control board. The two red lights start slowly counterclockwise. For the first time in untold millennia, the giant iron magnets are free to chase each other, started by nothing more than the natural forces of Zeon's rotation, polarity and magnetic field.

All in Scepter's party look at each other with an unknown dread of "What have we started?" There is a few seconds of silence, but then a deep, rolling sound approaches beyond the outer walls of their central cavern like a rumbling locomotive moving slowly from right to left. All stare in its direction and slowly turn with it as it works its way past them and recedes into the distance.

"That's it," declares Scepter. "They're rolling, and four more good souls are gone, and Dwell and Varo, their deaths mean you are the last two Farsiders alive on this planet."

"It's not your effort that released the second orb," as Yore's voice again bellows from Chronicle's mouth. "The release of the first one, released the second one. The two magnets weigh within ounces of each other and will *forever* chase each other, driven only by our planet's polarity unless the great timbers stop them, which brings the question; when do you want it stopped? That's my purpose and why this lever is here. Once clear of your system, does this lever get pulled to further extend the timbers, or do you want Zhama to run forever?"

"Whoa, is there any way to live through it," asks an astonished Scepter.

"No one lives through Zhama. What history do you have?"

"Only recent history. We can't find anything, far back."

"That's because Zhama destroys all. It flings *everything* off."

"We have people on the sixth planet. Is there any way to remain nearby," asks a hopeful Kairn.

"Like trying to stop a large ship, nothing happens quickly. Once Zhama takes effect, this world will again go far. The best you can do is live awhile longer . . . and enjoy the ride."

"Where can we do that? The surface is so violent. It heats up and spins in a blur. Where can we go?"

"To the only safe place possible: To the poles. You must go to the very top or bottom of our world. It is the only place the spinning is minimized."

"That's preposterous," exclaims Varo. "Our ice caps are much too thick. The top- and bottom- thirds of our planet are covered with ice."

"Not when Zhama gets going," proclaims a confident Yore.

"We've never ventured that far north or south. How do we get there, from here?"

"Take the path that rises behind me. After awhile, it splits. To the left is the South Pole and to the right is the North Pole. You'd better get going. It takes two days to get there."

"But even up there – with the spinning minimized - what will we find?"

"There is a large plate with grease under it. While the world under you spins, the plate does not, and you will remain still."

Another deep rolling sound approaches like a slow locomotive beyond the outer wall, again moving from right to left as the other giant ball rolls past their cavern.

"Hey kids, install that last lens in a nearby boulder looking at this area," as Scepter looks at Ogard and Trillo."

Ogard and Trillo jump down and do as they're told, drilling and installing their last lens far enough away to take in Yore's pool, the hanging pendulum, and the control board in front of him.

"Your people left you here when they went north and south," as Scepter again questions Yore.

"I am the Caretaker. The Engineer. Someone had to . . . stop the train, which brings us back to that question: we can either pull this lever to stop Zhama or let it run on forever."

"We have been repeatedly belittled hearing what the other planets have accomplished and how advanced they are," voices Varo. "If there is no living through it, I say we let it run forever and show the others our one little trick."

"Or do we deploy the timbers and maybe one day this planet will come to rest where another society can grow," offers Kairn.

Hep, with her broken arm still in a sling, "My tired and aching body says it's time for a little vanity. I say we let Zhama run forever."

As the others nod and agree, "Very well, then. We will let Zhama run on," declares Scepter.

Another tremor rumbles through, stronger than before. There is a steadily rising sense of urgency as the tremors indicate Tareon is getting closer, compounded with the added anticipation of what Zhama is capable of.

"We'd better uncouple Chronicle," advises Scepter as the others prepare to move on. "We have to get going."

Straining to reply in his own weakened voice, "Please, no. I am very old and my duty is here. I belong with Yore," responds Chronicle.

"Since we've decided to let it run forever, you can come with us."

"Thank you, but this is my place, my role, where I am meant to finish."

"Very well," responds Scepter as others' eyes start puddling up. "There *does* appear to be some remote lineage between you two. Yore, one last question: How will you and Chronicle know if Nozeon breaks free of orbit and embarks on its own course?"

"Is that pendulum still hanging, before me?"

"Yes."

"Momentum will cause it to rise and trail the direction Nozeon goes in, and it will no longer hang down."

"We have so much to learn from you, but time is of the essence. We must continue onward," concludes Scepter as they prepare to move on.

"Your voices echo of struggle and longing," notices Yore.

"We just want to survive, although for what, we do not know," responds Kairn.

"Maybe this will help. Before you go, are those doors in front of me still closed?"

"Yes."

"Open them."

Varo and Kairn jump down and unlatch the folding hinged doors and open them, revealing a screen and a video loop which begins playing. In it, lush hills and greenery give way to a healthy deep blue sea. Large whale-like creatures somersault above the waves while smaller flying aquatics buzz by in the air. A large Octo-dactyl flies loops overhead. It has a central mouth and eight eyes, four along the leading edge of each wing. Zooming slowly back, families resembling Yore play along a bucolic beach and coming into view is a timber so large, it towers up out of sight. Zooming further back, two other timbers also come into view. The timbers are very far apart, because the tree tops billow out over a hundred yards in each direction. Each tree canopy is an entire city of life. Roped elevators on pulleys lift beings resembling Yore up to the branches. Kids and families frolic on the lower branches while higher up, abundant life forms chase and court each other. The sky is very blue, filled with oxygen just like the deep blue cobalt sea.

"Wow, what place is that," asks an astonished Trillo.

"That is here, a long, long time ago, in another place and time," bellows Yore. "Soak it up as you wish, but you must get going."

They stand and admire it for a minute in splendorous wonder. Finally, Scepter admits, "I want to stay, but we must go, and Yore and Chronicle, something tells me we are in a way your distant children, and for that we owe you our lives. Stay alert, stay smart, and forward with brilliance!"

As another rumble from one of the advancing magnets rolls through – along with a stronger tremor - Chronicle again strains to get his weak voice out. "Forward with brilliance."

"Oh, Yore, one more question," asks Scepter. "How did you get the great timbers down into the planet?"

"We dug two great channels, one on each side of the planet. If you do not see them today, then Zhama caved them in. We regretted cutting all of the timbers, but if we had not, Zhama would still be running, meaning that none of you would be alive today."

With all of their questions answered, the last thing Scepter does is place Chronicle's Comstaff in the water next to him. The sorcerer's sword shall die with him.

Leaving the hinged doors open so the tape loop can repeat, they grab their belongings and start up the path behind Yore toward the distant poles, and Yore yells one last piece of advice to Scepter's departing party.

"Make sure you read the Longevity Stone, and grab some Nocab on your way out!"

Chronicle has a content look on his old face as if he is learning much from connection to a long-lost forefather, but deep within him, Yore said something of that resonates with a curious importance. What is the Longevity Stone?

A few minutes later, Garl and Hark arrive, cut and disheveled and covered with large splinters, but otherwise okay. They stop at the sight of the connected Chronicle and Yore, and then notice the tape loop of the past. After watching for a bit, they turn to Chronicle and ask, "Which way did they go?"

With a trembling arm, Chronicle weakly points in the direction of the back path. The old one looks as if he's in his final hours and is contentedly ready to die as Garl and Hark start up the rear path.

Up ahead, Scepter's party is approaching the path split when from behind they hear, "Scepter!"

All turn and "Garl, Hark, you're alive!" All hug the panting duo as they catch up, but can see that Garl and Hark are bleeding and have cuts.

"We heard your screams and your Comstaff being crushed. How did you survive?"

"When our giant ball started rolling, we were able to ride it down and fell into the tunnel floor channel. The ball rolled right over us, just inches away. We had a lot of splinters to remove, but we made it through the escape hole before the other ball came by. It took us awhile, but we followed the timber and blue hoses."

"Did you see Chronicle and the tape loop," asks Kairn.

"Yes, but we didn't stay. We wanted to catch up. What place was that?"

"We'll tell you along the way. Now here we are at the fork on the trail. Who wants to go to the South Pole and who wants to go north," asks Scepter.

"Poles? They're much too cold," replies an unknowing Garl.

"Like we said, we have much to tell you."

"Scepter, from two million, there are only eighteen of us left. Can we please stay together," asks a still-panting Hark.

"Agreed. The North Pole is closer. Let's go to the right. Who knows what we'll find?"

All turn and take the right path toward the north. As they walk, the tremors increase, occurring more often, reminding all that Tareon must be very nearby.

Also slowly increasing are the rumble intervals behind them of the giant magnets rolling through the planet tunnel, as each giant orb rolls through at a slightly faster speed than the revolution before.

On Tareon, the teams are in the top floor suite of the "W" building, preparing to head down the suite's escape elevator to the underground survival shelter. Three Transtubes hover outside their penthouse floor. In the sky, a huge Zeon approaches spinning ominously, and winds are blowing loose debris throughout the city below. Rayelle still scours old news records on a monitor, and an article about a traveler who crashed on a distant planet piques her interest.

"Drago, I think I found something."

"Not now! It's too late! We have to go down this escape elevator to the deep shelter below! Save it and bring it up later!"

She swipes the monitor away with her clicker and quickly gathers up her Comstaff and Evene. "Walking past the others and heading out toward one of the Transtubes, "I know where I'm watching from," she defiantly declares.

Drago and Othar look at each other but realize that she may have a better plan, and all then follow her out to the two other Tubes.

She flies just beyond the outskirts of the city to the seven opulent houses overlooking Infinity Lake and lands on the beach. The others follow her and Evene in the other two Transtubes, and also land. The angled concrete elevator box juts up just behind them, and the low-lying beach houses and low cliffs are just behind the sand. It's early afternoon, and the imposing Zeon is slowly working its way down toward setting directly beyond the watery horizon of Infinity Lake. The two other Tubes land near hers and all ten join Evene and Rayelle, who has stabbed her Comstaff into the beach sand.

Amid the dry warm winds, Rayelle emphatically declares, "I'm watching from here until the very last minute and when the winds get too hot and strong, the angled escape elevator down to the survival shelter is right here."

They agree that it's as safe as the elevator in the "W" building.

"What did you find in the news records," asks Othar.

"I found this," as Rayelle steps toward the shore and swipes her clicker to bring up a monitor with the old article.

"About a hundred years ago, an interstellar trader crashed on the outermost planet of the next solar system. He survived the crash. The people on that planet had not traveled much, but because his beings were longtime traders throughout the cosmos, he was asked what are the three greatest stories spreading throughout the stars?"

"Go on."

"The first story he told was about a great plague moving through the galaxy, the second was about a growing black hole, and the third and by far the oldest story - a story so old no one believed it anymore - said that hidden quietly in plain sight somewhere in the cosmos . . . was a planet . . . that could move . . . like a ship. No one knew if this ever happened or where this planet might be, and it was such an ancient story that it was dismissed as nothing more than 'space lore.'"

"Fascinating," responds Drago. "If we don't get killed by what's about to happen, we might be in for quite a show. We're with you on this. This escape elevator is close and we want to see all we can."

Deep within Zeon in the large circular tunnel, the two giant iron magnets are gradually picking up speed as they chase after each other like two mice in the same wheel; running, but never catching up to each other. Each revolution within the planet is faster than the previous, as each ball chases the magnetic tail of the one in front of it, and a tremendous rumble accompanies their endless chase throughout the tunnel; a rumble that reverberates and shudders through Zeon's dense granite frame.

In the control center cave, Chronicle and the ancient carcass Yore gaze up at the lights on the control board. The two red lights of the circulating balls chase each other counterclockwise on the large ring. While this happens, the slow decay on Yore's skin creeps up his hands and arms. While fixated on the task of monitoring the lights, Chronicle relishes in this contact with Yore. There is endless information being handed down in the final hours of Chronicle's long life.

Along the path to the North Pole, Varo leads as the eighteen Zeons are steadily tiring of the long trek. It's not only a long distance, but they have to fight to balance themselves against the nearly constant tremors, and the path ahead is uphill. Elixor carries the backpack he had removed from Chronicle, the one with the oozing poisonous soup in it.

"I'm feeling heavier," remarks Scepter's wife Norl, who is laboring and starting to fall behind. "The planets must be getting nearer and our rotation, speeding up.

"Tareon is going to be very close if we make it out of here," replies Kairn.

The rolling rumble of the magnets far behind them steadily increases in interval, but is not as loud now, as they work farther north and away from the planet's center. After a few more switch-backs and turns, "Scepter, there is a glow of light ahead," remarks Varo from up ahead.

A dim bluish light is becoming visible beyond upcoming bends, and gets brighter as they round each curve.

"I wonder what it could be."

The bluish glow gradually intensifies until its now quite bright, illuminating the darkened path as they round the final curve. Finally, they see them; off to each side of the trail and surrounded by boulders are pools of a bright blue gelatin-like fluid. They are the same color blue as the clear hoses seen earlier. There are a number of these glowing blue pools on each side of the trail, which jostle and shake with each undulating tremor.

"What is this stuff?"

"It may kill me, but I'm hungry" admits Garl, who reaches down and scoops up a glob of the glowing blue goo and ingests it.

"Hey, this stuff is good!"

The others all reach in and also scoop up handfuls. "Oh my, I've never had something so good."

Examining a sample closely, "With all the strange discoveries we've been making, my guess is that this is an ancient purified form of our green ooze," surmises Elixor.

"No way. It's much too good. It can't be."

"It's a bit different, but it has enough commonalities. I'm certain of it."

As the tremors continue, all except for Elixor, Hep, Stern, and Stip remove their backpacks and begin stuffing them with scoops of the gelatin, while also eating some. Others place some of the goo in the backpacks of Hep, Stern and Stip, as the injured ones chow down with their lone good hands.

In the blue glow emitted by the pools, their faces look long and drawn as their ordeals, hardships, and journeys are taking a visible toll.

They are the remaining-few of a once-great people, now relishing in the smallest bits of food they can find.

"Scepter, this nourishment is good, but my legs are more jittery than this goo and need a few moments rest before we continue," admits Kairn.

As the tremors continue, the others nod in agreement and sit atop the path-side boulders, greatly relishing their temporary nourishment, but Scepter's wife Norl can't hold back and starts to break down. "What if all this effort is for nothing and it just delays our demise?"

"Yore said things would be thawing ahead, but the way out may still be frozen over," adds Elixor. "We could be trapped in here."

"Then our final act will be to drink that steaming soup you brewed up," admits Scepter. "It will be a simple, quiet ending, and if this wonderful blue goo is to be my last meal, then so be it."

The lack of response from all seventeen others is telling, as none want to mention Elixor's silencing soup, which with each laborious step is becoming a better option.

Just then, another sizeable tremor and raining dust prods Scepter to conclude, "But we must push on. Come on and gather each other up."

The view in space again shows the planets – now on the opposite side of their sun from their last convergence – spinning relentlessly toward each other for one final time as their paths arc into alignment like two bulls staring each other down. All factors are ripe for a catastrophic acceleration and fusion of worlds, which will collide and congeal to create a young, lifeless, larger planet. The cosmos are ageless, yet events such as this impending collision only happen rarely.

On Tareon – on the beautiful beach at Infinity Lake – it's now late afternoon. Even though Rayelle's Comstaff stands impaled in the sand nearby, Drago – into his bracelet - makes a call to Zeon.

"Zeon, are you there? Hello Zeon?" After there is no response, "There's nothing but silence. It's getting windy here and it must be worse there, and I hoped to talk with my wife Hep and daughter Ogard again, one more time. They are either dead or somewhere still underground."

Evene tears up hearing this talk of death, but the only thing Rayelle can do is hold her tighter and reassure her that the survival shelter at the bottom of the deep elevator may enable them to live for a very long time.

Othar and three others emerge from the beach houses with modern lounges to place on the sand. Jurn, Plur and Virn have found beach-towel like materials, and lay them on the sand.

No one is there to see it, but on Zeon, the mid-latitudes are already a hellish place. The ice caps are again retreating. The winds are whipping violently and with no cover to protect the Nearside Sea, its wave's crash against each other in collisions of epic whitecaps which foam and evaporate into the warming dry air, just as the Farsiders lost their Sea. The seaside encampment has been blown away, and sand blows into the crater hole where all went underground. There are non-stop quakes as Zeon feels the incoming pull of the giant Tareon in the sky. Because of the quakes, many of the curled overhanging peaks break off and crumble below, but the granite Altai is a dust-blown mess and still stands tall.

Miles below, in the doughnut-ringed tunnel, the giant magnets are still picking up speed and the rumble that accompanies them has risen in pitch. In the entrance cave, the view through the slot shows the tunnel taking on a feint, eerie glow. Zhama . . . is just waking up.

CHAPTER 11

Topside

ALONG THE PATH LEADING TO the North Pole, Scepter's party has outlived the power of their illuminators and they've resorted to holding handfuls of the glowing blue ooze they found to light their way. The path incline has increased and switch-back turns highlight the elevation change. In addition, Zeon's shorter days and increasing gravity has them feeling heavier than ever.

Hanging down all around the path are the dead root systems of the tundra above. The roots hang like thick cobwebs, and all in Scepter's party have to brush them aside as they walk along the serpentine narrow path.

They have travelled long and far and each step on the rising path is more difficult than the one before. Their group has lengthened like a bicycle peloton succumbing to a great mountain climb, and Scepter is assisting his wife Norl, who is breaking down.

"I can't make it any farther! Go on without me," cries Norl.

"Yore said things ahead would be thawing, but what if it's still frozen over and we're all trapped," Elixor mutters to Kairn.

"Then it'll be time to go quietly, with one final sip of your soup," admits Kairn, who is too sore to care what Trillo hears.

Walking behind Elixor are the three young couples, who now stare longingly at the steaming backpack he is carrying, which represents instant relief from constant pain.

"We can't go on like this. What is all this for," as Hep and her daughter Ogard are also lagging behind.

Just then, "Scepter, I think there is light ahead," shouts Varo, up ahead of the others.

They have to round a few more turns and whatever it is is not bright like the glowing blue pools had been. It *is* light, but very dim, and it's just in time as all are spent from the long trek, even with the blue nourishment along the way.

Finally - nearing the source - a thin ray of light shines down from the perimeter of a rectangular overhead cover above the path.

"What is it?"

"It's a hatch. Some sort of cover."

The cover is just big enough for Elixor's monitor to fit through. There's just enough light shining down to see that next to the path on one side is a thick metal box with a lid.

"And what is this box? I want to open it," remarks a curious Elixor.

He lifts the lid on the box - which is hinged on the far side - and as it opens, a bright light inside comes on and temporarily blinds all of them.

"Hey, that's bright!"

After their eyes readjust, "It's a cooler and it's got stuff in it!"

Inside, there are pouches of bright blue sticks – a frozen, harder version of the blue gelatin they had consumed earlier.

"Didn't Yore yell something about not forgetting to grab some Nocab," recalls Scepter. "These sticks must be it."

After each grabs sticks and places them in each other's backpacks, the cooler light has illuminated the underside of the pathway overhead hatch.

"There is a handle on this hatch. Give me a hand pushing this open," orders Scepter.

Scepter turns the handle and Varo and Kairn help push the hatch upward. It would normally be covered by tons of thick ice, but all is quickly warming at the top of their world. It takes quite an effort, but the hatch breaks through a thin layer of melting ice and lifts, rising up and back over its hinge. Scepter sticks his head up through the opening and sees an area of their planet that no Zeon has ever seen.

In the thaw that is quickly advancing up to the pole, thin sheets of ice separate from layers below and slowly float upward. The ice sheets rotate in the air, slowly circling the nearby North Pole. More layers separate and also lift upward, a ballet of ice sheets at different levels slowly turning in choreographic unison above the nearby axis. The trapped water in each sheet causes a thousand prisms of mini rainbows, courtesy of light from the low sun on the horizon.

As each dripping sheet gracefully works its way upward and away from the spinning center, it crumbles, and droplets disperse in the warming air like tiny exploding balloons, and as quickly as they disperse, new sheets breaking off from the ground rise up and replace them. This beautiful ballet happens as the ground ice recedes toward the nearby North Pole, the very top of their world.

One by one, all in Scepter's party emerge from the hatch blinded by their first light in days. The floating ice sheets flicker in the waning sunlight, acting like hundreds of mini suns. When eyes are adjusted, all are agape at the beautiful sight, but Elixor soon reasons that this is not right for their planet.

"This is glorious, but our ice pack will soon be gone. After the last pass-by, our rivers still flowed, meaning our ice caps did not completely melt."

Because they are at the top of their world, objects usually high in the sky are now low, just above the horizon. Kairn turns and looks away from the late afternoon sun and "Scepter," as he points and yells at Tareon, its top one-third looming very large in the other direction and taking dead aim at Zeon.

All turn and are helplessly humbled by the sight of their incoming enemy. As the warm winds cut across their pole, "Two days, no more, but they'll be so short, it'll seem like later today," as Kairn states his estimate.

Hearing this, Scepter eyes Elixor with a helpless look. He doesn't ask his question but Elixor knows his thought, and briefly lifts the backpack carrying the smoldering, poisonous herbal soup. It's the only option to an infernal fusion of their world with Tareon.

"Scepter, the floating ice circles over an area in that direction. That must be the true North Pole," notices a pointing Varo.

"Right. That's our calling. Let's see if we can make it."

As the tremors continue, all eighteen make their way toward the only sign of structure in the area. As they walk, the receding ice uncovers low hills in the background and barren tundra now exposed for the first time in eons.

There is a minimal structure ahead, but the retreating ice is now replaced by windswept dust which partially obscures the scene. In addition, the world they walk on is spinning from their right to their left while the structure they're aiming for is not, so they *think* they have to take one step right for every step forward, to aim for their target.

As they get closer, they see a very ancient and minimalist scene. Twelve stone towers jut up from the ground arranged in a large circle and spaced perfectly apart. It's not unlike Stonehenge, but these stones are not smooth or perfectly carved. Their raw, jagged columns are rich with veins of granite and natural metals, and each stone column is spaced evenly from the other eleven. They are also not "standing" on the ground, but disappear into it as if connected to the planet.

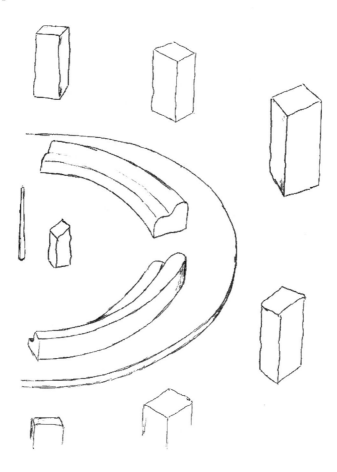

They surround – by a few yards - a 30-yard diameter sandstone plate that sits at the very top of their world. The plate resembles a large merry-go-round platform with a small space under it. Oozing out from under the plate is a thick layer of shiny blue-black grease. As Scepter's party approaches it, the last layer of ice attaching the plate to the surrounding ground melts and shatters, and the plate stops rotating, while the planet under it continues to slowly spin. Now, the ground they are approaching on spins, but because of the slick oozing grease underneath, the plate does not.

"Wow, that's a lot of grease," observes Elixor.

"And our slowly spinning around this plate is making me dizzy," adds Scepter. "Let's step up on it."

Once up on the plate, all eighteen are still as the columns and planet behind spin slowly under the platform. At the very center of the plate, a pole sticks up about three yards. The pole is connected to the plate, so it does not spin. The top of the pole is shaped like a spout toward the backside, as if for some fluid to come out, and further down, three chalices are curved to nestle tightly against the pole, to possibly catch fluid.

About 10-feet in front of the central pole is what appears to be a small stone podium, as if someone might stand behind it and speak or read from it. Etched into the top of it are ancient symbols similar to those seen in the entrance cave. The etched symbols are highlighted by a faded purple dye. Below the last symbols, there is space for a few more, which Scepter approaches.

"This must be the Longevity Stone Yore spoke of," as Scepter looks down at the podium symbols.

Almost unnoticeable in the late afternoon sun is soft mood lighting on the platform surface. As the sun sets, the soft lighting will slowly become more visible. The rotation of Zeon below the plate, powers the lighting.

About 10-yards out from the center, a curved stone bench extends fully around the platform and center pole. There are four openings at points along the bench for access to step through. The stone bench is built into the platform stone, and sitting silently on that bench . . . literally . . . are the skeletons of their distant past.

All twenty four skeletons sit stoically facing the central pole. Most appear adult, but there are a few children. There is no flesh, but their skeletal thinness and height look like both Yore's frame, and those beings on the video of the past. Stretching across their laps and running all of the way around the bench is a thick heavy piece of the bright blue Nocab. Like a roller coaster safety bar, it appears to have been a weight to hold them in place on the bench, and it also has bite marks in it as if it also was to snack on.

"This Nocab is clearly related to our green ooze," as Elixor notices the texture of the Nocab cord. "Look how similar this blue cord is to our Great Elastic."

Each skeleton's feet end in open-toed stone boots. The boots are heavy, but not part of the platform, indicating the old ones were allowed to walk as long as they wore the boots.

"Between the lap cord and the boots, I'd say these were to weigh them down, to keep them anchored to the platform and not flying away," observes Elixor.

"Fascinating," remarks Scepter. "They've been frozen up here under our thick ice cap for untold centuries, but I think it's time we free up our long-lost relatives."

Scepter, Kairn, Varo and others carefully remove the stone boots from each skeleton's foot. They then lift the thick blue cord from the skeletons' laps and gently, each skeleton rises upward, briefly circling around the center pole just as the ice sheets had before moving up and outward into the heavens, never to be seen again. "Sorry to take your seats, but it's our turn," remarks Kairn.

"Trillo, Ogard, Stern and Stip, you kids are the lightest ones here. Put your feet into these boots and have a seat before you all blow away," advises Scepter.

The kids do as they're told and take up positions on the bench, securing themselves in place. The big feet of current Zeons seem to match the feet of their ancient ancestors and fill the stone boots, nicely. The adults also step into the stone boots.

The bench is angled so that those sitting on it can see up as well as forward toward the central pole. As the low sun sets on the horizon and the first stars appear, Trillo notices the different sky compared to where they live.

"Father, the stars up here do not rise in the west and set in the east. Instead, they spiral slowly overhead."

"That's because we are at the very top of the world. The stars we see up here do not go out of view. Since we are at the top, *our* planet's turning makes them look like *they* are turning."

"The sun is setting and we've work to do," as Scepter issues commands for what's next. "Elixor, can you, Garl and Hark affix your monitor to that pole, and can you float an aerial relay antenna? Maybe we can see what's going on back where we live and have one last conversation with our teams on Tareon."

"Yes, Scepter."

Garl and Hark remove the monitor Elixor has been lugging and mount it on the center pole, tying it in place with green strands. They then attach a small lens to the monitor, aimed at the podium, stone bench, and stone columns beyond. Elixor removes a deflated green balloon from his backpack, a small patch of dried reeds, and two flint stones. He blows up and ties off the balloon and in the hot dry wind, gets a spark with the first stroke of the stones, and lights the reeds. He lets the heat rise into the balloon and soon ties the balloon around a small metal relay dish. When Garl and Hark have the monitor mounted, Elixor throws them a long green strand from the old Sea Cover.

"Here, tie this around the monitor."

Garl does as he's told and soon the wind quickly takes the small balloon and relay dish aloft. It would be too windy anywhere else, but this is above the exact North Pole, so the balloon maintains its position tethered directly above the central pole.

While this is going on, Scepter takes a look at the symbols on the top of the Longevity Stone. "Damn, if only I could make sense of these. All I can make out is the Zhama symbol," as he is frustrated by his inability to make out a language so old that it is completely foreign.

As Scepter rubs his head in confusion, Norl approaches to secure his necklace of polished metal stones around his neck.

"What's this for?"

"We have no idea what for, but if this is to be a special occasion, I want you to wear it. And anyway, if *our* skeletons are one day found here, I want whoever finds us to know who lead us; who got us here." Norl hugs Scepter, and couldn't be more proud of him. He has lead them long and far through calamity and pain, and discovering the skeletons makes her feel that this remote pinnacle will indeed be their final resting place.

Elixor pulls a simple one-button remote switch from his backpack and twists two long electrical wires from it to wires on the monitor. As the planet jostles below them and after a few seconds of static snow, he steps back and yells "Scepter, we have a picture!"

The view is from the lens the kids installed part-way up Altai, looking out over the lower curved mountains. It's an endless mess of blowing dust and little is clearly visible, but some of the curled peaks have broken off and fallen below. All can plainly see that conditions where they live are much worse than where they are at, now.

Elixor switches to a lens overlooking their sea – which with no cover to protect it - is raining upward into the hot dry atmosphere. The giant floating leaf pads again take flight, flapping briefly in the air before drying and crumbling into nothing more than a memory. Yet another lens shows one of their old cave entrances with sand pouring into it and forever covering it up. Every lens view is bouncy and shaking.

"This is what it was like during the last pass-by when we were hiding in the caves," clarifies Elixor. Elixor then switches to a view looking at Altai, whose summit pulsates in a strange amber glow.

"Look at Altai, and the glowing pulse of its crown," notices Scepter. "What could be causing that?"

"It may be that as each magnetic ball rolls deep under the great mountain, a wave of electricity shoots up to the summit," guesses Elixor. "It's the only possibility I can think of."

"If that's the case, Altai's pulsing every two seconds means those magnet balls must now be rolling at a very fast pace." Scepter has no idea what lies ahead.

Norl hands Scepter his small metal relay dish and he quickly mounts it to the top of his Comstaff. He points his Comstaff skyward toward the teathered relay-and-balloon and yells above the wind, "Tareon teams, can you hear us?"

On Tareon along the small beach on Infinity Lake, it's also twilight as the sun has just set. Zeon looms huge in the low sky, reflected in the glistening waters of the lake, and on both planets the winds are whipping. As Scepter's wind-whipped voice echoes from their bracelets and Rayelle's Comstaff, all twelve jump to attention.

"Scepter, you're alive," responds Drago. Yes, we hear you. We are all here."

"We have a monitor positioned, with an aerial aloft," responds Scepter.

"Give us a moment and we'll draw up our own monitor and maybe you can see us," replies Drago.

Rayelle takes a few steps toward the shore and with a swipe of her clicker, produces a monitor. The view is looking out from a lens on the Zeon North Pole monitor. Spinning by in the background are the twelve stone monolith towers and the planet below them. On the stationary platform, the curved stone bench, boots, and blue cord are visible, with the Longevity Stone podium standing in the foreground. All eighteen in Scepter's party gather in front of the monitor; even the kids get up and join the others, stepping forward in their stone boots.

On Tareon, "They're alive! They're alive! Our brothers are still alive," yell Wren and Zoree, seeing that their brothers Hark and Garl didn't die chopping the timbers. "They didn't die, after all."

"Hey, that's my boys, but why are you wearing slings," as Othar quickly notices that his sons Stern and Stip are seriously injured.

"Hi dad."

"Our arms were crushed when a giant boulder fell on us."

"We were ready to amputate their arms off, but Mr Varo here was able to move the boulder just enough for us to get your boys out. Your boys are alive because of him," adds Scepter.

"Where are you," asks Rayelle above the wind.

"At the very top of our world, at the North Pole," answers Kairn.

"Everything is melted?"

"We just looked at views of our homeland," responds Scepter. "It's already being overcome. We took a long journey inside our planet and ended up here. We freed up the giant magnets buried deep under our crust. They're gaining speed now, but we don't know if there's enough time."

As Rayelle counts the heads, "There are only eighteen of you left?"

"You are looking at all of us," humbly admits Scepter. "If we don't live, the journey through our world has been wondrous. Our planet once had a glorious past.

Realizing the unknown history that Scepter is about to convey is important, Rayelle quickly taps her clicker to start recording the conversation. "Recording" flashes on the monitor, and she reminds the eleven others, "Remember this part. This is what we've always searched for."

"We met a long-dead being named Yore," continues Scepter. "He was totally unlike us, taller and with no fur, but there was enough flesh left for Chronicle to achieve a link. We learned that Nozeon – as they called it – was once far far away, and was planet three in a system of five. It was lush and green then, the tall timbers were teaming with life and oceans were of the deepest blue, but they were getting close to planet four and built Zhama to escape that planet and system. Our planet *did* have a long history, but because Zhama destroyed it, that history was flung off, erased. Yore deployed the buried timbers that stopped Zhama, and the planet drifted and came to this system, which is why your old Tareon cave map only had eight planets and did not show Zeon. Only long after that did our culture grow, connected in some distant way to Yore, because he had silver eyes. And so Rayelle, Yore and Chronicle may in some way be your very distant great, great grandfathers."

Rayelle and Evene look at each other and Rayelle asks, "Where is Chronicle now?"

"Yore gave us a choice of deploying the buried timbers to some day stop Zhama or to let Zhama run forever, and we chose to let it run forever. Chronicle insisted on remaining with Yore, saying that his destiny was to end his life linked in that way. Yore told us of the path toward each pole, and we followed the one leading here, to the North Pole. There were skeletons like Yore still on these seats, but we released them and they rose into the heavens. We needed their stone boots to weigh us down and keep us from flying off and doing the same. We wish we had time to tell you more, but I'll now step aside and let all who are disconnected, say a few words with each other."

Scepter steps away and tears up, and Norl has to comfort him. All disconnected get one final brief moment together. Kairn and Trillo talk with Rayelle and Evene, Varo with his daughters Jurn and Plur, Garl and Hark with their sisters Wren and Zoree, Othar with his sons Stern and Stip, Elixor with his brothers Ingot and Spike, and Drago and daughter Virn with his wife Hep and daughter Ogard.

When they're finished, Drago – with his hands on daughter Virn's shoulders – asks, "Jurn and Plur, is Varo your father?"

"Yes," nod Jurn and Plur, wiping away tears.

"If I may, on a personal note," volunteers Drago, "To the one there named Varo, Rayelle and Kairn have told me you are a good man and father. For your last hours together on Zeon, my wife Hep and daughter Ogard should not be alone. Please hold them close and live out your lives, as one."

On Zeon, Hep and Ogard step closer to Varo with a look of great relief.

Othar then chimes in with a similar request. "To my sons Stern and Stip, with your mother dead and my being here on Tareon, please get close with Varo and Hep. All of you should be together in these final hours."

On Zeon, Kairn senses that now is the time for a reciprocating request. "To Drago, Rayelle, Othar and the others there, Hep and I have talked and we have a similar appeal. If you all survive this collision of our worlds, feel free to pair up and unite as you wish. The survival and growth or our species are more important than . . . taking sides."

"Understood," responds Drago. "Scepter, we are watching tonight from this beach on a lake, and when Zeon gets too close, this elevator behind us goes down to the deep sustainable shelter. When our worlds fuse together and if we survive it, we will likely live the rest of our lives, down there. What about you? You all look pretty exposed. Where are you taking shelter?"

"You are looking at it," humbly admits Scepter. "This circular stone plate here atop the North Pole has grease under it. It maintains position as Zeon spins under us. When things get too intense, we will pass around Elixor's silencing soup and that will be it. It'll be a nice, quiet way to go."

Hearing this talk of suicide, the eyes of Rayelle and everyone on Tareon puddle up, and Rayelle holds Evene, Jurn and Plur close.

Drago then asks, "So, from two million Zeons, there are only eighteen of you, left?"

"Remember your observation about thousands of Tareons stepping into death boxes, so that a few others could fly away and live on," asks Scepter.

"Yes."

"Well, that sounds like us."

After a short pause of reflection at this humbling similarity, "Is there anything else," asks Scepter.

"One more thing," adds Drago. We learned in searching Tareon's records and history that a hundred years ago, an intergalactic trader crashed in a neighboring star system. He lived and was able to tell of the three greatest stories spreading throughout space. The first two stories were about a spreading plague and a growing black hole. The third story . . . was about a planet . . . that could move . . . like a ship. The story was so old and its origin unknown, that no one believed it anymore."

"Really. And what did he say about the planet-ship?"

"He said the story claimed if the planet ship ever starts up again, that wherever you are, you don't want to be near it."

CHAPTER 12

Taking Over

"**G**REAT, AND HERE WE ARE atop it with no place to go," replies a sarcastic Scepter. "As your larger Tareon overcomes ours, things will quickly fly off our planet. We must now prepare for this day of reckoning by taking our seats around this bench as our forbearers did. I'll leave the view connected for a moment before cutting off, and to my brother Nax, carry on. Good luck to you all and stay alert, stay smart, and forward with brilliance."

As the Tareon twelve respond "Forward with brilliance," all eighteen in Scepter's party take up seats along the platform's curved stone bench. They position the heavy blue cord across their laps, don goggles over their eyes, and pass sticks of Nocab among each other. Next to Scepter on one side is his wife Norl. On Scepter's other side, Elixor removes a sealed green pouch from the woven backpack he's been carrying. Even unopened, the pouch emits an eerie vapor, which can only be their death juice.

On Tareon, all watching the seaside monitor notice the smoldering pouch in Elixor's lap before Scepter terminates the message. Rayelle, Wren and Zoree turn away, not wanting it to be the last image of their disconnected families. In disgust, Rayelle swipes the clicker back with one arm to extinguish the monitor above the shore.

"What do we do now," asks Othar. "Isn't it time to ride the elevator down to the shelter below?"

"I'm staying here until the very last minute," sternly proclaims Rayelle, who plops down with Evene, Jurn and Plur in the swoopy modern lounges brought out from the beach houses. The warm winds blow in from the lake, toward them, so the sand blows toward the houses and hills. This leaves the view of Infinity Lake crystal clear, as their lounges are near the waters' edge on wet sand.

The billion-star sky is doubled by the reflection in the shiny black lake. The day's sunlight is now completely gone and Zeon looms large, just above the watery horizon. "What's going to happen tomorrow," asks Evene.

"Zeon will set in front of us below the lake tonight, pass around Tareon to the other side, and rise above these hills behind us even closer, tomorrow," replies Rayelle. "You kids can ride down that elevator to safety whenever you want, but I'm staying here until the very last minute."

The others in their party hear her determination from their own lounges along the wet sand.

"We're staying with you," respond the three girls in unison.

On Zeon at the North Pole, seventeen sit about the curved stone bench with their boots on and heavy blue cord across their laps. Only Scepter is standing, in his stone boots at the Longevity Stone. He rubs his head, frustrated at not being able to make sense of the ancient symbols.

Trillo has been watching the blur of the distant hatch light spin by. They left the cooler lid below the hatch open, and its light shines up out of the hatch opening. On one of the revolutions of the light spinning by, the light shining up is obstructed, as if blocked by something. "Dad, I think someone's coming," as he points toward the distant, spinning hatch light.

Kairn and others all look toward the hatch light. A lone hunched silhouette slowly makes its way toward the platform under the windy, starry night.

"It's . . . it's Chronicle!"

The old man has limped and made the long journey alone. Yore's skin and DNA deteriorated until Chronicle could no longer maintain the coupling, and he set off on his own. His weary focus is such that he left his Comstaff in Yore's watery pool.

"Should we help him?"

Although all sitting want to help the weakened Chronicle, they remain seated under their cord as the old one steps up on the platform and hobbles toward the Longevity Stone where Scepter extends a helping hand, but Chronicle coldly pushes him aside. Chronicle is running on automatic now, a zombie with purpose, keeping himself going.

"I get the feeling that this is something, only *he* can do," Kairn quietly admits to Trillo.

As Scepter takes his seat on the bench next to Norl, Chronicle steps behind - and looks down at - the symbols atop the Longevity Stone podium. In the sky above, the first northern lights of arcing between the planet's poles start to flash, and hot dry winds whip across the ancient platform. Chronicle slumps forward briefly as if in a state of momentary meditation, and then deep within him summons a force which he has always been told he's had, but never used . . . until now.

He straightens up, as if filling with great strength to perform one final act. His eyes open to reveal a bright flaming silver, charged with energy, and focus down toward the stone symbols. Silver Eyes pick up traits from everyone they connect with and because of his link with Yore, he now knows the language, and for one last time, Yore's deep baritone reverberates from Chronicle's mouth, echoing throughout the flickering, starry heavens.

"It took all we had, to build Zhama, and if you have found us, you have found our secret. We used it, but once. If it is ever started again, hold on, my children. Hold on."

Calling on all the energy remaining in his soul, Chronicle's increasingly charged eyes build in strength and burn two focused beams onto the blank space under the existing symbols, deeply etching new symbols in their current language. The eighteen others are mesmorized as they have heard tales that Silver Eyes could do this, but have never seen such concentrated power. Under the arcing heavens as the winds increase, the light flickers and smoke flies like he's welding in the dark.

When finished, his eyes slowly cool to their normal silvery state. He pulls out a sharpened stone and slices open a cut in the palm of his opposite hand. He then allows his blood - of the deepest purple possible - to trickle down his fingers and drip into the new etchings, filling them with the same permanent purple dye as the older symbols. Under the arcing heavens, he concludes by reading his new final sentence for one last time, in Yore's booming voice.

"Destroyer and savior of worlds, we saddle upon you. From the Nozeon of yore to our Zeon of today, take us, Zhama! Take us!"

With lightning thundering overhead, the silver lights in his eyes slowly extinguish to a darkened lifeless state, and Chronicle crumples and falls to the platform just in front of the Longevity Stone, not unlike a salmon which has spawned before dying. His long life is gone and his last act, done.

All seated tear up at Chronicle's passing. He's filled in the blanks, before departing. In the sky above, the auroras increase because of the nearness of Tareon, its top one-third looming large on the horizon. It's the northern lights on steroids.

On Tareon, with Zeon's last glow dimming beyond Infinity Lake's horizon, the arcings from both planets' aurora lights flash across the sky and are doubled in the reflective black night-time waters of the lake. All twelve sit close together on their beach chairs and towels. Amid the blustery warm winds coming their way, Othar is the only one standing. He's off to one side looking at a monitor screen he's swiped up of the view of Tareon and Zeon. The ghoulish umbilical of dust again connects the planets as they converge toward each other.

"Why don't you take that down," asks a grumpy Rayelle. "It reminds me of what we face."

Just before doing so, by chance, Othar zooms out to a wider view of their solar system. Around the three outer planets, thousands of tiny bright lights are visible.

"What the . . . ", as he zooms in closer and can't believe what he's seeing.

"Scepter," as Othar thrusts his arm and bracelet skyward and yells.

"Zeon here," yells back Scepter amid howling winds across the North Pole platform.

"Planets seven, eight and nine; ships leaving! Thousands of them! They're all very advanced, but something about that machine you fired up is scaring them off!"

"Did they know we were the planet ship?"

Looking at the old news records, "Negative! In the panic of a hundred years ago, they set up sensors to monitor all planets in this part of the cosmos. They had no idea it was Zeon."

"Check the transmissions. What are they saying about us?"

"They can't believe it's the dumb one. The simpleton."

With her clicker, Rayelle steps forward and brings up a monitor showing the platform on Zeon. All eighteen are sitting and goggled on the windy platform bench, and Chronicle's body lies in the foreground next to the Longevity Stone podium. At the same time, an image of all on the Tareon beach appears on the Zeon monitor.

"Is that Chronicle," yells Rayelle. "Is he dead?"

"Yes, and we now know our story," yells Scepter in response. "He made the long trek here alone and lived just long enough to tell us our history."

"And what did he tell you," asks Rayelle, who clicks *"recording"* on her monitor.

"Chronicle learned from Yore that Zhama has only been used once, and for those of us remaining to hold on, because it's going to be one hell of a ride," responds Scepter. "That is of course, if it's not too late and we don't first careen into your world."

While Scepter is responding, Rayelle notices Elixor handing out capped green beakers of the frothing death soup, which are passed to all along the curved stone bench. Seeing this - after a brief pause - she can't hold back.

"You're not going to drink that stuff, are you," as all on the Tareon beach gather closely behind her.

"It's getting hot here," responds Scepter in a hopeless tone. "Very, very hot."

Leaving their seaside monitor on, Rayelle and the others return to their lounge chairs looking defeated. They always held out hope to somehow end up together with those remaining on Zeon. All on Tareon's beach remain awake as the last faint glows of Zeon set below the shining black night-time waters of Infinity Lake.

On Zeon, miles below the Zeon North Pole platform, the two giant iron magnets chase each other frantically. Their entire tunnel now glows in amber - as do the two blurry speeding balls - from the friction heat of their speed. In the entrance cave's horizontal slot - where Scepter's party first entered the tunnel – the slot now also glows in amber, and the two giant balls speed by the opening so fast that they're not clearly visible as each ball passes the wide slot two times per second. They're covering hundreds of miles every second. In addition, every time a blurry speeding magnet rolls past the slot, an amber wave of electricity spreads through the walls of the entrance cave, causing a pulsating glow that highlights metallic veins within the rock walls.

High above on the North Pole platform, all eighteen hold their sealed death beakers while trying to ride-out the lightning, wind and rumbling. The increasing heat is apparent as all are now sweating profusely. Even with goggles on, many have their eyes closed to keep from getting dizzy. But Trillo - ever the inquisitive one - gazes straight up at the stars spiraling above.

"Father, the stars are slowing."

Kairn initially thinks his son must be joking, but looks up and realizes the kid is right. "Scepter," as Kairn points skyward.

All look up and can't believe that their planet's rotation is slowing. It should continue speeding up as it has been for days, just like leading up to the last pass-by.

"How can this be," asks a confounded Scepter.

"And Scepter, look at the stone columns surrounding the platform," adds Elixor. "They are also slowing."

All on the curved bench are confounded that the stone columns and world under their platform are slowing in rotation.

"Our world's rotation is slowing down," replies Scepter. "That shouldn't be happening. We're still getting closer to Tareon. Our rotation should be speeding up."

As the planet spinning below them continues to slow, "The wind is also slowing," notices Varo.

"What strangeness is going on," asks Scepter, as all eighteen are wide-eyed at the unusual happenings.

Within a couple of moments, all wind - and the rotation of the planet under the platform - has come to a halt. There is an eerie surrealness under the now-motionless stars. The moody platform lights are aglow and the northern lights arcing above still flash, but all is otherwise quiet.

"I don't understand this. The winds should still be increasing. What could cause all of this," asks Scepter.

Below them, they start to feel strains and pops in the planet's crust. These strains and moans seem to come from different directions, and pass through the platform they sit on.

"What's that," asks Norl, feeling a strange sensation coming up through her stone boots.

"What's what?"

"That low buzz."

"I feel it too," replies Garl.

"As do I," adds Scepter.

With the planet no longer spinning – but still being pulled toward Tareon - Trillo asks, "Should we step off?"

"Our forbearers stayed on the platform, so I think we should stay on," responds Kairn. "And anyway, look at the dome of Tareon, low on the horizon. It's getting bigger and we are still being pulled in."

The humming below them slowly grows, gradually tingling up their legs and into their torsos as Trillo is again gazing up at the stationary stars.

"We're starting the other way."

Like a huge locomotive reversing direction, all on the platform gasp as the planet below their plate starts turning in the opposite direction. The stone columns and the hills beyond have begun a complete reversal. "My gosh, what's happening," as Scepter can't hold back. "The stars and the columns around the platform are now turning the other way. How is this possible? Time still moves forward, yet our planet now rotates backward."

Because they sit at the top of their world where rotational forces are minimized, they are not fully aware that what's going on below is a colossal war of physics on an interplanetary scale. Tareon and Zeon's closeness tends to stretch each planet outward, toward the other. Each planet is a magnet of its own, attracted to the approach of the other, but for this final convergence, Zeon has one other factor as Zhama now spins hysterically around Zeon's core, tightening Zeon's center and making it denser. The very structure of Zeon is being ripped apart. Zeon's outer crust could separate from the inner core. The strains and moans from each planet are because two titanic forces are in a tug-of-war, but Tareon is still winning as it and Zeon are still converging toward each other.

"Scepter, the arcing between the planets is getting worse," observes Varo.

Viewed from space, each planet's poles are now zapping the other furiously, a war of electric attraction and disturbance as the accompanying lightning and thunder returns, between the planets. In the silent vacuum of space, the lightning war is all-flash and no-noise, but within the atmosphere of both planets, thunder echoes with a constant deafening bombardment from all directions. In this twice-yearly war of worlds, the aligned, final tango is on . . . with nothing to stop it.

Amid the noisy racket, Elixor brings up a lens overlooking the curled hills of their homeland and it's a shaking reverberating mess, even though things seem calmer at the poles on their accelerating, backward-rotating planet. He changes to a lens overlooking the now-dry sea and there is more horrendous shaking, with faults opening and cliffs jutting upward. The landmasses jostle, rise and fall among each other like calving icebergs fighting for room.

"Fascinating," observes Scepter. "And at the bottom of our world is another platform and stones just like this one, with our forbearers still in their seats."

In the tunnel of the giant iron balls, the siren of velocity has risen to the pitch of a maniacal roar. The view through the entrance cave horizontal slot is now of an eerie orange glow. The tunnel has become so hot that heat ripples and distorts everything within as the giant magnets scream through the tunnel at such a velocity that neither ball touches the greasy tunnel walls. They each weigh 100 million tons and they're moving so fast, they are now weightless. It's an endless levitated velodrome of speed; a speed so great, that Zeon's core is no longer its primary magnet. The two speeding orbs are now the primary magnets. Zeon has fed Zhama, and now Zhama is taking over.

"Scepter, the spinning stone columns, they are starting to glow."

The twelve ancient columns surrounding the North Pole platform are now a blur as the backwards rotation increases, but a glowing hue is enveloping them. From the ground up, each column is turning yellow, then amber, then orange, and finally, glowing red. At the South Pole, the same thing is happening around a similar platform still holding the skeletons of yore.

"Scepter, there is a fluid coming out the top of the center pole and trickling down the backside." The clear fluid collects in the three chalices tightly nestled on the backside of the pole.

Scepter gets up and shuffles forward in his stone boots, and touches and sips the trickling fluid.

"Its water, being pumped up from below. Our ancestors thought of everything." A sizeable tremor then jostles him and he quickly waddles back to his stone seat. He *thinks* the water is for sustenance and thirst, but has no idea that it has a more immediate life-or-death purpose.

"Scepter, the flow of water is steadily increasing."

As the stream of water cascades down all sides of the central pole, it spreads out in a growing circular puddle in all directions until it reaches the platform edge and gently trickles off, fizzing into steam as it touches the glowing hot grease underneath.

"Dad, my feet are getting hot," notices an uncomfortable Trillo.

"Mine too."

As all start to fidget and squirm from the heat, "Everyone, lift your feet and allow the water to flow under your boots" advises Elixor with a hunch.

All do as directed and "Good. Now set them back down," concludes Elixor. "Ah, that's better. Scepter, the water has some cooling effect. Reposition your feet whenever they get hot."

The spreading water puddle, however, does not make its way under Chronicle's lifeless body and his corpse starts to smolder and sizzle from the heat, and some of the parents try to cover their kids' noses and goggles.

"Ooh, what's that smell?"

"Chronicle's flesh is starting to burn. But don't worry, he's dead and in a few minutes, we'll all get used to it," bluntly reasons Scepter.

In the control cavern deep within Zeon, the now-nearly skinless corpse of Yore stares straight ahead at the control board. The two red lights are circling counterclockwise in a blinding blur, tracking the giant magnets within the planet, and the pointed pendulum hanging down quivers on its chain, but does not move. Tareon is still winning.

Topside, on the North Pole platform and with no stone boots on, Chronicle's lifeless- and smoldering- body slowly lifts from the platform, and all eyes stare as it rises into the night sky. As it rises, his black, charred face stares ominously down at everyone seated on the curved bench. His body briefly circles around the center pole – just as the ice sheets had done – before floating upward into the flashing, arcing sky, never to be seen again. The importance of the stone boots is now readily apparent.

Next to appear is a thin trail of white steam vapor from the top of the central pole. It rises upward and snakes into a slowly-widening smoke spiral around Elixor's tethered balloon relay as it broadens away from the center axis.

Amid violent arcing between the planets' poles, the stars overhead are now spiraling rapidly backward. The dome of Tareon has become very wide, its top one-third just above the horizon. The spinning stone columns glow cherry red and the winds are getting very hot.

The thick layer of grease under the platform is now glowing red from friction heat as the planet below continues to accelerate backward, and the platform edge takes on a charred, blackened look. The intense heat causes thin, eerie curtains of smoke to rise from the platform perimeter. Those atop the platform are cocooned in a circular ground zero of everything happening on their overheating world. Soon, the entire platform is a steam bath as the sizzling water underneath, rises upward.

"Scepter, if this film of water wasn't flowing under us, we would already be dead," correctly reasons Elixor.

Even the stone bench all sit upon gets too hot to touch. As all are tiring and sweating profusely, "Scepter, is it time," yells Kairn in a helpless tone. He's asking about their poison, and Scepter knows it.

"To each, his own," solemnly mutters Scepter while looking skyward.

Elixor knows his concoction tastes good because the smell is good. He has no family left, and his brothers might be safe on Tareon.

Scepter's wife Norl is also looking overheated, and stares at her beaker with a deafeated look mixed with a tempered hope that life may finally be painless. A small trickle of ominous steam floats upward around the green cap covering her beaker.

Varo too, is feeling his life is done as his girls might be safe on Tareon. Amid the thunder and lightning overhead, he raises his beaker as if to toast, and "Scepter, it was the right choice sending my daughters on the last launch. I'm sorry Kairn, but that's what I think."

"Rayelle is an exceptional mother," responds a tearful Kairn as the platform and planet undulate below. "If they live, she will raise them, well." Trillo is also weeping, and Kairn and Varo have become the closest of friends in this last half-year of their shared loss.

"Scepter, Norl, I know this doesn't help, but its best that your son did not live to see an end like this," as Elixor has final words for Scepter and Norl.

Garl and Hark are crying, as are Hep, Ogard, Stern, Stip, and the three young couples; and in the echoing cacophony and maelstrom, all are ready to go.

With no future to worry about, each has dropped all internal barriers as the few still alive have become an intimate confessional group. All are now willing to freely speak their feelings without later worry, since there is no later, and as they face their frothing final cocktail, each has brief flashbacks of a more pleasant, simpler time. For Scepter and Norl, it's playing with their son Effy. For Kairn and Trillo, it's the frollocking fun of a once-complete family - including Arn, Kairn's parents and Rayelle's parents. For Varo, it's images of his beautiful wife Vellane before she was taken away and their two infant twin daughters.

The personal seriousness of this moment is highlighted as each – with their free hand – grabs and holds the hand of the one sitting next to them for support. The three young couples turn to face each other and wrap the crooks of their arms around each other in a final linked-arm death-toast of togetherness. All eighteen are tearily ready; finally a future without pain and hardship.

Others – mostly the young – are bawling uncontrollably, feeling their lives are being cut short and wishing they had been born sooner, when the planets were further apart. With lightning flashing overhead, the planet shaking and quaking below, and steam rising all around them, the agony is deeply etched into their sweaty, anguished faces.

On such a remote outpost of their nearly enveloped world, their bodies will likely never be found. It took millions of years and sheer chance and luck to come upon the skeletal forebearers originally on their stone bench.

"It's a shame we've come so far only to end up this way," admits Norl, while shaking and staring with blank exhaustion at her poisonous green beaker.

Taking a deep breath, Scepter then decides it's up to him to give the order and he holds up his smoldering beaker, as do all seventeen others.

"Right, then. Everyone, caps off!"

All others remove their caps - releasing more of the sinful vapor - and resume clutching each others' hands for togetherness and support.

On Tareon – with tears streaming and seeing the oozing potion - Rayelle covers the kids' eyes and quickly turns off the monitor. They can't bear to watch, and all on Tareon defeatedly plunk down on their beach lounges. Who could stand watching family members in the prime of their lives, poison each other?

On Zeon, those encircled look like an overheated therapy group bonded in agony, with no one to guide them. From two million, they are the eighteen remaining, each one representing over 200,000 of those killed along the way.

There is no turning back now. If any of them on the bench touches the slightest amount of tar resin to their lips, it goes straight to the heart and kills as quickly and quietly as it killed Krale.

"We of Zeon, our lives have been good, our families have been good, and our planet has been good," as Scepter continues, echoing Krale's last words before he took his final sip. "Now, all together on my count: And ten . . . nine . . . eight . . . seven . . . six . . . five . . . four . . . three . . . two . . . one . . ."

As each raises the smoldering beaker up toward their lips, "Kaboom" as a deathly explosion from one of the glowing red stone columns deafens everyone on the bench, and launches a night-into-day lightning bolt, skyward. It's not like any normal lightning bolt. It goes straight up high into the night before arcing gently outward.

"Kaboom," as another column sends a similar bolt skyward. The planet heaves and convulses with each mighty bolt.

The jolts are so severe that half of those on the bench have dropped their poisonous beakers, and the few who have ear muffs are passing them to others. The columns are only yards away and the deafening sound is increasing. "Kaboom!" "Kaboom, kaboom!" Kaboom, kaboom, kaboom!" The entire planet hemorrhages with each shattering blast.

The columns aren't blowing up. They remain in place, still glowing cherry red, and the frequency of explosions increases. Even with earmuffs on, the sound and thunder is too much as all cover their muffs with their hands.

Next, from the perimeter of the platform, a circular light shoots skyward and a few seconds later is followed by another, massive halo rings of energy pulsing upward into the heavens.

At Zeon's South Pole, the same thing is happening. Bolts blast down and outward from the cherry red stone columns, jolting the skeletons of yore in their stone seats. These strange arcing bolts are so powerful; they extend far out into space. Smoke spirals downward from the south center pole, and the same curtains of smoke and powerful halo pulses shoot down from the platform perimeter, as the grease and stone columns glow cherry red.

"Scepter, the metal ore in the columns is now charged with electrons," as Elixor has figured out what's going on and tries to yell. "Each column is releasing electricity in amounts never seen! We're making our own power now! The columns must be connected to the very backbone of Zeon! It's the only way!"

The planet rocks heavily from blasts of the surrounding cannons. All on the platform are cowering from the noise and flashing thunder, but with their hands over their ear muffs, Kairn and Trillo know where to look. They intently watch the wide top dome of Tareon, still firmly above the horizon. Despite all the explosive thunder at both poles, Tareon is still winning as deep in the Zeon control cave, the hanging pendulum in front of Yore, does not move.

The control center cave rumbles brutally. Dust and rocks rain from above, down into and around Yore's water bath, and the red pointed pendulum hanging in front of Yore quivers on its chain in this imperial war of worlds. The shaking and quaking are both constant and catastrophic as the two planets maintain their collision course against Zhama's violent, increasing heft.

Viewed from space, it's a dazzling light war. Bolts of fury fly between each planet's poles, as well as Zhama sending streamers up and down from Zeon's caps. The funnel-shaped dust cloud connecting both planets is thick with destruction and death and from Zeon's equator, strange pulses of energy fly out to the side in all directions. Can the awakening little dynamo escape the pull of the larger Tareon?

The magnet tunnel deep within Zeon now glows cherry red, and what looks like a train of many balls passing a given point in rapid succession, is in fact just the two giant balls at an incredible rate of speed. With no timbers to block their way, each revolution within their tunnel has been quicker than the previous revolution, as each ball chases the magnetic tail of the one in front of it. They are now much too fast to visualize, but the two giant balls have assumed the look of fireballs; flaming meteors within the planet.

In the entrance cave where Scepter's party entered the tunnel, the cave walls are now frantically pulsing red, which accelerates to a constant glow as the magnets keep speeding up, and the same color radiates the walls of the foundry cave, the manifold cavern, and Yore's control center cave. The intense temperatures generated by Zhama have heat-soaked throughout the granite framework of the planet as Zhama threatens to melt Zeon like a microwave; from the inside, out. There is nothing in nature that resembles the snarl of Zhama in anger.

With Zeon now spinning rapidly backward and continuing to accelerate, "Scepter, the ground beneath the spinning columns is also turning red. The entire planet is overheating."

The intense crimson hue in the spinning columns has seaped down into the planet's crust as all of Zeon has become scorched from the internal heat below.

Deep within, the heat from the magnet tunnel is now so intense that high pressure flames spew out of the slot and into the entrance cave, explaining the scorch marks on the backside of every boulder. A similar flamethrower jet blasts into the giant foundry cave, scorching its boulders as well as the giant hanging stone bucket on huge chains. Every time Zhama couldn't get more hellish, it rises to an even more incendiary level.

Millions of centuries before, in a place far far away, Zhama was built to do just what it's trying to do now, but in a better-planned execution. The opposing planet was not so much larger and Zhama was started up, sooner. The giant magnets never made it to the speed they are at now before Nozeon escaped its orbit and Yore extended the timbers that stopped them. Now, with Tareon being so close and so much larger, Zhama continues to accelerate far beyond its design limits, an internal firestorm of insane hysteria, velocity and power.

With the planet spinning frenetically backwards and explosions going off all around, "Scepter, so is this how it ends, with all of us shaken and bombarded to death after such a long, painful journey?"

In Yore's control center cave, the falling rocks, quaking and shaking have increased over the last shortened days to a blurry sustaining crescendo. The planet structure pops and cracks loudly as the gravitational war between Tareon and Zhama threatens to tear Zeon apart. Zeon reverberates with the moans, strains and ghastly echoes of a ship's structure being ripped apart. Hell knows no bounds when gods war.

This deafening resonance and distruction seems to last forever, but in the raining double-vision shakiness in this war of worlds, suddenly, the entire control center cave seems to rise upward as if being pushed by a new, stronger force. The whole cavern – and indeed the entire planet around it – seems to thrust slowly upward in a boost of gargantuan strength and as the Herculean groundswell increases - with the right side of the floor rising more than the left - the glowing red pendulum in front of Yore's Jacuzzi eerily swings out from hanging down toward six o'clock, to pointing at eight o'clock, while the chain it hangs from remains taut. It's a heavy, powerful lifting of a force beyond Atlas cubed.

An even stranger similarity is occurring in the huge underground foundry cave. As the grand cavern quakes from both Tareon's nearness and Zhama's power, the same upward tilting thrust causes the giant stone bucket hanging from overhead chains to also swing out to eight o'clock, as have the loose chains with nothing attached. Heaven's heaviest rocket has just been thunderously relit. Lift offffffffff!

The rumbling, racket and tremors continue, but now a substantial push has been added, as if being shoved upward on a strong, rising wave.

The North Pole platform is a maelstrom of deafening lightning bolts, thunder, quakes, winds, and the backward blur of the landscape beyond. It's a multi-sensory hell as sparks and embers from the nearby lightning bolts cascade down around all sitting on the platform. There is the high-level lightning caused by both planets' arcing, coupled with the nearby columns' adjacent lightning and thunder shooting high into the night. The effect on those seated on the platform is horrendous. Brains shake within their skulls, organs slosh between ribs and skin, and teeth and bone joints grind painfully against each other. Adding to that now is a reverberating sonic roar from all directions accompanied by the upward thrust of an entire world rumbling up off a launch pad. With their hands over their earmuffs, Trillo and Kairn keep their eyes on the domed top of Tareon, now menacingly huge on the horizon. The width of Tareon's dome above the horizon has been growing steadily all evening as the planets grow closer, but now, that widening starts to lessen as Tareon starts to slowly sink down toward the shaky horizon.

"It's getting lower, going down. We're movingggggggggg!"

Everyone else concentrates on the top of Tareon. "But we're getting closer," notices Scepter, who dejectedly adds, "Where's my poison?"

It's deafening, chaotic, thunderous and powerful, and they are powerless.

On Tareon, amid the quiet, starry black night, all twelve are asleep on their lounges and towels on the shore of Infinity Lake. Zeon set below the waters of the lake a couple of hours ago, and there are creaks and groans from deep within Tareon. The only ones awake are the girls; Jurn, Plur, Evene, and Virn, their minds deeply etched by the poison seen on Zeon, earlier. They are unable to sleep, so they do what all kids do on a sleepless, starlit night; they watch for distant shooting stars.

"Dad and the others on Zeon must all be dead by now. I hope that poison took them quietly," surmises Jurn.

"So do I. Oh look, there goes another shooting star," observes Plur. "I wish I could go to sleep. They say tomorrow's going to be a big day." Jurn, what do you know about shooting stars?"

"No more than you. Oh look, there's another! Let's ask Evene. Evene, did you say your parents talked to you about shooting stars?"

"Yes."

"And what did they tell you?"

Evene is finally getting tired and answers with her eyes closed, but gestures upward with one arm. "If the stars shoot from up high to down low, they're going away from us. And if they go from low to high, they're getting closer."

Pausing for a moment to take in the affect they are seeing, "Then, there are a lot of stars coming at us," observes Jurn.

Evene opens her eyes and together, all four girls sit up and notice sporadic stars shooting up from beyond the distant, dark horizon of Infinity Lake. Each rising star's trajectory is reflected downward in the glistening blackness of the waters below, doubling the effect. Gradually, there is a steady increase, and strangely – except for this one area - there are no other shooting stars anywhere else in the billion star sky. As it continues and increases, the girls notice that the stars come from beyond the horizon in a wide, fan-like pattern. Some shoot toward ten o'clock while some shoot toward two o'clock, and some in between. Some also shoot further away from their beach, while others come their way, arcing up over their heads. It's a three dimensional spray of streaming lights, but that's not all. As the effect slowly seems to rise in height, it becomes clear that the entire spray may be coming from a source that just might be rotating; a growing fountain of unreal beauty, and as the four girls watch, the fountain grows steadily upward.

"Mom, mom, wake up!"

"Let me sleep. Tomorrow's a big day."

"But mom, wake up! There are a lot of stars coming this way!"

Rayelle sits up and looks to take in what they are seeing. Soon, the stars rise in height and intensity, fanning out higher and higher, further skyward, and there are gentle arcs at the top. It's a blossoming vase of stars erupting into the night sky.

"What's going on? Stars only go straight," wonders Rayelle. "I've never seen anything like this. Drago, Othar, everyone, wake up!"

Next, at a point just above the center of where the stars are emerging, a thin spiraling telltale light curls upward, and as it climbs high up above the lake's dark horizon, it dissipates, but is replaced by another spiral, and yet another. The sparks and streamers increase, fanning out before their eyes, and are accompanied by halo rings which pulse upward and widen every few seconds, emitted from some powerful force.

Along the night's dark invisible horizon where stars reflected on the lake meet those up in the sky, a single solitary light emerges, moving steadily from left to right, and back to the left. It skitters back and forth horizontally at a steady tempo, spanning nearly twenty percent of Infinity Lake's far-off width. As the left-right-left light thickens on the distant horizon, it reveals more of itself, and finally, crowned by blossoming lightning bolts fanning high into the heavens, Zeon rises, but no planet . . . has ever risen . . . like this.

As Zeon slowly rises, it now spins in the opposite direction than when it set hours earlier, and its rotation has accelerated to an impossible one full revolution per second. As it continues to slowly rise and uncloak more of itself, the reason for the initial left-right-left movement becomes clear as there is no definite top point due to a *pronounced* wobble, like a lopsided ball oscillating while it spins. In addition to wobbling and spinning rapidly, Zeon's entire surface is now an intense red sphere. It's a swollen, pulsing, throbbing, egg-shaped power generator. A very ancient engine has been brought back to life.

"Oh no! It's so close, and huge," yells Rayelle. "And look at that red color! The entire planet is overheating."

"Something's wrong," as Drago can't understand what they are seeing. "This is not right. Zeon set there just a couple of hours ago. It should be coming up back here behind us, tomorrow."

Seeing this, all twelve on the Tareon lake beach drop to their knees. It's awesome, powerful, and tears start to flow.

As the top twenty percent of Zeon's dome rises up above the horizon, the rapidly flickering protrusion of Altai explains the severe wobble as the granite weight of the great mountain has caused a huge imbalance to one side of the planet.

"Rayelle, don't you think it's time to go," as Drago and the others gather near the angled elevator doors.

As Rayelle closely watches Zeon's widening base, a tidal wave from the distant end of the lake rises up so high, it blocks out much of the spreading Zeon and aims straight for their beach.

"Now," she finally replies. "It's coming at us! It's time to go!"

"Everyone into the elevator," forcefully yells Drago.

As the huge wave advances relentlessly toward their beach, all twelve rush into the fortified concrete elevator car. Just as the doors start to close, Rayelle turns and notices that sticking out of the sand is her one remaining Comstaff.

"Wait" as she starts to run for it, but Drago and Othar quickly react and grab her, holding her back.

"No you don't! It's too late!"

"Noooooooo" she screams as the elevator doors close just before the tsunami slams into the beach houses, the three Transtubes, and elevator box. She starts to cry but abruptly stops as the elevator car shudders, sways, and bounces among the shaft walls on its way down, and a menacing roar is heard from above. As the car picks up speed and accelerates quickly down the deep shaft, torrents of water gush in around the inner door jambs and cascade down the vertical shaft. It's a race to the deep survival cave as the descending car is followed closely by the waterfall avalanche chasing it. Inside the elevator car - as all twelve look up and hear the advancing roar just above - their fur is white with fear.

"We're about to be drowned!"

CHAPTER 13

Total Annihilation

S EEN FROM SPACE, ZHAMA HAS now freed Zeon of its natural orbit arc and deflected it 45-degrees onto a straight path angled further away from their sun, but the larger Tareon is closing quickly and they are clearly on an intersecting collision course.

On Tareon, the angled elevator has finally reached the sustainment shelter, miles deep within the planet. Just after the twelve get out - with the elevator doors still open - torrents of water gush down between the elevator car and the shaft wall, and spread out into the shelter cavern. The flood immediately advances and overtakes all twelve, and shoves them forward on a strong wave. Many are separated and sloshed into different rooms. They bounce off walls and equipment as beds, chairs and other accommodations are sloshed around the survival cave. All twelve are too busy to notice that since a signal was established with Zeon, one of the control room monitors displays the view of the Zeon North Pole platform, but as the planets get closer, that screen goes blank. Moments later, Drago finally manages to grab a desk in the control room - with many monitors above - and hangs on. The others slosh around and look for anything to hold onto - sometimes even each other - until the rush of water subsides. Only the enormous securely-sealed plant nursery is safe.

As the floodwaters gradually lower and begin to drain away, Drago then brings up views on the monitors above. The wide center portion of Zeon now lifts slowly above the horizon, looking like an oversized belly darkening the stars in a gigantic eclipse, and its rotational wobble is substantial, caused by the weight of Altai on one side of the planet.

"We are going to be crushed!"

Amid the shaking and rumbling, all twelve crawl to gather up and sit against a back wall of the control room, clutching each other in fear.

"We should've prepared our own poison."

Zeon is coming straight toward them with the cold purpose and intent that can only be simple physics. The only question now is *"will their deep shelter sustain them long enough for untold generations to live below ground until the air above is once again breathable?"*

The overhead monitors show views of Zeon, the seven large cities, the forest, the ocean, and Infinity Lake. The tall city buildings and levitated buildings swing and sway in tornado-velocity winds. In the forests, some of the tallest trees succumb to the high winds and topple over, exposing massive root systems that cannot withstand Zeon's overhead closeness and siphoning power, and entire forests are being felled by waves of blasting heat. Many smaller trees are pulled upward into the sky, as are entire clumps of wild grasses. The same destructive scene occurs across the farming belts surrounding each city.

Atop Zeon's rumbling and thrusting North Pole platform, amid the battleship cannons surrounding them, "Can you bring up our lenses? If it's this bad here, it must be worse back home," as Scepter yells to Elixor.

Elixor does as told and the first thing they see is a bouncy view of daylight quickly changing to night and back to day, as Zeon's rapid backward spinning is accelerated farther away from the poles. "Look at how fast the sun speeds by. How could a full day spin by in only one second," wonders Scepter.

"And look at the red landmasses. The whole planet is now a burning red fireball," exclaims Kairn.

Amid the quickly-scrolling light-dark-light sky, the next shaky view looks at Altai, its red summit now flickering faster than a frenetic disco strobe, with scattered molten avalanches cascading down Altai's flanks.

"My world, look at Altai," exclaims Scepter. "If Altai is flickering at such a rapid rate, the giant magnets below must be going insanely fast."

"And it's all caused by Zhama," asks a disbelieving Elixor.

Their faces are in confounded at the scale of Zhama's chaotic power.

The next rapid light-dark-light view looks down into the sandy burial crater and it shows a sickening sight; the skeletons of their buried ones rising up through the red sand and being whisked up into the sky, never to be seen again. The Nearsiders have used it as a burial crater for as long as they can remember, and thousands upon thousands of skeletons rise up and are cast off. Watching this recalls Yore's words; that Zhama "flings *everything* off."

The next shaky, oscillating view is looking out from the lens partway up Altai. It shows that all of the lower curved mountains have transformed into a moving, swirling ocean; a red earth sea of undulating fluid rock. Waves of sand and boulders collide and pound into each other just like water waves.

"So that's why all of the other mountains are curled."

Elixor brings up the lens looking at the entrance cave slot and all get their first look at Zhama in anger as the red glow and heat waves distort the view of the ominous slot. The boulder blocking the floor channel was never put back, and the intense rumbling causes the remaining stone carts to roll steadily down toward the fiery slot. The carts merge into the central floor channel and just before reaching the jet flame from the slot, some divert into the left direction while other carts swerve right. Each cart then disappears into the flaming cauldron to be crushed by the speeding giant balls and never seen again.

"Incredible! That thing must be beyond hot. Zhama is overheating the entire planet!"

Deep within Zeon, the giant timbers swing and sway against their support rods as dust and rocks rain down from above, and some cave supports, collapse.

The long manifold of blue tubes shakes and quivers on the upsetting planet. Rocks fall all around the blue tubes and manifold, and finally, a large boulder falls and penetrates the manifold, springing a high pressure leak that spews blue gelateneous fluid throughout the cavern, the same blue ooze as on the path to the North Pole. The leak reduces pressure in all of the blue tubes and they deflate from lack of fluid.

In the huge magnet tunnel, the loss of fluid causes the teeth holding the inboard side of each timber, to retract. With the teeth retracted, the huge timbers start to drift out into the magnet tunnel, but the speeding giant balls bash through the impeding timbers like they're the ends of toothpicks, as Zhama's huge magnets have become battering rams from beyond the devil, high-balling locomotives of stampeding fury obliterating all in their path. The shattering impacts happen relentlessly over and over until every inch of all forty lengthy trunks are broken off, pulverized, and burned to a crisp in the magnet tunnel cauldron. With the buried timbers no longer in place, Zhama will never again be stopped.

A view from the lens in the underground control room shows it collapsing on itself. Boulders fall onto Yore's bathing perch, crushing both him and it. The video screen doors - which were left open - swing wildly and fly off. Strangely, the video continues, still showing the nirvana of a bygone era until it too is knocked to the floor by a boulder. To move Zeon, Zhama must destroy Zeon.

In the cavernous underground foundry where the giant orbs were born, the enormous blast furnace teeters, its substantial moorings separating from the cave wall structure. Huge chunks and boulders fall from the ceiling, crushing the giant stone bucket on the floor. The suspended giant bucket – still hanging strangely from its chains at eight o'clock - bounces in its chains until they snap, and crashes to the floor and shatters. The giant hanging chains ebb and sway wildly back and forth, and some fall. Rocks rain down onto the floor below and finally, giving in to the relentless quakes, the enormous blast furnace falls slowly forward like a giant redwood being felled, crashes to the floor and destroys the entire cave.

Outside, under the quickly-scrolling light-dark-light panorama, the soft sand crater is now a swimming ocean of sand, and the quakes' next victim is the rocky outcropping as the top half breaks off from its base, pivots nose-down, and plugs the entrance hole at the base of the outcropping, sealing it for eternity.

Back in the rollicking underground control cave, the only constant is the sharply pointed glowing pendulum, maintaining true at eight o'clock, the wake and weight . . . of a planet on the move.

The only certainty topside is Altai, its granite permanence anchored securely to the rest of Zeon, and its glowing summit rapidly strobing red.

Through it all and atop their rumbling North Pole hell, the eighteen passengers can only watch helplessly from their stone seat. Their poison beakers long ago rolled off of the circular platform. Since they are stuck at the top of the world, only the top of Tareon has been visible, but as it slips below Zeon's heated red horizon, all have figured out that Zeon is about to crash into it. Where's that poison when you're ready for it?

The view from the underground monitors on Tareon is of a daunting monster eclipse. Zeon is not that big, but up this close, it's a huge menacing balloon covering nearly all of the sky. There's nothing left on Zeon to destroy as both Tareon and Zhama have seen to that, but Tareon has thousands of years of development to demolish, and Zeon is taking dead aim.

Swooping in low for the impending hit, Zeon does to Tareon what Scolios did to Zeon, but on a much … larger … scale. The fast spinning of Zeon's superheated surface creates intense temperatures, sucking up all water out of Tareon's healthy oceans. As the deep purple seas rain upward and quickly evaporate from the top down, huge undersea creatures emerge and are sucked up into the sky. Inlet Pods under various coves, enormous fanged rays, and 300-feet long winged whale-like creatures are sucked up into the superheated sky and explode in mid-air, as do thousands of smaller Sizors and other small species.

As the huge planets roll near each other and Zeon moves from over the oceans to over land, all of Tareon's forests and vegetation are set ablaze. Tree-born creatures such the IrisCatchers and others lose their grip on branches and sail upward to be quickly incinerated, and the old small vacant towns explode like dried match sticks.

As Zeon's bow wave of fire approaches the first of the seven great cities, a shockwave of blasting heat advances over Tareon. The farming and vegetation quilts surrounding the city are torched into oblivion, and as the inferno wave blows into the first city, Transtubes floating at various levels explode in place as the shockwave of blasting heat blows through every structure. The levitating buildings detonate in midair and the gleaming tall buildings which stood so high, curl and twist to become melted stubs of their former selves. This sequence repeats as Zeon and its fire wave advance over the rest of Tareon and each of the remaining six cities. And finally, Worthland – the city high above their deep fortified survival bunker - is the last to be incinerated, centuries of modern development torched in mere seconds.

The flames and embers destroying Worthland extend down the W building suite back elevator, and leap out into the underground bunker, but the survival shelter's sprinklers activate, putting the flames out. It's a wide path of destruction that continues as Zeon is now very close. So close, that Zeon's wobble and the protruding Altai are about to strike Tareon.

In the rumbling deep underground shelter, the twelve Zeons struggle to hold on as dust and rocks fall all around them. On the monitors overhead, they can see the dark red giant shadow of death approach, and new vibrations and motions are added every minute. They also see the rapidly flickering mass protrusion of Altai coming in, each time it quickly spins by in the sky above.

"What's that sound?"

With each passing revolution of Altai over Tareon's crust, there is a sickening, repeating, gale force *whoosh* coming down the elevator shafts, as in just missed, just missed, just missed.

"And look at that glowing mountain spinning by on the monitor. That must be Altai. It's all lit up and flashing and getting closer with each revolution!"

Every time the great protuberance of Altai spins by in the sky just above the surface, another daunting *whoosh* from its wake is heard coming down the elevator shafts, with each passing occurance getting louder. The walls of each open elevator car buckle with each whoosh as each car slams within its shaft walls, and a plume of dust cascades down each shaft and out into the survival cave. Even buried miles underground, they can hear each escalating near-miss *whoosh* coming down the elevator shafts, and all look up to the cavern ceiling with dread.

Rayelle holds the girls close, Wren and Zoree hug each other, as do Drago, Virn and Othar. All eyes are closed and hands are clenched. "Please don't let this be the end?"

"It's coming in, right at us and getting closer. It's going to hit!"

And finally, it happens: After 24 near-misses of increasingly-tense closeness, Zeon comes around again and Altai slams into Tareon hard, pulverizing off the top 1000-feet of the giant peak. The intense dust created doesn't settle as Zeon's rapid spinning flings the earthen matter into space like a spinning pinwheel. The underground bunker heaves with a giant rocking motion and the lights go out, but the monitors stay on. All twelve are thrown violently about the darkened cavern and attempt crawling back together.

The impact has no effect on Zhama's momentum and Altai comes around again, with a second impact breaking off another 1000-feet from Altai's summit. Each successive revolution results in another impact, with massive amounts of dust being repeatedly flung into space by Zeon's fast rotation. The dirt flies into space like a badger burrowing a den, a pinwheel of sediment being flung far out from the nearly-siamesed planets.

The impact on the survival cave is devastating. Pipes are bursting, steam gushes from cracks in the walls, fires erupt behind the control panel and sprinklers activate, trying to put the fires out. Large chunks of cave ceiling break off and slam onto the floor, causing the twelve below to dodge them, just like in the life-or-death caves on their home planet. Rocky outcroppings suddenly pierce upward through the cave floor, and some areas of the cave ceiling protrude down lower and lower into the cavern. All twelve are thrown violently about the underground control room, and some are thrown through glass partitions. The flames come perilously close to those huddled nearby before sprinklers douse all with water and reduce the flames, and many of the twelve have again become separated.

The impacts are relentless as - with each revolution of Zeon - Altai again strikes Tareon hard. Every time those hiding below hope *"This is the last of it,"* there is another impact from above. The entire planet is being repeatedly punted. With each impact, the twelve Zeons are thrown further apart, and more of the survival cave is shaken into a mess. The 3D fabricator printer topples to the floor, breaking into many pieces. In the football field-sized plant nursery, the smaller plants in front are securely held in place, but the taller trees in back tip over or jostle left and right with each impact, and the burlap containing the broken Comstaff pieces falls to the floor.

Wren is pinned to the cave floor by a falling boulder stretching from her chest to her knees. The boulder is heavy, but she's still breathing. With the boulder on top of her torso and upper legs, further down behind her left lower ankle, a rock pinnacle starts protruding up through the cave floor. With each successive belt by Altai, the pinnacle pushes upward a little more, applying more and more stress to the bones of her knee and lower leg. With the tenth hit from Altai, her lower leg snaps suddenly forward as the bone breaks, and she screams in agony. No one can help her because the gravity is so strong that all are pressed against the survival cave floor.

The belts from Altai separate Virn from her father Drago, and a falling sharply-bladed stalactite severs her left arm at the elbow. Drago crawls toward her and pulls from his side-pack a strip of the old sea cover material, and ties it tightly around her upper arm to stop the bleeding.

Elsewhere, Scepter's brother Nax has been trapped between two outcroppings coming up through the floor, and from above, a sharply pointed stalactite grows down toward him. He's unable to move his head or shoulders and with each impact from Altai, the protruding rocky ceiling spike extends further down toward his captive face.

"Help me! Someone help me! I'm trapped!"

The others hear him, but sucked to the floor by the gravitational pull, no one can reach him. With each belt from Zeon, the rocky spike from the ceiling juts down a few more inches, growing larger and larger, and his big eyes couldn't be bigger from fear. After 20 strikes from Altai, the spike's sharp point is within three inches of his left eye.

"Get me out of here!"

He screams in fear and with the 24th impact from Altai, the sinister protrusion's sharp point stabs his left eyeball, spewing vitreous eye fluid up around the rocky spike. He screams in agony as the rocky tip pierces three inches into his eye, and with 25th passing of Altai overhead, there is an accompanying *whoosh*, but no impact, followed by another *whoosh*, but no impact.

The whooshes continue, but the impacts might be done, and Ingot has managed to crawl to the screaming Nax.

"Is it in your brain or your eye?"

"I don't know! I think my eye. I can only see out of one!"

"Try to turn your head and I'll see if I can pull you out!"

Nax turns his head to the side slightly and Ingot abruptly yanks on his pelt, which pulls Nax's head away from the sharp point. His left eyeball is tugged from its socket and remains stuck on the end of the stalactite tip, and the attached optic nerve stretches and snaps like a rubber band. Nax screams vehemently and reaches up to cover his bleeding, empty eye socket. Ingot pulls Nax from the rocks that are trapping him and together with Othar, they crawl and pull Nax toward the control room on the shaking, quaking planet. Nax is in too much pain to know how lucky he is. One more impact from Altai, and the rocky tip would've entered his brain.

Returning to Wren, Spike has managed to crawl to her and rolls the large boulder off her stomach. Her broken left lower leg and foot have flopped horribly off to one side of the pinnacle which came up from below. Zoree crawls to reach them and together, they pull Wren toward the control room.

As all twelve again crawl toward the control room to unite, the mayhem is not over. As each reaches the control room on the rollicking planet, all watch the overhead monitors in horror. Is the rest of Zeon next to hit?

The monitors show an ominous view of the giant bottom of Zeon spinning just 200 yards above Tareon's surface, since Altai has been chopped off. Nearly all sunlight is blocked out and the two passing giants look like enormous ships inching closely by each other, leviathans in the night. There are bellowing moans and groans from both planets and some moans are from frequencies so low, they rumble completely through the structure of each planet. As the two spinning giants roll just by each other, Drago and Othar watch the monitors with a look of contorted disbelief.

"How could a machine be so powerful that it not only moves a world, but also keeps a nearby planet, away," asks Drago, while cradling his one-armed daughter Virn."

"And to think, all our generations walked above something so huge and powerful without ever knowing it was there," adds Othar. "Zhama is beyond evil. It's madness."

Just then, the blank monitor regains its signal and the view of the Zeon North Pole platform reappears, and with winds howling and explosions going off in the background, a few sitting atop Zeon look up through their goggles toward their lens and monitor.

"They're alive! They're alive! They didn't drink their poison after all," roars Rayelle.

All twelve on Tareon perk up at the sudden visual and on the other monitors - as Zeon seems to roll forever face-down in the sky just above Tareon's mountains - the bow wave of fire continues to precede it, a planet-wide firestorm still advancing over Tareon's entire surface.

Next, as Zeon rolls in the low sky past the distant Tareon launch cave hangar, the heavy black death-boxes Tareons stepped into skitter across the floor and are sucked out of the hangar opening, and each box explodes above the canyon floor. The valley below is completely torched and thousands of blood worms and other creatures are sucked up and explode in the flaming air. Inside the hangar cave, all of the metal supports and structure melts, and finally, the earthen roof caves in and collapses the hangar shut. No one will ever launch from Tareon again.

On the underground monitors, as soon as the narrow gap between planets starts to widen, "It's . . . it's leaving," notices Rayelle. With the intense gravity now lessening, she grabs Evene and runs toward the angled elevator.

"No, it's too soon! You can't go," Drago and Othar roar in unison.

Drago and Othar run toward the angled elevator after her, but the doors close just before they get there. They pound on the doors in disgust, and tears start to fall.

"You'll be killed up there! We need you down here! It's too soon! You'll be fried to a crisp!" They turn and sit against the elevator, crying and defeated as the six able ones run up behind them. All eight watch as the rising lights next to the door trace the car's upward movement, and none of them expect to ever see Rayelle and Evene again.

Inside the elevator, Rayelle is antsy, her blood racing from the visual that Kairn and Trillo are still alive on Zeon. She restlessly paces back and forth with a focused stare and furrowed brow of pent up emotions which are about to erupt, and the long ride up hightens her tension.

"Mom, what's gotten into you," as Evene has never seen her mother on such an edge. "Zeon is still too close! Are you going to get us killed? I don't want to die! I like this planet! I could learn to live here!"

Panicking that their lives are about to be incinerated, Evene frantically starts pushing and kicking at the *down* arrow button, hoping to reverse the rising elevator car's direction.

"Mom, make it go down! Make it go down! I don't want to die! Make it go back down!

Suddenly, occasional thumps strike the top of their rising elevator car from above. What they can't see is that at the top of the elevator shaft, the outer door perimeter glows and flickers from a fiery exterior light, and small flaming members at the top of the shaft break lose and fall toward their rising elevator car, striking and bouncing on its roof.

"Oh no, what's that," as with the first thump, Evene looks up in horror.

That sound is followed by another thump, and then another.

"It's destroyed up there! You're taking us up to oblivion! Let me out! Let me out! I don't want to die!

The thumps have no effect on Rayelle, who focuses an intense, wound up stare through the closed elevator doors.

"Mom, I beg you, don't take me with you! We're going to be killed!"

Nearing the top, the elevator finally slows and – touching the doors and sensing an increase in heat - Rayelle quickly pulls Evene away from the about-to-open door.

The thick doors open to a sudden blast of incoming heat and wind, which slams Rayelle and Evene into the elevator back wall. The roar is deafening as Rayelle crawls to cradle Evene in the near corner protected by the short wall next to the door. Mother and daughter scream in agony at the intenseness of the heat, which singes their fur black. It's the biggest ever jet engine, roaring hotly into their elevator.

After enduring the blast until it subsides slightly, she and Evene step out onto the sand amid the loudest roar ever heard. The doors close, as Drago has summoned the elevator back down.

It's a scene of total annihilation. The Transtubes and seven sprawling beach houses are gone, only foundations are left as the houses were plundered through by the giant tidal wave. The trees behind the houses are burning stubs of their former selves, and Infinity Lake is now an empty, muddy bog. A similar fate has decimated Rayelle's lone Comstaff. The tidal wave broke it off a couple feet above the sand, and the remaining stub now smolders from being burned in the roaring heat. The elevator thick outer concrete door was left open and has been nearly ripped off its hinges. The previously white concrete elevator box is now scorched black, and its top corners and edges still glow with burning embers. An intense windtunnel of beach sand blows furiously inland, driven by tornado velocity winds.

Holding Evene and shielding their eyes from the blasting heat, Rayelle backs toward the shore, which is the direction of the oncoming wind and heat. While protecting Evene with her arms, they turn toward a bright light in the night sky, low above the horizon beyond the lake, and as the brightness lessens, they slowly open their eyes and both behold the departing *Roman Candle* of their home planet.

Pirouetting rockets of lightning shoot spectacularly upward and downward from both of Zeon's poles as bouquets spray incendiary bolts far into the heavens. Helixes spiral mightily up and down in both directions, as do halos of incredible power from a planet so glowing in red heat, it resembles its own sun. Tentacles of lightning streamers in a giant spinning hourglass shape for all of humanity to see. Peacock feathers of pulsing lights in full plumage, erupting with untold fervor in both upward and downward sprays in a display of ebulent gallantry. In a galaxy filled with interesting planets, Lady Zeon wears an ornate spinning headdress, two of them. The mundane little simpleton has become a turbocharged fireball.

The small puddles remaining at the bottom of Infinity Lake reflect- and double- the dazzling lights of Zeon's power as it slowly, majestically spins and propels itself away. It's a powerful and beautifully-lit finality: a finality that soon sets in. There is no longer a wobble, and a dark blurry circle spins around Zeon's mid-section, a permanent battle decapitation from the now-headless Altai.

Rayelle and Evene kneel in the sand at the sight of their departing home world. Nearside Zeons were always uniformly humble. They never knew how little they had, but now, jealousy overcomes the normally steadfast Rayelle. She was always able to conceal hope that somehow she and Kairn would reunite, but now she caves and yells through a torrent of tears, "Why can't I be with you? Why can't we be there?"

The elevator doors open behind her and nine others get out, all except for Othar, with Virn missing an arm, Spike carrying Wren on his shoulders, and Nax's optic nerve ending dangling from a bloodied, empty eye socket. As all squint toward the heavenly light show, Jurn and Plur run up to Rayelle. She has become their mother away from home. They join her and Evene on the sand, all eleven kneeling and watching their formerly mundane little planet spin powerfully away, and from big eyes rain big tears, even from Nax's lone eye.

Drago gets up and takes a few steps toward the old shore, swipes up a monitor with his clicker, and quickly clicks "recording," which flashes on the monitor.

The view shows the eighteen Zeons in their stone seats riding the candle onward as the blurry glowing stone columns fire off lightning bolts in the background on the fast-spinning, red hot world. With goggles on and their fur blowing, all eighteen look up toward their lens-and-monitor mounted on the center pole. It's not easy for those on Tareon to watch, but at least it's one last look to remember all, by.

"None of us are ever going home, and none of the eighteen remaining on Zeon, will ever join us."

Miles below Infinity Lake in the damaged Tareon survival shelter, Othar opens the sealed door to the enormous climate-controlled nursery where food and vegetation is grown. The back portion of the forest is a toppled-over mess, but the smaller trees near the front are undamaged. He finds a toppled cart and rights it up, and five modern shovel-like devices, and steps toward some saplings bearing small fruit which look ready for planting.

"We are going to need you now."

On his way out, he also finds and collects the burlap containing the broken Comstaff pieces. He seals the door shut and rolls the now-laden cart toward the angled elevator. He rides up to the surface, the door opens, and he rolls the cart out and stops it off to one side and joins the eleven others along the shore. Zeon is not quite as large now, but is as glowing- and lit up- as ever, and clearly spinning majestically away on a new path of its own making and direction.

They weep and yet marvel at the ornate sight as the streaking lights of a thousand suns spins brightly away, but just when they start to think that all alive on both planets have lived through this catastrophe, the other devil reappears, as something streaking in from the right catches their attention and is aiming straight at Zeon.

"What's that incoming object," asks Drago, who is the first to turn his head.

"It looks like a chunk of Scolios – one of the pieces that broke off," responds Othar. "It must've orbited far out into our system and is now coming back, and it's headed straight for Zeon!"

"Don't tell me they lived through everything only to be killed by this," adds a still-sobbing Rayelle.

"It's headed straight for Zeon's center!"

The eighteen sitting atop Zeon don't even see the streaking meteor's approach, which is coming in from behind them. It's still a sizeable chunk and is taking dead aim at Zeon, and it's large enough to destroy Zeon for centuries and all riding atop her.

Zeon's powerful lights are emanating from her poles. If this assassin's missile was approaching from the top or bottom, Zeon's lighting bolts might take it out, but the incoming killer is approaching from the side and heading straight for Zeon's mid-section.

"This can't be! They can't die now," as Rayelle continues to crumble at the helpless sight.

This is much more personal than seeing other Zeons getting killed. As luck and fate would have it, every one of the twelve on Tareon has family members atop Zeon; brothers, sisters, mothers and fathers centered in the cross-hairs of an executioner's incoming bullet.

"Please, no!"

As the streaking invader nears Zeon's atmosphere, it heats up and becomes a flaming fireball, and all twelve crying on Tareon vehemently roar "noooooooooooooooo!"

At the last second - just before impacting Zeon's mid-section - all get one last glimpse of Zhama's power as Zeon's fast-spinning energy and red-hot surface causes a bright flash of light and pulverizes the invading meteor into millions of small rocks, which splay out around the departing Zeon broader than the rings of Saturn. Zhama isn't just awake; it's pissed!

The twelve on Tareon are front-and-center for this beautiful sight, but then shield their eyes from the incoming rocks, some of which splash into the sand and Infinity Lake, which is slowly refilling from underground springs. They use the angled elevator box as protection as rocks impact the sand, all around them.

"What in the hell just happened," exclaims Drago. "One second, a piece of Scolios was incoming, and the next . . ."

"I think Zhama . . . blew it apart," guesses Othar.

With raining rocks hurtling their way, all twelve defiantly return to the shore, draw up a monitor, and see the following scene: Scepter rises from his seat and – with his stone boots on - steps forward from the stone bench. The seventeen others shuffle forward and join him, connecting hands and forming a circle in front of the small podium where Chronicle scribed his last words.

The twelve on Tareon see this and with tears still falling, quietly understand, forming their own hand-held circle on the beach sand, with Wren hopping on her one good leg and Virn using her one remaining hand. Each group quietly begins performing the departed waltz, which ends with the hands starting low and then spiraling skyward. They are not *burying* each other. They're saying *goodbye* to each other. It's all each group can do. When done, each group assembles in front of their monitor to be seen by the other group. For Wren and Zoree, its one last look at their brothers Garl and Hark. For Ingot and Spike, one last look at their brother Elixor. For Drago and his one-armed daughter Virn, one last look at his weeping wife Hep and daughter Ogard. For Othar, one last look at his sons Stern and Stip. For Scepter, one shocking last look at his now one-eyed brother Nax. For Jurn and Plur, one last look at their father Varo, and for Rayelle and Evene, one last wave to Kairn and Trillo. Kairn holds up one hand in the shape of the family half-circle salute, and seeing this, Rayelle responds with her own half circle. Trillo holds up his half circle salute, and Evene matches his. "Good bye my loves, but I'll always be with you."

It's akin to being at a port and seeing loved ones off on an epic voyage of a great ship that is *not* coming back; families to be forever torn apart by luck, cataclysm and awe. The long goodbye seems to last forever as the great vessel-planet churns brightly away in a display of flamboyant and erupting power.

With final waves and big tears, the eighteen on Zeon then step to the edge of the platform where Tareon is slowly retreating beyond the gaps of the spinning stone columns. With the symphony of exploding fireworks and thunder continuing above, they can finally see all of Tareon as it recedes on the horizon. They hold hands and embrace in a shared closeness of those who've been through not just one war together, but many wars together.

Standing just behind Trillo – with his hands on Trillo's shoulders - Kairn asks one last question as they look back at the departing Tareon.

"Son, do you feel like you're flying?"

"Amongst angels; thousands and thousands of angels. We're soaring."

"Each one of these bright explosions above is for those who have passed and not lived to see this spectacle as we have," replies Kairn. "Assign a face to each beautiful light whether you knew that person, or not."

"In this last short half-year, we've skirted death, how many times," asks Scepter, staring out at the retreating Tareon, numbed but with a degree of calmness. "And here we are amid all this explosive majesty and glory. Why are *we* the chosen ones; the ones to have lived through something so harrowing and epic?"

"You can't keep beating yourself up over what happened," answers Kairn. "We have no control over chance. Rayelle and I were mere inches from the boulder that killed our parents. The same goes for you, Norl, and your son. Whose caves collapsed, or who was lucky enough to be at the bottom of Altai when Scolios flew over, are things we had no control of, and we launched as many as we could. To constantly dwell on what might have been will only shorten our lives. I wish I could be there with

Rayelle, one more launch and Trillo and I would have been, but all of us alive on both planets have stared death in the face, are still here to talk about it, and with the heavens we are now passing, I want to soak up every mile."

They all turn in their boots and slowly shuffle to their seats on the stone bench and place the heavy blue Nocab cord over their laps. As they do, there are only the shortest of glances back toward Tareon, retreating slowly above the horizon.

Soon, they will no longer be able to hear as the nearby repetitive thunder and lightning will render them deaf, but they quickly become adept at reading lips. They pass chalices of water among each other and enjoy bites of the wonderful blue Nocab. There is a quiet contentment on their faces as if all stress has been lifted off, because for the first time in over a half-year, there is no ticking clock to beat, no long trek to make, no hard labor to perform. They even toast each other before drinking water on the undulating ride of a lifetime atop the spinning generator formerly known as "the simple planet."

High atop the underground magnets forever racing below, it's easy to forget that Zeon is still a planet. It's now a thoroughly destroyed ecosystem, as thoroughly as once before, but Zeon still has its atmosphere. Kairn and Elixor will inform Scepter that if Chronicle had stayed in the control cavern and extended the timbers to stop the giant magnets, the outcome would be the same. Even if stopped, Zhama's momentum would've hurled Zeon so far across the cosmos that its journey would long outlive their lives.

The three married young females – Jin, Vail, and Wee, are now showing the protruding bumps of coming childbirths and the platform they all ride atop will be an island prison, but for the time-being - with blowing fur and contented smiles showing through those green goggles - it's more than the ride of a lifetime; it's the ride of a people.

For the Tareon twelve, it's *their* turn to worry about survival. On their obliterated beach with rocks still raining down around them, all turn, and Othar and a seated Wren hand out tree saplings and shovels. In teams of two each, they gaze at their saplings as the life ahead and look for places to dig. Each can't help but take glances outward at their fleeting, fiery home planet, but if they are to survive, they must start now. Their new home - the one of tall green forests and deep purple seas - has been summarily laid to waste, but the conditions will soon return for a vibrant renewal. They will make many trips bringing up saplings to plant from the nursery deep below. It's not their world, but they can build their own.

After planting their first sapling – spurred by nothing more than a spontaneous hunch - Rayelle takes one last look up at the shoreline monitor, which has been left on. She and Evene see the following: Kairn is lying prone atop the Longevity Stone, facing the monitor with his arms outstretched wide and stone boots on. Trillo lies on Kairn's back, arms outstretched in the same way. Each is giddily living a lifelong dream pretending they are flying through the heavens. In another view, Kairn, Varo and the kids have stepped down just off the platform and are equally spaced apart on the spreading insulating grease, surfing around the platform on the fast-spinning world, happily chasing each other. And in yet another view, they've taken the Nocab cord from the other half of the platform and extended it between two non-adjacent stone columns, which has shorted out and darkened the column in between. Once that column has cooled, Kairn, Trillo and Varo have climbed atop it and surf around the platform on the dynamo world. Kairn figures their platform may be an island-prison, so they might as well enjoy it.

On Tareon, the beach monitor will be left on for all separated to see each other as often as they want. Rayelle, Evene, Jurn and Plur will huddle daily on the beach to wipe away tears and say "I love yous" to Kairn, Trillo and Varo, standing in front of their own monitor. Varo and Kairn will have to be satisfied with watching their girls mature from afar.

In the Tareon deep survival shelter, Drago and Othar will piece-together- and fix- the damaged 3D fabricator printer and bring it up to the beach. Soon, they will figure out that by putting sand and water into the printer, it will produce extrusions and members of great strength, and begin building huts along the shore. The printer will also make a walking cast and splint for Wren's broken lower leg, and they will also learn that by placing Virn's good arm and Nax's good eye on the printer and hitting *"mirror opposite,"* the printer will spit out a new arm and eyeball.

After attaching Virn's new arm, Spike and Ingot will implant Nax's new eye and within a couple of days, remove a patch and get a look and hug that makes their perils and permanent separation from Zeon seem fully worthwhile.

Spike and Ingot will also concoct- and stir up- a strong adhesive, and using the remaining broken pieces, will glue together one complete Comstaff, and all will soon realize why the Comstaff means so much to Rayelle.

She will explain that if she and the girls are expected to birth children to prolong their species, these offspring will ask questions about Zeon, and the only remaining piece of their former world those parents have to share is that Comstaff. It's something only a mother - or any forward-thinking parent - would understand. As such, it will quickly be revered and become so important, that it will be kept in the climate-controlled underground nursery, the lone cherished artifact of an entire society.

The disconnected families will talk and lip-read every day as long as the monitor signal will last. Those on Tareon will realize that although the eighteen atop Zeon are trapped on their platform, they couldn't look more content and free of stress. For those atop Zeon, they will watch the Tareon seaside encampment grow daily, with beach huts expanding and plants and crops sprouting upward.

Scepter will stay in touch with his brother Nax and the bond between Scepter and Norl will grow stronger than ever. The loss of any child is bound to bring parents closer together, but Norl will remind Scepter that it was his prodding of Elixor's knowledge which figured out what Zhama was built to do, and although they lost their son Effy, Scepter's leadership has saved all eighteen still alive. She will also point out that more than once during their arduous perils and journey, she and the others were ready to give up and drink their permanent sleeping potion. It was a common will to follow Yore's direction and somehow talk to loved ones again on Tareon, which kept them going long enough for Zhama to spool up and save them. As they grow old, they may one day yet drink Elixor's life-ending soup, but for now – with the contentment showing through those big-eyed green goggles – that soup couldn't be farther from their minds.

Kairn and Rayelle – wiping away tears and with their kids at their sides - will have one final lip-reading conversation. It's an achingly personal send-off as each stands so close to their monitor that they can reach out to touch the face and features of the other, one final time. As they talk, each has flashbacks from their first meeting where Kairn noticed the unusual young Silver Eye swimming in their sea, to their leaf pad marriage on a beautifully rainy night, and to the births of Evene and Trillo.

"I miss you terribly, but short of being together, this is the best possible outcome," observes Kairn toward Rayelle on his monitor. "We both somehow lived through it and each of us can talk and see that the others are well. You and Evene and the others have a special responsibility there to live on and grow our kind. Take it as seriously as any other role, and you will all do well. Those of us here atop Zeon may not last much longer, but after all of the slaving and hardship we've been through, we just want to celebrate."

"Which of us is luckiest," asks Rayelle, with tears but now accepting of their outcome.

"We all are. We all are," as Kairn concludes with holding up their half-circle hand salute. Instead of ending with the customary words of send-off, he choses to finish with the more personal "Carry on, my loves. Carry on."

Rayelle responds by holding up her own half-circle salute. "Carry on, my loves. Carry on."

Aside from the repaired Comstaff, only the brief recorded footage of Scepter explaining Zeon's history and showing the eighteen atop Zeon, will be all that the Tareon parents have to pass on to their children, and to their children's children; but oh, what a tale do they have to tell, about the mundane little planet not known for much. A planet with seemingly no ancient history that turned out to have *two* histories; one more recent and another that was very far back; each with separate peoples and environments and most astonishingly, at two different places in the cosmos.

They can also pass along how this unadvanced little world harbored a very ancient secret: a deeply-buried simple machine waiting for untold millenia to diabolically roll again; a machine so powerful that it cannot only move a world, but that it can also careen its way through any planet in its path.

And finally, they can also tell how this incredible machine saved two blessed groups of people – one group on each planet – by narrowly preventing the destined impact of these two determined worlds. The laws of magnetic physical attraction did their best to bring these two approaching planets together, but the enormous hidden reactor named Zhama would not allow it, and as Zeon now spins brightly onward, it ebulliently warns all others that the queen of the skies is wide awake and on the move, and to give her a wide berth.

From a population of two million Zeons, they are the lucky thirty remaining; eighteen atop one planet and twelve on another world. Having lived through this last half-year of dodging one killer threat after another, there is no fear of death now. Bring on the future - however short - for the spectacle I have lived to see, is wondrous.

In the end, the giant magnets within Zeon will over-rev and over-heat to the point where their solid iron makeup will melt into the tunnel walls, spreading their formerly massive weights throughout the planet. This dissolving of their mass will put an end to Zhama's powerful propulsion, and Zeon will once again drift across the heavens, although much farther than the first time. Where Zeon settles next is another far-off tale, but after slowly losing momentum, Zhama will never be used again.

But in the near term, Zhama's reciprocating energy and dazzling lightshow will propel Zeon on a path past the orbits of planets seven, eight and nine, and as it glitters gallantly onward, it passes thousands of assembled ships far off to each side, like escorts greeting a new ocean liner entering New York Harbor for the first time. Those ships aloft will quickly send word throughout the stars that the legend of the planet-ship, lives. The thousands of assembled vessels are aloft to avoid her wrath, wonder at her beauty, and behold the greatest show in the cosmos as the monster within her spins the planet-ship . . . forward . . . with brilliance.

Made in the USA
San Bernardino, CA
16 November 2017